Helpless and Alone . . .

Reata heard the clang of the rifle, monstrously loud, and felt the sting of a bullet that drove through his left thigh cleanly.

He fell forward on his hands and his right knee. Even in falling he had snatched the rope out of his pocket, but it slithered out of his hand and dropped—not over the edge of the cliff but down a ragged gap in the floor of the trail.

He was helpless, and from the other side of the ravine a beastly, booming voice was roaring down at him . . .

Books by Max Brand

Published by POCKET BOOKS

MAX BRAND

RAWHIDE JUSTICE

PUBLISHED BY POCKET BOOKS NEW YORK

POCKET BOOKS, a division of Simon & Schuster, Inc.
1230 Avenue of the Americas, New York, N.Y. 10020

Published by arrangement with Dodd, Mead & Company
Library of Congress Catalog Card Number: 75-31967

ISBN: 0-671-41589-1

First Pocket Books printing July, 1977

8   7   6   5   4   3

POCKET and colophon are registered trademarks
of Simon & Schuster, Inc.

Printed in the U.S.A.

RAWHIDE JUSTICE

Part One

CHAPTER 1

From his head to his ankles, Reata looked the perfect cow-puncher. His whitish felt hat was the sort of a "genuine Stetson" that might have been bought ten years before; the wind and the rain had worked on it; its uneven brim had been tied down to make ear flaps; it most certainly had saved part of Reata's anatomy from the cold and damp of winter ground. His flannel shirt, too, was a checkered pattern, and the stuff of it had been rubbed and worn out of color rather by much wearing than by many washings. His trousers had the sleek of the saddle inside the knees; down on his heels were a pair of beautiful spoon-handled spurs, enough to stir the heart of any range rider; and, as if to show the authentic label, the little round tag of a sack of smoking tobacco hung from the breast pocket of his shirt. His face, too, was coated with that brown varnish which is laid on in successive coats only by many exposures to the scorching sun of the southern deserts and the winds of the northern mountains, and he was of the rider's ideal build, lean in the hips, light and sinewy in the legs, with all the weight where it was needed, in the arms and shoulders.

However, there were details in the picture that a very clever eye might notice. The eye of old Pop Dickerman, nevertheless, was the only one in that rodeo crowd which took heed that the feet of those riding boots were not as the feet of the boots of the average cow-puncher, who drags on a fitting a couple of sizes too small, with a high heel behind it which, to be sure, keeps the foot from becoming too dangerously and deeply committed to the stirrup, but also forces a man to walk high on his toes with the stilted gait of an old woman. Instead, the foot part of Reata's boot was made of the most comfortable and supple leather, the heel was low, and plainly it was designed for the convenience of one who is much upon his feet—and sometimes has need of their utmost in agility. And in that smiling, good-natured face the eyes, as Pop Dickerman saw, were a little too bright and too changeable. Sometimes they were bluer than gray; sometimes they were yellower than hazel.

Otherwise there was nothing particular about face or features, and in height, weight, and general looks, one might have put Reata down as simply the average man, most readily lost in a crowd of people whose hair is blond and whose eyes are blue-gray or green-gray.

There was a pause in the rodeo entertainment, and Reata had chosen that occasion to start his own little performance. Before he had made three flourishes, a circle had opened before him, and people were packing closely around to see tricks as clever as were devised on the range by idle men with plenty of wits in the head and in the hands.

The tool of Reata was, in fact, the thing that gave him his name, but it was such a reata as never had been seen before. It might be the full length used on the southern range—forty feet—but it was a "rope" no thicker than a lead pencil. Yes, or even thinner. It seemed to be made of finely braided rawhide. It had the snaky suppleness of rawhide, and it could be made, by Reata, to drop out of the air into a pile in his hand, and thence shifted easily into one coat pocket.

Though it seemed to be rawhide, even the power of that tough leather was not enough, a man would have sworn, to explain the strength of this material which Reata used. Some people suggested that into the fabric, or serving as a core, might be a braid of intensely strong wire. Piano wire, for instance, is capable of enduring a great pull, but this wire would have to be more subtle and more supple by far. One thing at least was true—that just as a length of good twine will hold a man, so that very slight rope of Reata's would hold a strong horse! Another thing was patent to all who handled the rope—it was heavier than leather ought to be.

It was a joy to see what Reata could do with that slimsy length of mystery. As for the "rope dance" that a good many clever cowboys have mastered, every feature of it was simple to Reata. He could make his lariat into a walking wheel, into a double and a triple walking wheel, or a wheel that spun with dizzy speed in the air. The crowd gasped and laughed and pressed closer, and little men gripped the shoulders of luckier beholders and pulled themselves up on tiptoe to see Reata throw his lasso into complicated and intertwining curves through which he leaped and danced. For a feature of his performance was that he was rarely still, but seemed as lively, as supple, as lithe as the rope he used.

Now the loop head of the lariat rose suddenly, like an angry snake. Now it coiled its length under that raised head like a snake about to strike. Now the rope stood up its whole length on revolving serpentinings, and formed rapidly into various figures, until there seemed to be a stiffening material in it, for the master wielded it so that the rapid ripples which he threw up in it were able to maintain it in almost any position above him.

What it could do in the air was wonderful, but that was hardly anything compared with the patterns which it made on the ground, when it slithered about in such a snaky way that one or two of the wide-eyed women gasped with something akin to fear.

And it all seemed so easy when one glanced into the laughing face of Reata!

He made a deft loop that picked the hat of a man off his head, jerked it high in the air, caught it, and then, most marvelously, restored that hat to the man's head, though a good deal awry, to be sure.

And as the crowd fairly shouted applause after this master stroke, Reata tied into the single end of his rope two bits of lead and asked anyone to throw something into the air.

A half-drunken cow-puncher responded, in the midst of his excitement, by letting out a loud whoop and hurling his good Colt revolver high into the blue.

As it descended, the crowd scattering back a little from that dangerous fall, a slim streak of shadow darted out of the hand of Reata. It was his rope, the double-weighted end of which struck the gun in midair, wrapped instantly around it, and allowed Reata actually to jerk the big gun back to him without allowing it to touch the ground.

The reata had done the trick, but so swiftly, so subtly, that it really seemed as though a stroke of magic had made the weapon leap into the hand of Reata.

9

There was a thundering applause for his feat, which might have made some of the people think of those natives of South America who, in the old days, were able to throw a bit of rope weighted at both ends so accurately that they could entangle the legs of running game with it. Reata now caught the gun in a new loop of his lariat and swung the Colt out to the easy reach of the cow-puncher who had thrown it into the air.

Then Reata took off his hat from his blond head and waved the sombrero to indicate that the performance was ended. Several of the men told him to pass his hat and they'd make his show worth his while.

"I'm just a puncher having a holiday; I'm not a beggar doing tricks," said Reata. And he laughed and nodded at them. Then he went off through the crowd, leaving a murmur of delight and wonder behind him.

Only Pop Dickerman looked after him with a glimmering light of real appreciation in his eyes. And old Pop Dickerman put up his hand over his beard, so as doubly to hide his laugh.

In the meantime, getting to the outer edge of the rodeo grounds, young Mr. Reata paused behind a tree and began to produce some small articles from his clothes. He had not devoted all of his attention to his art with the rope. In fact, to see his collection, it appeared that the rope work must have played a very small part indeed in occupying his attention.

He had two wallets. One contained only ten dollars, but the other held nearly three hundred. He had a roll of bills that once had been coiled up in the vest pocket of a wealthy cattleman who had been staring, like all the others, at the antics of the rope high in the air, unaware that ambidextrous Mr. Reata could continue his rope work with either hand, leaving one set of fingers free to wander and explore—not blindly!

Besides the wallets, he had submitted to temptation and extracted from rather deep in a pocket a fine pearl-handled knife. He had selected for his victims only the most obviously well-to-do of his spectators, and from these he had drawn as contributions no fewer than four diamond tiepins. One of them would be worth fifteen hundred dollars if it was worth a penny!

That was by no means all, for he had picked up a pair

of watches, both gold, and one of them of a very fine make.

When he snapped it open, the picture of a very lovely girl looked back at him.

Reata frowned. He remembered the fellow from whom he had taken that watch—a big, darkly handsome, proud-headed fellow in the middle twenties, a fellow who was so assured in his position that he was able to venture knee-fitted riding breeches instead of the proper range garb.

And out here in Rusty Gulch, people would not ordinarily dare to infringe on the old customs.

No, that fellow was a person of wealth, of holdings so large that he could afford to do as he pleased while the rank and file of ordinary men, never knowing when they might need a job on his place, had to treat him with respect.

For that very reason Reata had picked on him as a perfect victim. He never used his talented fingers to empty the pockets of hard-working cow-punchers. He only took where it seemed that there might be profit for him and no heartbreak for the loser.

And for the second reason, he now regretted having taken the watch. No matter how high-headed and stiff-necked that cattleman seemed to be, the fact was that he had won for himself—or else why the picture in the watch?—a very lovely girl. And the more Reata looked into that pretty face, the more he was stirred. He was, in fact, one of those fellows who lose their hearts as easily as they lose their hats. A pretty face set his blood singing in an instant. And he was as gullible about women as he was keen and sharp about men. Now he drew one long sigh and instantly decided that, for the sake of this charming girl, he would have to return the watch to its owner.

So he returned straightway into the crowd. When he had been a performer, a mere tilt of his sombrero to the back of his head and a flash of his eyes had been enough to attract attention to him. Now, as he slipped quietly along, finding interstices in the thick groups where none would have appeared to ordinary eyes, rarely jostling so much as an elbow, but melting, as it were, into the mass, he who had been so observed a moment before was now totally unremarked—except by the hawk eyes of old Pop Dickerman, who was able to see the very thoughts that stir behind the foreheads of wise men!

11

Coming quickly to the tall and handsome fellow in riding breeches, Reata slid the watch back into its proper vest pocket.

Fate, at that instant, tricked him. It made the big fellow glance down in time to see a slender brown hand with his watch dripping from the fingers. The wrist of Reata was caught, and he was flung heavily to the ground.

CHAPTER 2

Perhaps Reata had been just a little clumsy. Perhaps the charming face of that girl and that delicacy of modeling about her mouth obsessed his mind too much. Perhaps he was a little bit dreamy. But as he was caught and hurled down to the ground, with the bulk of the big man on top of him, his mind was working cleanly and quickly, like the flashing of a shuttle flung through the intricate shadows of the loom.

There were a lot of things that he could do.

If he had educated hands, he had educated feet, also. He knew that with a slash of his spurs he could open up the back of the other fellow's leg. Or with his upjerking knee he could paralyze his enemy; or with a cunning stroke of his elbow he could practically obliterate one eye of the other. But all of these methods were brutal, and he hated brutality. When he used any means, it was always just sufficient, no more and no less.

So he considered each of these possibilities for perhaps the tenth part of a second, and then drew from his pocket that end of his reata to which the two lumps of lead had been tied. With them under the tips of his fingers, he slapped the side of the head of the big man just hard enough to collapse all of his strength like a spilled house of cards.

From under that burden of loose flesh, Reata arose to find that a veritable forest of hands were reaching for him.

They caught him, too, but it was like catching a snake.

People were shouting "Thief! Thief!" Those nearby

were reaching with their hands, and some of those at a little distance had drawn guns which they poised in the air above their heads, waiting for a chance to shoot, as Reata dived through a pair of legs, rose like a swimmer a little ways off, and had suddenly twisted into the open.

If he ran in the clear, he would be blasted to death with a volley of revolver shots, he knew. Instead, he headed straight for the nearest hitch rack, where stood a long line of horses. The men would not fire at him, probably, as long as he was directly in line with horseflesh.

They would rather trust to their speed of foot to catch up with him, and in that matter they would have a lot to do.

Most of them were in riding boots, but a few were not, and of those few, one pair held almost even with Reata. It was plain that he could not distance them easily. It was also plain that men would soon be in the saddle to ride him down. Again he had to find an idea in his fertile brain and a trick for his clever hands.

He drew a knife. As he ran, he shouted, and the horses at the rack reared back in violent fear, trembling, striving to flee; and as Reata went by, with a powerful, swift slash of his knife he severed several lead ropes by which the mustangs were tethered.

They were off immediately, snorting, scampering. Fast as he ran, of course, he could not possibly overtake them, but he had a tool that would bring one of them to a halt.

That was the reata, which now shot out, bullet-fast, from his hand, and dropped its noose neatly over the head of the nearest mount.

The range horse, knowing well the first lesson of the cow pony—don't pull against a rope—came to a sliding halt. Yet it had not fully lost its momentum when Reata flicked aboard it as a cat might jump on a fence. In half a moment he had that mustang stretched out like a string and sprinting as if for its life. Reata, bending low over the pommel of the saddle, looked back and saw men hastily untying horses, mounting them for the pursuit, heard them shouting, heard guns exploding, heard bullets sing for a few instants in the air about him.

He laughed. For he felt his luck on him, and he despised the bullets. A moment later he was crashed through a high thicket, and he was well out of revolver range before the riders ever came in view of him again.

A good many of them were better mounted than Reata. A number of them were very excellent riders, and not a whit heavier, and yet he managed to keep that mustang going a bit faster than anything that came behind him. He burned up the first three miles, jumped a fence, caught a loose horse of promising appearance in the corner of the great field, and, shifting only the bridle—there was not a second to change the saddle—sped on bareback into the hills.

Behind him the pursuit drew away and away and away. They had burned their horses out in the first stage of the race. Now they would have to settle down to trailing and to patient nursing of their mounts.

But they *would* be patient, and Reata knew it, for by this time some of those men had discovered the loss of their wallets, and others had missed scarfpins, and besides, every man in the crowd must have felt that he had a personal obligation to run down the thief.

So Reata rated the speed of his horse to trot or canter, and made steady instead of brilliant progress. To save his mount, he did what few Westerners would ever think of doing. For when, among the hills, he came to a steep rise, he dropped to the ground and ran beside the gelding; and when he came to a steep down slope, he did the same thing.

That was why the gelding, though it was by no means a fine animal, got through the first canyons at a remarkable rate of speed and was still fairly fresh as Reata came to the bank of a stream, up which he could ride with a fairer footing, and afterward he would cross it when it grew shallow near the headwaters.

He was so entirely confident now that he gave up jockeying the horse to get greater speed out of it. Instead, he rolled a cigarette and jogged on in comfort, and, to ease his position, threw one leg over the withers of the pony and rode aside. For by this time he and the brown gelding were very good friends.

A horse knows a master by those vibrating messages which run down the reins, and by qualities of voice and touch which would never appear to ordinary human audiences. The brown gelding did not feel that it was being forced to labor. It was rather out on a lark.

And then, when all was going so well, trouble dropped suddenly, like a spring shower, on the head of Reata.

He was too far away from the pursuit, by this time, to be hindered by it. The thing that injured him was, as usual, his foolishly sentimental heart. For as he jogged the mustang up the bank of the stream, he saw a few bits of wreckage that clung to a rock in the center of the stream, and on top of the wreckage there was a little mongrel dog, making itself small, with its tail between its legs.

"The devil with it!" said Reata.

For he had recognized the terrible, hot thrill of compassion which darted through his heart when he saw the poor little beast, and he knew that the impulse to go to the rescue ought to be handled firmly and quickly, and put behind him.

If he wasted time riding through the width and the danger of that strong current for the sake of the dog, the pursuit would almost certainly catch up with him and bring rifles to bear! They themselves might have fresh horses by this time, and then things would be very bad for Reata indeed.

That was why he said to himself grimly: "A little mongrel! Not worth five cents. Ugly little fool of a mongrel—better in the river than out of it!"

He kept his eyes straight ahead of him, like a soldier marching at a review; but all the time his heart was being tugged at, and finally his glance went aside again.

For the little mongrel dog, which was perched on the last remnants of a roof of some kind—perhaps that of a henhouse—was not in a blind panic, howling, but instead had braced itself on its spindling legs and was looking down with pricking ears to study the condition of its moored raft, and the strength of the current which was battering that raft to pieces.

It was like a little philosopher, capable of regarding death with a bright and earnest eye, gaining knowledge of the last breath.

Reata ground his teeth and pulled in a great breath. At that very moment the dog saw him, and stood up and commenced wagging its slender whip of a tail.

It was plainly a cross of many breeds. It had a body as sleek as the body of a rat, and a tail like a rat's tail, but its head was fuzzy, like the head of a very diminutive Airedale. In fact, the dog had not even a color. One could not say whether it was brown or gray or spotted, or roan, perhaps.

However, when it stood up and wagged its tail, Reata groaned aloud. He swore once, then he turned the mustang and forced it into the water. But even as he entered the stream, he could see, far, far away on the next ridge, a moving dust cloud that was sure to be composed of his enemies.

The mustang, as all mustangs will, swam with courage into the current. It had entered the river a good distance above the dog. Now, fighting bravely, striking out with a will, while Reata swam beside, the good gelding brought its master gradually nearer and nearer to the central rock where the mongrel waited.

That tail was wagging so fast now that the eye could hardly see it at all. And the eyes of the dog were jade, set in the ragged fur of the face. "Rags" was the name that came up into the mind of Reata. Throwing himself away for a handful of rags—that was what he was saying to himself as his hand reached the bit of life and lifted it.

"No bigger than a jack rabbit, and I'm a fool!" said Reata to himself.

He looked back.

That dust cloud which had poured over the ridge had now dissolved into a number of galloping riders, who were straining their horses forward.

Looking forward to the farther half of the stream, Reata saw at once that he could not possibly reach the farther side without coming under rifle fire. They would be shooting at him before he gained the other bank.

When he was sure of this, instead of attempting the impossible, he simply turned the head of his mustang and swam beside it back to the shore which he had just left. The little mongrel, Rags, he put on the back of his neck, where it stayed fast, riding him as a circus monkey will ride a horse.

So the three of them reached the shore, and, clambering up the bank, saw a charge of a dozen riders sweeping down, with the leaders hardly twenty yards away.

There was no use trying to escape by further flight. The gleaming guns that were ready for him told him that. So Reata simply began to take off his clothes and wring them out.

CHAPTER 3

Any Western sheriff has sense enough to know that he may be needed around a rodeo, for wherever horses run for money and bets are placed, there is apt to be trouble, and wherever there is trouble in the West, guns may work. So Sheriff Lowell Mason had been at the Rusty Gulch rodeo, and therefore he had joined the pursuit. He had not been able to ride so fast as the man who had lost the expensive stickpin. He had not been able to ride so fast as Tom Wayland, who had actually grappled with the elusive thief and brought him for an instant to the ground. But before the chase was over, the patient sheriff had saved his mustang so carefully that now he was out in front. He had not been tempted to urge his pony in that ruinous first sprint. The result was that he came first to the thief, with big Tom Wayland, handsome Tom Wayland, furious Tom Wayland, half a length behind him.

It was Tom Wayland, however, who got to the ground first. He hit it running and drove a fist with all his might and weight behind it at the head of Reata. He was so sure that he was going to knock the head of the thief right off his shoulders that the lips of Tom Wayland stretched a bit and his teeth set hard, prepared for the shock. But he only lunged his arm through the empty air.

Reata's head had dipped suddenly to the side, and the shoulder of Wayland, as he stepped in, bumped softly against the chest of the smaller man.

An unusually odd thing happened then.

Not with the keen spurs that armed his boots, but with his heel, Reata kicked Tom Wayland behind the knee, in that exquisitely sensitive place where nerves and tendons and straining muscles are laid in a shallow layer over the rounded bones of the joint. Straightway, as an insect is paralyzed by one sting of the wasp, so that leg of Tom Wayland was paralyzed by the blow. A mere twist and thrust then made him fall heavily on his face—so very heavily that he knocked the dust out in a large puff on either side of him.

As Wayland fell, as the rest of the charge pushed up, sliding their mustangs to a halt, the sheriff said, without drawing a gun: "Are you sticking them up, brother, or are you going to fight us all one at a time?"

Lowell Mason wore no badge, but young Reata, looking into that battered face, smiled and nodded.

"Hello, sheriff," he said. "I'm glad to see you."

"The thieving young rat!" shouted the whiskered man who had lost the big scarfpin. "There's plenty of trees over there. I dunno why we ought to take him back to jail. If we string him up right here and now, we'll be savin' the world that trouble later on!"

Rags squeezed himself between the legs of his rescuer and began to bark, suddenly and sharply, at the last speaker.

"You see why I'm glad to have you here?" went on Reata to the sheriff.

"Sure, I see it," answered the sheriff, dismounting last of all his men. "Got to say that you're a mite out of order, Mr. Thompson. They don't lynch gents in my county. Not except rustlers and hoss thieves, and they don't count as men! Just back up and give the prisoner a little air, boys, and somebody see if Tom Wayland has busted his face on the ground."

But Tom Wayland was picking himself up slowly, and, aside from a thin trickle of blood from the nose and that double lump on the side of his head, he was not injured. He was too dazed and breathless to speak for the moment, however.

"Horse thieves are not men, and this is a horse thief!" exclaimed Thompson, his whiskers bristling. "There's the horse that he stole, right under your eyes, Mason! What you got to say to that?"

"I dunno," answered the sheriff. He scratched his head, while Reata went on wringing out his clothes. "What you got to say to that, stranger?"

"This horse?" answered Reata, smiling. "Why, sheriff, this horse I simply borrowed to try him out. You know how it is. I needed a horse, at the time, and I didn't want to buy before I'd tried it out."

"Does he think we're a pack of fools?" shouted Thompson.

"No, but he thinks that maybe we know how to laugh at a joke." The sheriff chuckled. "What name might you be traveling under just now?"

"I never could see," said Reata, "why a fellow should go sashaying around the world with any set name. Now I leave it to you. Don't you wear a different suit of clothes for the summer than you do in the winter?"

Wringing his articles of clothing one by one, he now stood quite naked, and showed a slender body over which the sleek muscles were laid on in intricate entanglements. His stomach lay against his backbone like the middle of a wasp. There was no weight except at the top of the torso, and all the weight was whalebone and India rubber. He began to shake out his twisted garments and dress again, as the sheriff asked: "So you change your name the way you change your clothes, brother?"

"Why not?" asked Reata. "Down south they like to hear one kind of a name. And up in the lumber camps they're partial to something with a Swede sound to it. Why not make everybody as happy as we can, sheriff?"

"I'm going to make you happy by breaking your head!" gasped big, handsome Tom Wayland, wiping the blood from his face. "Sheriff, if the lot of you will turn your back for one minute, I'll give you a different-looking sneak thief!"

"How'll you change his looks, Wayland?" asked the sheriff a little sternly. "With your hands? You've tried your hands on him twice before this, and you didn't seem to have any luck! You—whatever your name is—Reata, I suppose I might call you—"

"Sure. Reata. That's as good as any," he answered.

"Where's my stickpin, you scoundrel?" shouted Thompson.

"It's here. I have everything you people could ask for," said Reata, cheerfully as ever.

He took out his spoils and handed them all to the sheriff.

"There's fifty dollars of my own," he said, "but I suppose you'll want that for my board and keep for a few weeks, sheriff?" He added a separate sheaf of wet greenbacks, and the sheriff took it with a grin.

"There may be some costs, or something," said Lowell Mason.

"Some people collect butterflies, and some collect

moths. Very pretty, but hard to catch. For my part, I prefer to collect stickpins and watches and such things. Easier to find, and they last longer, somehow. You know what I mean?"

At this everyone laughed, even Thompson putting back his head and shouting; only big Tom Wayland was silent, his dark eyes eating at the face and the soul of the thief.

"I wanta know one thing," declared the sheriff. "That's this: Why, when you had a long lead and fresh hoss under you, did you ride out into the river there?"

"Look yonder," said the thief.

He pointed to the last bit of wreckage which was now washing away from the rock.

"I saw a fool of a little dog out there, and just then I was feeling lonely. There was a whole lot of good company back yonder at the rodeo, and after I'd mixed around among all you people and admired you a lot, all at once I found myself riding alone through the mountains. Well, it was kind of a sad thing, and when I saw the pup out yonder, I thought I'd pick him up."

He added: "If I'd known that I was to have all this company right away again, I wouldn't have wasted my time, I suppose."

The sheriff lowered his head a little and stared at the prisoner through the thick brush of his eyebrows.

"It's true," he declared. "It's gotta be true, and it's the damnedest thing that I ever heard in my life! It's got me clean flabbergasted! You went and chucked your chance for this jack rabbit that's got the head of a dog stuck on its neck?"

"This dog?" said Reata, frowning seriously. "You don't realize what sort of a dog this is, do you, sheriff?"

"What sort is it?" asked Mason.

"This is a lion dog," said Reata. "This is the best kind of a dog in the world for the catching of mountain lions."

A rumble of chuckling greeted this suggestion.

"Runs the mountain lions right up trees, does he?" asked the sheriff.

"He doesn't have to," answered Reata. "It's this way: When he comes in sight, the mountain lion, that could eat a pack of ordinary dogs, just takes two looks and then sits down and laughs so hard that he cries. He laughs so that he can't run any more. It's a sort of funny nightmare for the mountain lion, if you ask me. And all you have to do is to come up and take that lion by the chin and skin him on the spot, because he'll keep on laughing till he's skinned and bare."

"All right," said the sheriff when a big, fresh roar of mirth had rippled away. "I'll have to ask you to climb onto the back of that horse you were trying out with an idea to buying him, and then maybe you'll come back to town with me. But what did you do with your gun, stranger?"

"Gun?" said Reata. "What would I be doing with guns in a world like this, where I can find towns like Rusty Gulch, all full of food and friendship? Why should I need to travel around with guns?"

"You do your job and never use a gun?" asked the sheriff dubiously.

"I never carried a concealed weapon in my life," answered Reata honestly, "unless you want to call this piece of string a weapon!"

He took the reata from his pocket and made it spring into the air.

They rode back in close formation to the town of Rusty Gulch, most of the men grouped as close as possible to the prisoner, chuckling at the nonsense he talked all the way. Only Tom Wayland rode in the rear of the party, with his face gray and as hard as stone.

That was how they passed into the little town of Rusty Gulch, where the people came out to see the horse thief pass, and where they came to stare and whistle and snarl, they remained to laugh and gape as Reata rode down the center of the street, surrounded by his guard, and keeping his length of rope jumping and playing and twisting in the air like a living snake.

In front of him, spraddling the withers of the horse, accurately keeping balance, with his ears pricked to the sharpest attention, was Rags.

CHAPTER 4

When they got to the jail, a considerable crowd had followed and collected in front of the entrance to the building, which was simply a low, squat hut, built of heavy stone. Here Reata dismounted at the command of the sheriff, and he made a little speech to the crowd which encircled him, after taking up Rags in the hollow of his arm.

"Ladies and gents," said Reata, "I am about to retire from you to a rest for I don't know quite how long. Fact is, ladies and gents, that the county *and* the state take a lot of interest in me. They don't feel that I ought to go around from pillar to post working for a living. They want to have me handy all the time, and they're likely to give me free board and room for quite a spell. Well, friends, it's the sort of attention that a man can't help appreciating. It's a real kindness, even though I've got to say that it has been forced on me. But before I retire, I'd like to lend somebody a mighty fine dog that I have here. Can you all see him?"

He held the little dog up in the flat of his hand, where Rags balanced with some difficulty until he managed to bunch his feet together, his front paws on the tips of the fingers of Reata, and his rear paws clinging to the heel of the hand. Once he was in place, he accepted this perilous position with a perfect content, his small red tongue lolling from his mouth as he panted in the heat of the sun, and his bright little eyes sparkling like black jewels from his furry face as he looked about him, wagging his absurd tail constantly. There was a general laugh at the sight of the mongrel.

"Here's a dog, ladies and gents," said Reata, "that you never saw the like of before. Here's a dog, I can tell you, that's worthwhile. Here's a dog with a lot of variety to him. If a cat sees him from behind, she thinks that she's seeing an overgrown rat; but when he turns around, he gives her the surprise of her life because she sees that it's a lion dog. A regular hunting dog that laughs the mountain lions to death. I'm asking you what you'll pay for him on loan. A low rate of interest is all that I'll charge. What am I bid! What am I bid!"

There was a good deal of laughter during this speech, but there was no answer.

The sheriff said: "He'll be all right, Reata. He won't starve to death, likely."

Reata put the mongrel on his shoulder, where the dog sat down. No matter where he was placed, he immediately made himself at home.

"Here's a dog," said Reata, "that you can put down a rabbit hole and he'll bring you back the rabbit. Gents, you wouldn't let a dog like that go without a home, would you?"

Even to this appeal there was no answer except noisy mirth for some moments, and the sheriff took Reata by the arm.

"We've gotta go in, Reata," he said. "Drop the dog and go in, will you?"

Here there appeared from the back of the crowd that keen-eyed, smiling old man, Pop Dickerman, whose business was that of junkdealer, and in whose junk yard one could find anything from old sacks to a broken-down combination harvester.

Pop put out his hand.

"I'll take that dog on trust, young feller," he said.

Reata looked for an instant into those clear eyes. They were too young for the grizzled, shaggy face in which they were set close together. It seemed to Reata that he never had seen a greater possibility of evil in any human face, in spite of the smile which, as a rule, masked the rodent qualities of those features. Intense dislike overcame Reata.

"Who makes a real bid?" he asked. "Here's a gent willing to take the dog on trust, but who's offering a hard-cash proposition?"

There was again no answer. And Pop Dickerman held out his hand.

"Come along and shake on it," he said, with a touch of meaning in his voice, "and you'll be glad that you gave the dog to me!"

Something made Reata put out his hand, though reluctantly. And as his palm met that of the junkman, he felt the cold, thin touch of a steel blade, and another flat bit of metal. Instantly, by an imperceptible gesture as he withdrew his hand from that of Dickerman, Reata made these presents disappear up his sleeve. His sensitive fingers had recognized the rough edge of a very fine saw!

So he picked Rags off his shoulder and presented him to Dickerman.

"Take good care of him," he said, "and he'll take good care of you."

"That's the funniest thing I ever heard of you, Pop," said the sheriff. "You got a house full of cats, and how you think that a dog will get along with 'em all?"

"Dogs is like humans, sheriff," said the junkdealer. "They gotta take their chances and live the way that they can."

Now that this transfer was made, Reata went up the steps into the jail, the door of which had been pulled wide. Already, before he entered the gloomy little building, he had slipped the saw, and what his touch told him was the flat stamp of a key, into the lining of his coat, through a small, imperceptible cut that was inside the lapel.

He was taken into the jailer's office and searched thoroughly. A pen, a capped pencil, the knife, a few scraps of paper, and odds and ends of a sewing kit wrapped in a bit of canvas, were all that the sheriff found on his prisoner, aside from the supple length of the reata. The other stuff he laid on the desk. The reata he dangled for a moment, surprised by the weight of it and the flexibility of the coils.

"Well," he said, "I guess you can't pull out the bars of your cell with this here, and you might as well keep it to amuse yourself, Reata."

"Thanks," said Reata. "It'll kill time for me."

"I've got to fill in the book about you," said the sheriff. "Will you answer questions?"

"Sure I will," said Reata. "I always answer questions. I was taught to be polite, sheriff."

The sheriff, with a faint grin, sat down behind the ledger. The jailer, a low-browed brute of a man who looked equal to his profession, gripped the arm of Reata as though to make sure of him without irons on his wrists.

"Nationality?" asked the sheriff, poising his pen.

"U.S.A.," said Reata promptly.

"What state born in?"

"The United States," said Reata.

"That's no right answer," said the sheriff.

"It's this way," answered Reata. "If I picked out one state, all the others would be so dog-gone jealous that you couldn't tell what would happen. All the other states would start in claiming me, and there'd be a ruction. You wouldn't want anything like that to happen, would you?"

"Sure I wouldn't." The sheriff grinned. "Dog-gone me if you don't pretty nigh beat me, Reata!"

"I'm sorry," said Reata, "but you see how things are? A real popular fellow like me can't play favorites. It isn't good manners."

"All right, then. Let's see—height about five ten. Color of hair, blond. No scars or distinguishing marks. Color of eyes. Hey, come a little closer with him, Bob. What color are your eyes, Reata?"

"Medium," suggested Reata.

"All right." The sheriff chuckled. "Kind of gray, I'll put down, but seems to me that they're changing about a good deal."

"They try to please everybody. You know how it is," declared Reata.

"Ever jailed before?" asked the sheriff.

"Let me see," murmured Reata. "Was I ever jailed before? Let me try to remember. Matter of fact, sheriff, I didn't bring my diary along with me. I can't remember."

"I'd bet that you can't and that you won't," said the sheriff. "But I dunno that I'll ever learn anything from what you say. We'll go and take a look at your quarters, I guess. If we can suit you here, I hope you might be making quite a stay with us, brother!"

He led the way into the cell room, which occupied the greatest part of the little building. There was one aisle down the center of the room, and three small cells on each side of it.

To the central one on the left went the sheriff and unlocked the door.

"Good, hard, tool-proof, is what this steel is," said the sheriff. "I thought I might tell you that to save you time if you wanta make inquiries for yourself. Walk right in and make yourself at home," he went on.

Reata walked in, put his hands on his hips, and slowly pivoted.

"Couldn't ask for a better place," he said. "Nice small bed so that it doesn't take up too much room. No strong light to bother the eyes. And lots of scenery."

He waved toward the forest of steel bars.

"I'm a nature lover, sheriff," he said, "and I'm going to be mighty happy in here."

The sheriff slammed the door; the lock engaged with a loud, clicking noise; the door shuddered for a moment and then was still.

CHAPTER 5

As Reata very well knew, "tool-proof" is a term, not a fact. The specially hardened surface of "tool-proof" steel will, in fact, turn the edges of ordinary instruments, but when Reata had worked out from the lining of his coat the little saw, he was delighted to observe that the edge of it was perfectly set and jewel-bright in hardness. Such a saw as that, he hoped, would be able to make good progress through the bars. But he did not intend to use the saw if there were any possibility of escaping with a light sentence.

It might be that his good-natured behavior, which seemed to have won over both the crowd and the sheriff, would gain for him a very light sentence. After all, everything he had taken had been restored. All would depend on who appeared to press a charge against him, and on the frame of mind of the judge. Tom Wayland, who seemed to be a man of power, might spoil the entire business by the weight of his opinion. But even Tom Wayland might decide to forget and to forgive. At any rate, it was better for Reata to take his term, of anything up to sixty days, rather than bring attention to himself with a jailbreak.

He examined the flat key. It was well filed, and was made to fit, obviously, the big lock in the rear door of the jail. The lock of the front door was of a huger size and a more complicated pattern.

After that Reata sat down to reflect upon the donor of these important gifts, that rat-eyed, wise-looking old fellow with the face as shaggy as that of a Scotty. The way the tools had been palmed into the hand of Reata meant a great deal to him, for he had recognized, instantly, the professional touch. There was no doubt in his mind that, as far as jails were concerned, Pop Dickerman deserved a place in one as much as most criminals in this world.

A profound sense of disgust troubled Reata. He was himself a criminal—but he detested his fellow crooks. He would hardly have called himself a thief. He was rather inclined to the idea that he was a mere opportunist who did what he could as chances were presented to him.

Well, if Dickerman was taking the dog to his hospitality and offering a prisoner a chance of escape from the jail, it was entirely plain that the old man would expect some return, and a great one. Already Reata writhed a little at the thought of what that return might have to be! He decided that he would take any sentence up to ninety days—yes, or even six months, rather than put himself under obligation to Pop Dickerman.

He was in the middle of these reflections when the sheriff returned.

His face was very sour.

"The Waylands are going to raise hell," said the sheriff. "Why did you have to let Wayland catch you when you were lifting his watch? Why couldn't it have been some other man?"

"He didn't catch me when I was taking it. He caught me when I was putting it back," said the thief.

"Putting it back? What you mean by that?"

"You wouldn't understand, sheriff. I can't explain."

"Try me."

"Well, there was a picture of a girl inside that watch," answered Reata. "You know how it is. She's a beauty, and I thought I was a dirty dog to rob a fellow who had a girl as nice as that. You won't believe me, but that was what went through my fool head."

The sheriff stared.

"I dunno," he said. "I've got to a point where I could believe pretty nigh anything about you after I've seen you slide through a crowd like a knife, and then chuck yourself away for the sake of a little guttersnipe of a dog in a river! I went to the judge and told him about you, and I laid on heavy the idea that you'd not managed to get away with anything, and that you'd got yourself into prison, when you were practically free and safe, all on account of a fool of a dog. He was beginning to say that a fellow like you just needed a good talk and a second chance.

"But right then, in comes Tom Wayland. And the name of the judge, mind you, is Lester Wayland. He's an uncle of Tom's. And Tom let out a blast about you that would 'a' rattled the sides of a mule. In two minutes he done away with all of my good work, and I seen the judge get black. In two minutes more the judge was talking about grand larceny, and a term that would be the limit. And there you are, partner. If you get out under eight or ten years, you're a lucky man! There ain't much forgiveness in Tom Wayland."

It was not of Tom Wayland, big and handsome, that the thief was thinking. He was remembering the ratty face of Pop Dickerman, and inwardly sickening.

But he came to the bars and shook the sheriff heartily by the hand.

"Mr. Mason," he said, "you're a mighty white man to me, and whether I have to wait eight years or ten before I get out, I'm going to find a way, someday, of repaying what you've done for me."

The sheriff seemed quite moved.

"You never would 'a' started doing wrong things except that you started young," he declared. "And if you get a chance to break away from the business, you'll do it. I think. A man with clean eyes, he's always clean-minded, too. I'm sorry for you, kid. I'm going to do what I can for you right to the end!"

But the best thing that he could do for Reata during the rest of that day was to give him fried bacon and eggs for supper, together with a big side dish of frijoles.

The huge jailer, Bob, came down the aisle, grabbed hold of the bars, and puffed on the cigarette that hung from his lips and breathed the smoke into the cell.

"Havin' it easy, ain't you, kid?" he said. "Well, you ain't goin' to have it easy long. They're goin' to sock you, Reata. You know that?"

"I know that," answered Reata calmly.

"Why, it makes me laugh," said Bob, sneering, "when I think of a gent like you, a kind of a half-wit. The only brains you got is in your hands. And it kind of makes me laugh, I say, when I think of you throwin' yourself away for the sake of a dog. And what a dog! It'd make me sick if it didn't make me laugh so hard!"

"I'm glad you can laugh, Bob," said the prisoner. "It must be a pretty sight to see you laugh. It'd do me a lot of good to see that maw of yours gap open and watch your yellow fangs working up and down."

"You don't like my mug, eh?" demanded Bob. "Well, I'm goin' to make you wish that you was in prison and out of this here comfortable jail before I'm through with you! If I get another word out of your trap, you get the butt of this in the middle of your pretty mug!"

As he spoke, he pulled out a big Colt and stared with hungry eyes at his prisoner.

Reata said nothing. He was too patently in the hands of Bob.

Moreover, night was closing down. The two wall lamps that lighted the room were blown out by Bob, and the place was left in darkness.

"You want a window open, don't you?" asked Bob before retiring.

"Yes, please," said Reata.

"It'll be closed, then," said Bob. "You can lay here all night and choke like a pig in a pen!"

And he laughed as he left the room.

Five minutes later Reata was at work with his saw. He would have to make four cuts, he knew, in order to get out. Even then, with two bars down, he would need to squeeze hard to wriggle through to the aisle. After that the key to the back door would immediately give him freedom.

Afterward would come Pop Dickerman, for, much as Reata detested the thought of the old man, he had not the slightest intention of avoiding his debt.

Once out of this mess, decided Reata, and he would keep his hands clean the rest of his life. It was not fear of the law that moved him so much as the consideration of that leaning figure, that ratty face of old Pop Dickerman. For his own future and the whole foul shadow of the world of crime rose over his mind like unclean water when he thought of the junkdealer.

In the meantime, the steel of the bars was tough, but so was the patience of Reata. And he oiled the saw with bits of the bacon fat which he had saved from his supper. If his fingers began to ache, and then his whole arm, he nevertheless continued. And in his patience, instead of scowling with the pain of his effort, he smiled a little.

An Oriental might look the same way when enduring a great agony, making his face bland while his soul was on fire. And life had taught Reata the same lesson. Under pain he grew still as a pool, and knew how to endure.

He endured now, cutting gradually through the one bar in two places, and leaving the bar attached in its place by only a shred of steel, so that it could be twisted away by his hands when he would. He attacked the next bar, finished the top cut, and was halfway through the second one when he heard the sighing sound of a door pushed open and then a light entered the place.

Reata slipped back to his cot and stretched himself on it. One twist of the blanket gathered it around him. There was only a faint squeaking of the spring of the cot. And now, composing his features, he saw the shadow of the approaching form upon the bars.

A moment later lantern light flooded the cell, and the gross voice of Bob the jailer exclaimed: "Wake up, thief. Stand up and lemme look at you!"

Reata yawned, rubbed his eyes softly with the palms of his aching hands, and then sat up. "What's the matter, Bob?" he asked. "Can't you get to sleep tonight?"

"Yeah, can't I get to sleep?" answered the brute. "I'm tellin' you to stand up. And when I tell you to do somethin', you hop to it, kid."

Reata rose instantly to his feet.

"You don't undress, eh? You turn in without undressin', do you?" said the jailer.

"A few new ways in a new place helps the time to roll along," said Reata. "You know how it is, Bob."

"You lie!" declared Bob. "You wasn't in bed. You heard me comin', and you slid in under the blanket."

Reata smiled at him.

"What was you doin', hey?" demanded Bob.

"Thinking about the old folks at home," said Reata, "and the dear face of old Aunt Sally, and the smell of the cornbread in the kitchen, and the sight of the thoroughbreds in the pasture."

"Shut your mug!" said Bob. "I got a mind to go in there and slap you with a gun right now."

"Have you?" said the prisoner. "Ah, but you're a good fellow, Bob. You have a good heart, I know, under your dirty skin."

"I'm comin' in now!" snarled the jailer, jangling a bunch of keys.

"Good old Bob! Come in! Come in!" said Reata. "I'll be glad to see you. Come in and make yourself at home."

"Yeah, and you'd like it, wouldn't you?" growled Bob. "But I've heard about your tricks. I'll wait till I get the irons on you tomorrow before I dress you down. Then am I goin' to beat the freshness out of you? You wait and see!"

"I'm glad to know about it," said Reata. "And I like to see a real hearty nature like yours, Bob. It does me good. Now, if you don't mind, I'll go back to bed again."

His calmness infuriated Bob more than before. And, grasping two of the bars, he shook them with an apelike burst of passion. Behold, one of those bars suddenly wrenched away in his hand!

He stood back, gaping down at the thing, stunned, bewildered, unable for an instant to understand the thing that he had discovered.

Reata, that instant, drew from his pocket the slender, sinuous coils of the lariat.

"You snake!" whispered the big man in the aisle. "I've found you out! Breakin' jail on me—breakin' jail on me—sawin' through the bars! I'm goin' to sound the alarm. And when I get my irons snug on your arms, I'm goin' to make a new picture of you, young feller!"

He turned, and as he moved, Reata glided a swift and soundless step closer to the bars. Through the gap made by the cutting away of the section of one bar he threw his rope. The thing hissed softly in the air, and Bob dodged as though he had heard a snake underfoot. But he moved too late, for the coil shot over his head, dropped, and was jerked snug just below the elbows of his arms. The powerful pull stiffened his arms against his sides. It jerked him off his feet and brought him with a thud and a jangle against the bottom of the bars.

Big Bob, parting his lips to screech for help as soon as he had caught breath, found a slender, steel-hard hand on his windpipe.

"I don't want to choke you," said the voice of his prisoner, as calm as ever. "But the fact is, Bob, that I'd rather enjoy it. And if you even try to yip, I'll throttle you!"

"Don't!" whispered Bob. "I'll lie as still as a stone. Don't strangle me, Reata. I don't mean no harm to you. I

31

wouldn't 'a' done any of them things. I was just tryin' you out. I was just talkin'."

"Shut up," advised his prisoner. "I don't like your voice even when you whisper. Lie still, and don't bother me."

He shifted a few rapid coils of the reata around the throat of the man, leaving just slack enough for poor Bob to breathe. Then, reaching for his saw, he fell to work on the one uncompleted cut with great rapidity.

"Where'd you get it?" whispered Bob.

"I wished for it, and it came," said Reata. "That's a great thing, Bob. Your mother must have told you when you were just a little chap. She must have told you that when you grow up to be a big man, all you need to do is to wish with all your might, try with all your might, and you'll get everything that you want out of this good old world."

"You got a funny lingo!" breathed the frightened guard. "But what'll the sheriff say when he sees what's happened? He'll think I been bought and sold. He'll think that I passed you the saw."

"Be still!" said Reata. "You fellows didn't search the lining of my coat, did you?"

"The lining of your coat? You couldn't—yes, you could, and you done it that way!" groaned Bob softly. "What a fool I was."

The last cut was completed, and a single twist brought the section of the steel bar away.

Reata wriggled through the opening like a snake and stood in the aisle above the jailer.

"I hate to do it, Bob," he said, "but I've got to gag you."

"Gag me? Don't gag me, Reata. Don't gag me and tie me, because I'll sure choke myself to death tryin' to breathe—tryin' to get the thing out from between my teeth. Just thinkin' of it makes me start in chokin'."

While he was still protesting, his own handkerchief was removed from his coat pocket and suddenly thrust between his teeth. And Bob drew up his feet in an instinctive gesture of protest.

The quiet, rapid voice of Reata stilled him.

"I know how to do this to keep you still and to let you breathe, too," said Reata. "But if you struggle, you *will* choke—and make a murderer out of me. It's a strange thing, Bob," he went on, as from the pockets of the jailer

32

himself he took some lengths of twine and began to tie the man to the bars of the cell. "It's a strange thing that the killing of a brute like you would send a man to the hangman's rope. I'd rather hang a man for killing a little dog like Rags than for killing you, Bob."

He stood up, dusted his hands, then rapidly disengaged his reata from the body of the prone man.

He saw the wild, popping eyes of Bob strain up at him.

"Lie still," he advised. "Don't struggle. Even if your throat grows a bit dry, you'll manage to breathe till they find you here in the morning, and when they see you, they'll never think that you were bought up for this job! Never in the world. So good night, Bob!"

He walked to the back door and tried the key. It fitted instantly and perfectly, and, pulling the door open, he stepped out under the free stars of the night.

The air was clean and good. He drew down a deep breath of it. There seemed to be in that sweetness a remedy for all the ten years of prison life which had been staining his mind and all his hopes of the future.

That terrible danger was banished from him, and he knew, when he thought back to the malice and watchfulness of Bob, and to the toughness of the tool-proof steel of those narrow bars, that only the forethought and the skill of old Pop Dickerman had saved him from the great disaster.

The Waylands were avoided for the moment, but what would lie in wait for the escaped prisoner when he put himself voluntarily in the hands of Pop Dickerman?

He took another breath of that pure, sweet night air and started away.

CHAPTER 6

All that Reata knew concerning Pop Dickerman was that there had been, behind him, when he had made the pause near the jail, an old wagon well piled up with junk of one sort or another, the sort of wreckage that accumulates around a decaying house. From his whole appearance, Reata felt sure that he had the junkdealer of the town to handle, and therefore he judged that he might be able to find the yard even by night.

He was right. On the edge of the town, a little set away from the rest of Rusty Gulch by a dry draw, with a narrow bridge across it, he came upon the high board fence and the tumble-down shanty which had a meaning to him as soon as half a dozen little phosphorescent lights ran in pairs across the road before him; then he saw the shape of a cat walking along the top of the high fence and looking down at him as though it were a beast of prey about to spring.

He had heard that there were plenty of cats at the place of Pop Dickerman; he closed instantly with the idea that he had found the spot.

The gate to the yard was shut, but not locked. He pulled that gate open and heard a thin sound of a bell somewhere in the distance. Before him he saw a wide sweep of ground inclosed by the fence on three sides and the house on the fourth, immediately opposite him. All of this ground was piled over with accumulations of junk. In the starlight he could not make out things very clearly, but he was able to recognize the combination harvester lying on the ground like an elephant with its huge belly up and its enormous trunk slanting stiffly into the air.

He saw the skeleton of a hay press, too, complete; and there were crowds and piled masses of single plows and gang plows all in one heap, and in another of mowing machines; and there were horse rakes in a third, their teeth making them look, in the starlight, like a vast entanglement of spiders' webs. But there were more piles of nondescript junk than of anything else. He saw the flats and the rounds of stoves and chimneys in one heap, but on the whole he got very little information out of the heaps except the distinct impression that Pop Dickerman must have worked busily for many years in order to gather such crowds of objects about him.

Among the huge heaps, which seemed like the relics of a ruined city, there were regular little paths laid out like streets, and a broader way, where a large wagon could have passed, straight up to the House of Dickerman itself.

A cat yowled from the roof. Reata looked up and saw

the beast, looking as large as a dog as it stood on the crest of the roof among the stars. And Reata recalled tales of witches and midnight evil in other days.

He came to the front door. As he looked about for a knocker and was about to rap, a voice said, in his very face: "Come right in, partner. There'll be a light as you open the door."

That was old Dickerman, speaking through a loophole in the door, of course.

Reata pushed the door open. He felt a delaying tug, as of a string; there was a sharp scratching sound, and then a light flickered and flared up, a sort of torch which had been ignited by the striking of a flint.

Dickerman, half dressed in a dirty undershirt and patched trousers, and with old, moldering slippers on his feet, stood with his leaning body near the door. His attitude was always that of a man midway in a bow. About his feet were half a dozen cats, some rubbing themselves against his legs, and one of them actually perched fondly on his shoulder. This beast now stood up—a scrawny, red-eyed female—and stretched itself and yawned, and showed to the stranger the pink of its mouth and the sharpness of the little white teeth.

"So? So?" said Dickerman. "I'm glad to see you, young man. You've come for your dog, of course?"

"Well, I've come for Rags, if you don't mind," said Reata.

"I'll get him for you. Come in and sit down," said Dickerman.

He pointed to a chair, and Reata went to it.

He was in the strangest room that he had ever seen. The place was so big that it must at one time have served as the mow of a barn. The uprights and the thick, squared cross-beams seemed to indicate that it had been a haymow originally. Now it was literally filled to the roof, not with hay, but with odds and ends. With junk!

The eye of young Reata wandered over the heaps of stuff on the floor in amazement. One could find a thousand things there—a heap of battered furniture, chairs here, tables there in a mighty pyramid that in itself almost reached the roof; a glimmering mound of kitchen tinware, another of great black pots and pans; a stacked confusion of buggy wheels in a corner; and, above all, all manner of things hanging in the air.

For the storage purposes which he required, Dickerman had had to throng the air, after covering the old wooden floor of his place. There were hanging, from ropes and chains, clusters of harness of all sorts, groups of saddles, snaky ropes, rawhide and hemp. There were carpets hanging like strange flags, and rugs, and shawls, and bed-clothes, and Indian blankets, and there was a strange, filmy float of color and illusion—party dresses that a woman would have loved to finger and turn over, breathing still a commingling of old perfumes which reached to Reata through the other smells like a ghost of dead de-light.

But all that he saw on the ground and in the air he could not enumerate. Wherever he turned his eyes, he found something new. He found, for instance, a bundle in which, suspended from various rings, there must have been literally tens of thousands of keys of all kinds, and yonder on the floor appeared a dim, crystal heap of glass lamps, while out of a corner was the smirched flame of a pile of copper articles.

No matter how cheap and tawdry many of the things were, one gradually began to have a feeling that all the wealth that a man could want in the world was here! An entire barbarian nation could have been enriched by the brilliances of glass beads that hung shimmering down through the torchlight, and greedy hands of men and boys would have reached to the cumbersome arsenal, in which there were revolvers, rifles, shotguns of all sorts.

He sat down under the suspended collection of lanterns, great and small. His chair had once been upholstered in good velvet, which was worn away at the curves. In front of him there was a little inlaid round table, and beyond the table a very low couch that squatted close to the ground.

He had no chance to see more than these details before there was a rustling out of a corner, and a whole herd of cats appeared—yellow cats, white cats, black cats, striped cats, pinto cats, Maltese cats, tiger cats, Siamese cats—an out-pouring of cats, a fountain of them bursting across the floor, leaping over one another, waving their tails in the air, or flickering them straight out behind. And at that moment came Dickerman again, with another group of cats, a sort of personal bodyguard of cats, all about him, and at his heels, with head and tail down, was Rags.

The poor little dog seemed so frightened that he was fairly crowding against the heels of the slippers as they rose before him at each step of the tall man. But when Rags saw Reata, as though he recognized an old, old friend, he streaked across the floor and leaped suddenly into the lap of the thief.

Reata put him on his shoulder. Rags laid his weight close against the face of his new master and whined with uttermost joy, while little tremors of delight kept passing continually through the small body.

Dickerman came to the low couch or divan on the opposite side of the table, squatted on it cross-legged, and picked up the long, rubber stem of a water pipe, whose glass bowl on the floor Reata had not noticed before. The first puffs that Dickerman blew out from his mouth refreshed and strengthened the oddest of the fragrances that hung in the air.

"I thought it wouldn't be till tomorrow," said Dickerman. "I thought that you'd wait till you got used to the ways of things in the jail."

"That would have been better," answered Reata. "But there was a thick-necked fool of a jailer who promised to make a lot of trouble for me. Account of him, I had to make a move tonight. This saw is a beauty. And the key is exactly a fit."

He laid the two on the table. The old man picked them up in his fingers and stowed them both in his trouser pockets. The torchlight threw shuddering shadows over them, and the eyes of Reata dwelt a little too long on the clawlike fingernails of his host.

"So here you are," said Dickerman, "and I'm glad to see you. Where would you reckon to be going from here, partner?"

"You might guess," said Reata.

"Guess? Now, how would I be able to guess, I ask you?" said Dickerman.

"Why," said Reata, "I suppose that what I have to do for you will take me pretty far away."

Pop Dickerman sat back on his divan and raised his eyebrows, but not his leaning face, and smiled up with his mouth and with his two close-set eyes. His eyes were too bright and young, and his lips were as though they had been freshly streaked with grease paint. The devil was in him, in his shadow, in his soul.

37

"Hello, there," said Dickerman gently. "What did you mean by that, anyway?"

"Why," said Reata, "it isn't something for nothing. I don't think," he added, waving around at the gigantic accumulation of junk, "that you're the sort of a fellow who gives a great deal away."

"No, I don't," Dickerman said. "Giving leads to thriftlessness. That's the terrible thing about it. But there was a minute back there when I couldn't help thinking that I'd hired you to do what you was managing, and that was when you were slammin' Tommy Wayland. Ah, son, that done my heart a pile of good—a whole pile of good! I loved you then, brother."

"Well," said Reata, "I'm glad that you liked that part of the show, but now you tell me what price I've got to pay to you."

"What price for you, eh?" murmured Dickerman. "What price for your life?"

"No, what price for getting me out of jail."

"Aye, but that's your life," said Dickerman. "There'd 'a' been a burned-out Reata after eight or ten years of prison. The surface and the shine of him would 'a' been all wore away, I'm thinkin'. It wouldn't 'a' been you that would 'a' come out of the prison, son! No, it's your life that I've given you."

"Well," said Reata after a moment of thought, "I guess you're right, in a way. Now what's your rate of interest?"

"High!" said Dickerman. "I'll have to get three lives for one."

CHAPTER 7

When Dickerman had made this pronouncement, as though in agreement or in praise of its master, a cat jumped into his lap and then bounded up onto his shoulder, where it took the exact position of Rags and stared straight across at the dog and Reata. Dickerman began to puff slowly at his pipe, his eyes quite closed, and the red-lipped smile lifting the corners of his mouth.

Reata, in the meantime, turned the last words slowly in his mind. As he heard them, and repeated them silently to himself, he had felt the sense of a trap closing over him.

There was an essential integrity about Reata—not that sort of honesty, unfortunately, that prevented him from putting his hands on the property of others, but the kind of straight seeing that enabled him to face an obligation at its full value. When Dickerman claimed the credit of giving life itself to him, he knew that he could have dodged the issue in one way or another, and he could have mustered up a virtuous indignation and revolted, forthwith, against the proposal which was made to him. Instead, he confronted the thing as a fact. That jail had been strong enough to hold him; the influence of Wayland would have been enough to secure the maximum penalty for grand larceny.

This part of the case was clear, and when he recognized it, he merely said: "Three for one is pretty high, Dickerman."

"There's always a price on rarities," said Dickerman. "You take a gent that asks for snow in the desert, and maybe he can get it, but it might cost him a thousand dollars a pound before he's through. Understand? And when a gent comes to me and asks for his life, well, he has to pay a price, and a big price. Three for one is what I'm chargin' you."

Reata again allowed a pause to follow. And about him he felt hands of impalpable but unescapable force closing in.

At last he said: "Put it your own way, then. Tell me what you want me to do."

"I want three men that I've lost," said Dickerman.

He took out an envelope. From the envelope he produced three pictures and tossed them across to Reata, who caught them out of the air.

"The one on top is Harry Quinn," said Dickerman.

"Tell me about him," suggested Reata.

He was studying a broad, rather good-natured face, with a small nose and eyes surrounded with heavy bonework in the brows and the protuberances beneath.

"Quinn's a useful man," said Dickerman. "That's all that you need to know. Quinn's a mighty useful man. I want you to get Quinn first. Afterward Quinn and you might get hold of Bates, who's the next of those pictures."

Bates was an opposite type, one of those men whose features are so extremely thin that it seems to be only half of a face that one looks at. A nervous energy, even from the picture, seemed to radiate out toward Reata.

"Bates," said Dickerman, "is a mighty lot more useful than Quinn, but he's just that much harder to get at. But you and Quinn might work together and get him. And then the whole three of you could combine on saving Salvio. He's the third man."

"All right," said Reata.

He looked into the third face, and it seemed to him, at first, that it was the most handsome face of a man that he had ever seen, and the smile that played on the lips increased its attraction. However, there was ground for a further inspection, and that was to be found at the corners of the mouth and the eyes, and in something sneering that one perceived without being able to place it exactly.

"Gene Salvio," said the junkdealer, "is far and away the best of the three. He's the fine sword, all right. He's the sort of steel that you might bend, d'you see, but sooner or later it'll straighten itself and run its point between your ribs. Understand that, partner?"

"Aye," said Reata. "He looks sort of like a knife in the ribs. Will you do something for me?"

"What?"

"Stop smoking that perfumed tobacco for a minute. I'm getting dizzy with it."

"Sure, I'll stop," answered Dickerman, with his smile that lifted slightly the corners of his mouth.

"These three used to belong to you, eh?" said Reata.

"They used to belong to me."

"What price did you pay for 'em?" grinned Reata.

"There's prices and prices," said Dickerman. "I'll tell you what—you buy one man by giving him hard cash; and another gent, you do him a good turn and he never forgets; and another gent, you give him the thing that he ought not to have and he keeps coming back to you to get more of it."

This indirect answer was, after all, enough for Reata. He could use his own imagination in order to fill in the details of the facts.

"You break away and outline what's coming to me,"

said Reata. "You tell me what I have to do, and then I'll have to see whether I can tackle it or not."

"No," answered Dickerman, "you'll gimme your hand that you'll go through, no matter whether it's hell in particular and earnest. You'll shake hands with me on the thing, or else I don't talk no more."

"All right," agreed Reata. He got up and moved slowly, with short steps, toward the old man, and felt those bright, snaky eyes, which never winked, fixed steadily upon him. He leaned and held out his hand; at his ear, Rags shrank and shuddered, and began to whine pitifully.

"I'm wrong," said Reata to himself, "but I'll tackle the thing, anyway."

He put out his hand, and it closed over the cold, hard, dry claw of Dickerman. And at that moment a wicked triumph burned up in the eyes of the junkdealer and made them flame brightly.

"Maybe I've been a fool," said Reata. And he drew back.

"Maybe you have, and maybe you haven't," said Dickerman. "But where there's many a good man that'll fail you, I'll never fail you so long's you're my man. You hear me, Reata?"

"I hear you," said Reata solemnly, for suddenly he knew that he was now hearing truth, and real truth, and nothing but the truth. "And I believe you."

"I'll join to you, son," said Dickerman, "closer'n iron was ever welded and heated and hammered together, so long's you're workin' for me. There ain't no hell you can slip into that I won't find you and pull you out ag'in by the hand. I'll find you and I'll save you when you get into trouble. The money that you need you're goin' to have. The horses you'll want you'll ride. And everything that a man could ask for and want, I'm goin' to find it for you, Reata. You been havin' your ups and downs, but you ain't goin' to have nothin' but ups while you're with me. You're goin' to be like a gentleman. You hear?"

"Thanks," said Reata, and something made him smile quickly, brightly, with a mirth that came deeply from the heart.

"Now then," went on the junkdealer, "there's another side to this here business. The other side is what happens to you if you double-cross me or step out of harness. Other gents have tried it, Reata. And those other gents

41

have died. If you try it, you're goin' to die as sure as if you drank poison, slow poison, the minute that you done the double-cross."

He went to the heap of cutlery and pulled out of it a little straight-bladed stiletto.

"Take this here," he said. "I went and pulled it out of the side of an old partner of mine that was givin' me the double-cross. I didn't stick that point into his heart, but I was able to name the gent that done it. And so I'm tellin' you, Reata, that if you come in with me, you gotta stay till the job's done. Understand me?"

"I understand you, all right," said Reata. "I could understand you if you didn't show me the knife even. I can see the idea in your bright eyes, Dickerman."

"Aye," said Dickerman with his smile. And he passed his hand over his grizzled, shaggy face. "Aye, I reckon I'm the most ugly man on this earth." He went on: "Folks is simple things; simpler than rabbits, or chickens, or such. They believe the words they hear and the smiles they see. But me, I prefer to have cats around me that always like you for the fish they eat and the milk they drink, and they thank themselves for all the rats they're able to catch. My cats live on rats. They don't thank me for them rats, mind you, but they thank me for the fun that they got with 'em."

"Rats," said Reata, a horrible interest overcoming him. "You can't have enough rats on this place to feed that whole tribe of cats!"

"Aye, and sure I ain't got enough, but rats is easy fetched. You come and see."

He led the way through the big room, Reata swaying his head this way and that to avoid great bundles of cloth or of metal or of glass that hung down from the beams above his head. They passed out of the main room and into a small chamber beside it, where a close, foul, damp odor was in the air.

Pop Dickerman lighted a match and held it up, sheltering the flame inside his dirty hands.

"Look at 'em!" he said.

Reata, looking, saw half a dozen great wire cages which were filled with rats. As the beasts saw the light and the men, they began to swarm into life, running around and around like the whirling of foul waters, and running up on the wires with their handlike feet, and now and then one of them would pause in the ugly race and look with bright little devilish eyes at the men.

"There!" said old Pop Dickerman. "You see 'em? What you think of 'em for cat food, eh? Fightin' cats is the only kind that I keep, Reata, and fightin' men is the only men that I keep. What you think of that little show now?"

"It's a pretty show," said Reata, with cold running through his veins.

As for his real thought, he kept it to himself. But what was most strongly passing through his mind was the similarity between the rats and the long, downward, hairy face of Pop Dickerman. He, like a rat, a great king of rats, was keeping cats about him and feeding into their mouths his own race.

There was something in the simile that rang profoundly true in the heart of Reata; he felt sure that time would enable him to prove what his instinct announced.

CHAPTER 8

When they returned to the main room, Reata simply said: "You tell me where to look and I'll start for Quinn."

"They're somewhere around Horn Spoon. That's where they want me to send the money, anyway," said Pop Dickerman. "The idea is that Quinn is my last good man, and I sent him out to get hold of Bates for me. You know where Horn Spoon is?"

"I know where it is," said Reata. "The railroad goes through there."

"Quinn got that far, it looks like, and then he got drunk in a gypsy camp, and when they threatened to use their knives on him, he tells them—the fool!—that they can turn him into money. And so they try the idea out and they send word to me that they've got a man of mine that says he's worth twenty-five hundred dollars to me, but they'll take nothing under ten thousand. And if the ten thousand ain't in their hands inside of ten days, they'll take and slit his gullet for him. That's the news that I get from a dark-skinned hound that shows up down here one evening a week ago."

"It'll take me two days to ride across to Horn Spoon," said Reata. "That'll leave one day for the spotting of Quinn and the saving of him. It's a short pinch."

"Sure it is," said Dickerman. "It's a short pinch."

"Quinn means a lot to you," answered Reata. "He's one of your three good men. Isn't his life worth ten thousand to you?"

"There's a value on things, and only fools spend too much," said Dickerman. "Five thousand, six thousand, seven thousand, even—but not ten thousand for Harry Quinn. I added him up a good few times this last week, and he never come to ten thousand dollars. Here, Reata. You step over here and pick out the guns and the knives that you want."

Reata went to the heap of guns and looked them over with a shake of his head.

"I won't have one of those," he answered, but, going to the cutlery, he picked out an ordinary horn-handled hunting knife. "This'll do," he said, glancing down the blade.

"You don't never travel with no guns?" asked the old man.

"Never," agreed Reata. "I hate to carry a load."

"Aye," said Dickerman harshly, "and I know a lot of gents that would like to drink, but they're afraid to carry whisky. What'll you take? Just your hands and that reata? Well, you work it your own way. You ain't got more'n one chance in a thousand of saving Quinn now, anyway. Come along and pick out a hoss, will you?"

He led the way out of the house to a small shed. In the distance, across the night, Reata could hear the swift beating of hoofs coming and going. Far, far away there was a rapid barking of guns.

"They've found your ghost," suggested Dickerman, "and they're pumpin' a whole lot of lead into your shadow, brother! Here's the hosses."

He opened the door to a long, low shed, and Reata took the lantern out of the hand of his host and stared down a line of a dozen horses.

"You're a horse dealer, too, are you?" asked Reata. "Trade with the thieves and sell to the honest men? Is that it?"

Dickerman laughed. He was capable of laughter, but

44

never of letting the sound finish itself naturally. The laughter always died out with a sudden shock in the very middle of its course, as though danger had suddenly looked him in the face.

Reata, with Rags still on his shoulder, looked over the horses rapidly. Two or three of them were ordinary mustangs. The others were "blood horses" of more or less quality, and one of them, a big and beautiful gray gelding, was a picture that stood out from the others as though sunshine, not lantern light, were falling on it.

Reata stepped back and shook his head.

"You've got a better one than this," he said.

"What makes you think so? Who—" began the junkdealer. He checked himself abruptly. For an instant a dangerous fire had glimmered in his eyes, but it went out again. In that instant both of the men had faced one another, and the gleam of danger was as bright in the eyes of Reata as in those of Dickerman.

"Well," said Dickerman, "I didn't think—"

He left that sentence unfinished, also. Then, going to the end of the stalls, he opened a door set very closely into the wall, and Reata walked into a narrow corridor behind three big, roomy box stalls. There was a silken, polished black stallion in the first stall. There was a golden bay gelding in the second with the bony head of a thoroughbred. In the third stood an old-looking roan mare, not an inch more than fifteen hands in height, built rather long and low, and with every rib plainly discernible.

The door to her stall, nevertheless, was the one that Reata opened. For the first thing he guessed was that the sunken places above the temples did not truly speak of age. And neither did the hanging head and the hanging lip of the mare. The first thing that he did was to part the lips of the roan, and then he found that the teeth were short, and she was not above five or six years old. At that he put back his head and laughed.

For the instant that he knew her age the rest of the picture burned into a bright light for him. She was covered with a stringing of powerful muscles, not big, but ropy and individually developed. And though her withers stuck up high as a knife and her hips were like two projecting elbows, she had one really beautiful feature—shoulders perfectly sloped and intricately muscled.

"What's the name of this one?" asked Reata, still laughing.

"Yeah, she's a funny-looking old thing," said the junk-dealer. "But there wasn't no more room left in the outside stalls, so I put her in here. Sue is her name."

"You're kind to the old, I see," said Reata. "You gave her a good blanket for cold weather, and while you feed barley to the rest, you give her oats, don't you?"

"How'd you—what makes you think that?" asked Dickerman.

"By the smell," said Reata shortly. "This is the nag for me."

"You can't have her."

"Give me a mule, then. I don't want the rest of 'em."

"Well, take her, then," said Dickerman with a snarl. He came into the stall and ran his hands over her bony ribs. She lifted her head and made it beautiful suddenly, as a horse knows how to do when it pricks its ears and brightens its eyes. She loved Dickerman, and, seeing that, Reata was stunned. We cannot have affection except where we give it; plainly Dickerman loved the mare, also.

"She's gotta be used sometime," muttered Dickerman. "And by a gent that knows hosses."

He helped in the saddling silently.

Afterward, when the mare had been led outside and Reata was in the saddle, he said: "If you're lost in the desert and don't know the chart of the water holes, give her her head and she'll take you to a drink. If you're out in bad country, she'll watch you like a dog all night long. If you can't find a trail, she'll smell it out even if the last hoofs went over it a hundred years ago. She'll never fatten up on you, but she'll keep strong on cactus and the smell of gunpowder."

He rubbed the head of the mare between the eyes.

"So long," said Reata.

"So long," said Dickerman. "Good-by, Sue. Good-by, girl! Be seein' you again one day!"

CHAPTER 9

Horn Spoon had been called Great Horn Spoon in the old days, but after the mining booms it shrank to a half-dead village, and the name shrank, also, until the point of the old joke was almost lost. Reata rode through that town with no one paying the slightest heed to the down-headed rider who slouched in the saddle on the old, down-headed mare, with the little ragged mongrel dog trotting just ahead of the reaching hoofs of the horse.

Beyond the town, beyond the railroad, he found the creek which still wore the name of Great Horn Spoon, a little trickle of water that wound among the pebbles and boulders of the dry bed. And here, in a semicircle of meadow hedged in by a great thickness of shrubbery, he found the gypsy camp. There was a string of wagons which served as shelter, also, because canvas covers were stretched over them so that they looked somewhat like the old prairie schooners. Half-starved mules and horses grazed the grass—they were starved by years rather than by the lack of fodder. It seemed to Reata that there was not ten dollars' worth of horseflesh in the lot. And mixed with these wretched creatures there was a liberal sprinkling of little velvet-coated, deer-eyed mustangs. One could trust the gypsies to pick out the best of the horses wherever they were to be found.

Would they recognize the qualities of Sue? he wondered.

The gypsies lolled about under the shade. In the center of the meadow smoked a fire over which hung several pots attended by one bulky female who wore a man's sombrero and smoked a cigar. On all the others, men and women and children, there was always some slash of color, one single, bright note, at least. Only this heavy creature showed not the least decoration.

Reata noticed these things as he came through the shrubbery by a well-trodden gap and rode the mare at a

47

walk across the green, with Rags trotting a little in advance.

Instantly a dozen savage mongrels rushed out. Rags had learned much during that two-day journey, however, and now he turned, leaped up onto the foot of his master, and so gained a place of refuge on the withers of Sue. Into the midst of the yelping dogs, Reata dismounted without taking the least heed of them.

It was a pleasant place, this green meadow. At one side it opened back in a long, green strip down the bank of the creek. Some goats were grazing there.

But the pleasure might soon be spoiled, he observed.

For as he appeared, all the chattering of the ragged children ended suddenly, as though at a signal, and all the women arose, and all the swarthy-faced men stepped out and shifted quickly into various places so that they ringed in Reata.

He could not escape now if he wanted to.

The dogs backed away and lost interest in a man who was not even afraid of them; that permitted Reata to walk on toward the cook, who presided over the black pots. He could ask of her the name of the head of the tribe.

She had the face of an Indian squaw—or an Indian chief. It was a massive pyramid, built up from great jaws, across a huge nose and mighty cheekbones, to a rapidly receding forehead. The cigar she carried in a corner of her immense mouth. The ashes from it, unheeded, had fallen across her man's coat and down onto her short, wide skirt. The moment that Reata had sniffed the fragrance of that cigar he changed his mind and his question.

"Madame," he said, "I'm looking for a place. I think I've found it here. Will you take me on in the gang?"

She looked him over without the slightest interest.

"Go talk to the men," said she. "I'm only the cook."

He did not hesitate. Much might depend upon his accuracy in this first guess of his.

"If you're only the cook," said he, "I'll be only the roustabout. I don't want to come any nearer to the head of this tribe than you are, Ma'am."

"There's one," said the woman, staring at him in some surprise, "there's one so dog-gone much higher than me as I'm higher'n a grasshopper."

He had seen the glint of a wedding ring, a big, golden ring, on her hand.

"Aye," said Reata, "but he's dead."

At this the immobile face froze into astonishment.

"Who are you?" she asked suddenly, ominously.

Her head jerked back. He became aware that men were approaching him stealthily from the rear. And perhaps he was close to his last glimpse of the blue and the white of the great mountains which soared into the sky all around him. They had him totally in their hands.

"Who are you?" she demanded.

"I'm a lazy man," said he.

"Who told you—about *him?*" she asked with a heavy emphasis.

"Nobody," said Reata.

Her face blackened at once.

"Nobody," he repeated.

"Hi! Nobody, eh? And nobody told you that I was Queen Maggie, neither, I suppose?"

"Nobody told me," he replied.

"I think you're a spy!" exclaimed Queen Maggie. "But you're a fool, too. And there ain't no place for fools around here. You tell me what made you think that I was the head of things around this camp!"

"The smell of your cigar," said Reata.

"How come? What you talking about?" she asked.

"You wouldn't be smoking Havanas," said Reata, "in any gypsy band in the world outside of your own band. Some man would be on deck to give you a beating for daring to put your teeth in one."

She stared heavily at Reata, her eyes opening little by little.

"Who told you, though," she demanded, her anger and her doubt returning in a flood, "that there was somebody bigger than me—that he was dead?"

"There's a ring on your hand, and you're wearing not a slash of color. You wouldn't be gay with him underground."

"Underground, you fool?" said the woman. "He's in the air and all around me. The fire that burned him took him into the air, and I ask you why he ain't in every wind that touches my face?"

"I care what I eat and drink, and where I sleep," said Reata calmly. "I don't care what you believe."

This moment of high insolence he chose even while he felt with quivering nerves that men were softly closing in

49

on him at either shoulder and at his back. But he kept himself smiling a little as he looked into her angry eyes.

Her lips parted. The angry shout did not issue from between them, however.

"You ain't a fool," she said. "And maybe you ain't a spy. And maybe you're a part of a man. It's a long time since I seen one. Now, you tell me what you'd do with this here band of mine?"

"Sleep in the day, gamble at night, drink when I please," said he. "I'm tired of working, and I'm tired of jail."

She grinned. "Well," she said, "you'd get all of this for nothing?"

"I'll do tricks when you give shows."

"How do you know we give shows? Ever see one?"

"I never saw one of your shows. But you have horse tricks, and I'll do rope tricks such as you've never seen."

"Horse tricks? What do you mean?" she asked.

"Why, when you come to a new place you put on your show—you have card tricks and fortunetelling, and then you have bareback riding to bring down the house at the end. Isn't that right?"

"And you never seen one of our shows?" she asked him. "You never seen one, and still you know these here things?"

Again he felt, like weights upon the spirit, the presence of the men at his back.

He said: "Every lot of loafing gypsies can tell fortunes and do card tricks. And I see where you've been galloping the horses for the bareback riding."

He pointed to a circular track, so well worn into the turf that in many places the grass had quite disappeared.

"That might be a ring for breaking horses," said Queen Maggie.

"Gypsies never break horses that way," said Reata. "They live with 'em. And the horse dies or learns. That's the way it goes."

She stood quite immobile for a long moment. Then she suddenly asked: "What kind of tricks do you do, eh?"

"Rope tricks," said Reata.

"What's your name?"

"Reata."

She scowled again.

"Fetch me a chunk of that wood for the fire, and then show me one of your tricks, will you?" she demanded.

The rope came out of his pocket. A flying coil of it caught the end of a heavy chunk of wood and jerked it to the feet of Queen Maggie.

She looked down at the wood, at the rope that had slunk back like a snake into the hand and then into the pocket of Reata, and last she stared at Reata himself.

"That's something," she said. "Anything else?"

"Like this," said Reata, and, producing the rope again, he swung its slithering length suddenly around his head so that it flew straight out in a whistling line.

There were three or four loud yells of pain and rage as the rope flicked like a whiplash across the faces of the unseen men. Then snarling voices ran in at him. He did not turn.

"Do you like that trick?" asked Reata, smiling.

She flung up one grimy hand, big as the paw of a man, and shouted out three or four words in a harsh tongue, a language which Reata had never heard before, and not a hand touched him. He heard the breathing of those angry men almost on the back of his neck. But then he felt, rather than heard, their withdrawal.

The woman spoke again. An angry muttering answered her command, but the sounds withdrew.

She smiled at Reata her horrible smile.

"They'll hate you now," she said. "So will all the other men in the tribe. They'll hate you because you have a white skin, because you've been able to talk to me, and because you've put the whip on some of 'em. All of Romany bleeds when one gypsy loses a drop of blood."

"Well," said Reata, "Queen Maggie is worth all the men. If I couldn't talk to you, I wouldn't want to be here, easy life or none. And as soon as I could talk to you, the rest of 'em would hate me, anyway."

"You can stay if you please," she said. Her eyes looked him over with a partially amused and a partially cold calculation. "But I'll tell you this: If you hope to live with us, you'll have to have a skin tough enough to turn the point of a sharp knife."

"I've seen your men," said Reata calmly, "and I don't think that their knives are made of good steel. I'll stay, Maggie."

"Get out of my way, then," she answered him. "I'm busy here. If you had half an eye, you could see that."

"Where's my place to sleep?" he asked.

"Any place you can find—and keep!" said Queen Maggie, turning her back on him.

He had taken from Pop Dickerman a thin roll of a blanket and a tarpaulin for bedding. Now, as he unsaddled the mare and let her graze unhobbled—for he knew that she would not stray—he threw the bedroll over his shoulder and walked around the semicircle of the wagons with Rags jogging before him.

It seemed as though the men of Romany understood exactly what was in his mind—perhaps the bedding itself was a sufficient hint—and everywhere he went he found a man at the head and at the tailboard of every wagon. They folded their arms, and when he asked them if there was room in each wagon for another sleeper, they gave him for answer an utter silence.

That meant fighting.

As he realized how certainly he would have to battle his way, he sighed a little. There was little pleasure for him in the thought of the fighting—his hands and his reata against the knives, perhaps the guns, of the gypsies.

He went back to the fire.

"Maggie," he said, "will they use guns on me—or only knives?"

"Go find out. Don't ask me, like a sneaking fool!" said Queen Maggie, stirring some pungent seasoning into the contents of the largest of the pots.

Reata stood back and looked around him at the thin blue of the sky, the deep blue of the mountains, the shining green of the brush. He sighed again, and then picked out his man.

There was that strange something in Reata which made him inevitably select the largest of the crowd and the most ferocious in appearance. This fellow had a pair of bristling mustaches that made his face look like that of a cat—a huge, six-foot-three cat, with leonine jaws and a lion's power, and a lion's triple wrinkle in the center of his forehead.

He wore a shirt of red silk, a yellow sash around his hips, and a sort of turban of blue silk twisted upon his head, while great green brilliants hung down from his ears.

This was the man that Reata chose and approached.

CHAPTER 10

The big fellow was stunned when Reata stepped up to him and simply said: "Walk into the brush with me, you big, cat-faced brute, and I'll show you reasons why I'm to have a place in this wagon of yours."

Then he turned on his heel and went quickly away into the shrubbery, which closed in rustling waves behind him.

From the rear he heard a yell of rage. That insult had been so great, so effective, so unexpected, that the gypsy had needed a moment or two to allow it to soak into his inner understanding. Now he came with a roar which extreme rage made not deep, but shrill. Reata, turning in a ten-foot clearing, stood like a statue while that monster rushed out at him with extended hands.

Reata ducked those formidable hands, and since there had been a knife in one of them, he dropped the loop of his rope over the bulk as it rushed past him. The flashing arc which the knife had struck through the air still lived like a solid bit of burnished steel before the eyes of Reata. He jerked on the rope as the gypsy turned, and bound those arms helplessly against the ribs of the giant. He sent a swift, wriggling shower of loops through the air and bound his man hand and foot.

Utter despair, utter terror, utter rage convulsed the face of the gypsy, but the rage was greater than the fear. He uttered not a single plea as Reata snatched the knife from the nerveless hand and raised it. But Reata had never intended to do more than break the spirit of the man. Now, shrugging his shoulders, he tossed the knife on the ground, and with two or three swift gestures made his captive free. Through the brush, an instant later, burst a tide of half a dozen of the tribe. The big fellow, catching his knife from the ground, leaped, not at Reata, but at these newcomers, and his howl of rage sent them scattering.

They fled away through the brush, and the man with the knife turned slowly about to face Reata again. He was

53

purple with extreme passion. His face was swollen, as though strangling hands were laid about his throat. And these checked and raging forces inside him made his great body waver a little continually from side to side.

At last he put up the knife with a brief gesture.

Reata waved a hand.

"Nobody needs to know," he said. "I never talk—about friends. Make a place in your wagon for me and I'll give you the bedroll to put in the spot."

That was what happened.

There was no further speech from the gypsy. He merely stood for a long moment, re-collecting himself, calming himself, seeming to realize that his disgrace might still be covered from the eyes of men. Then, taking breath, he put back his head and burst into a powerful, full-throated song. With that music he marched back into the clearing. With that song on his lips he climbed into his wagon—the largest of them all—and presently was seen to be flinging blankets, a saddle, a bridle, clothes, boots, in a shower upon the grass.

A slender youth came running, dancing, yelling with rage, picking up one piece of his goods only to have to dodge another bit of his worldly wealth. At last passion got the better of his discretion. He leaped into the wagon, and for a reward he received a driving blow of the fist that catapulted him out and laid him breathless and flat on his back on the green.

Above him stood the giant, laughing. The entire tribe took up the jest.

At last, pale, gasping, but with his wits about him once more, the youth regained his feet and came slowly up to Reata.

"You buy *him* with a little money; you will have to pay *me* with your blood!" he said, and went away, limping.

That was how Reata "bought" a place in the tribe.

He had hardly installed his bedding roll before Queen Maggie shouted out orders from the central fire. Reata went out, and in the golden light of the late afternoon saw the gypsies rehearse their "show." Altogether, it was quite a performance, and Reata could not help counting the dollars that such entertaining must win out of Western wallets when the tribe moved on to a new town.

There was a little orchestra of three violins and a flute, a drum, and a strange horn which kept up a rapid, gay music throughout. To it, in the opening, an old man with flowing white hair and a glossy black beard danced like a Cossack, leaping, spinning, dropping to his heels and shooting his legs out before him in rapid alternation. For all his age, he seemed to be muscled with watch springs that would not wear out.

He finished and walked off the center of the grass, hardly panting from his exercise. And not a single ripple of applause followed him. Only Queen Maggie shouted some harsh words at him.

She sat in a canvas chair beside her cookery, and, with a fresh cigar stuck in a corner of her mouth, and a long iron spoon in her hand like a scepter, she ruled over the performance and was chief critic. Now and then Reata could understand the remarks of the people around him. And never once did they protest against a judgment of their queen, whom nothing seemed to please.

After the old dancer, out came two gypsy girls and two youths, limber as willow wands, with feet as light as the wind, and went whirling and bounding through another dance that made the little children laugh with delight.

The cat-faced man was next, now stripped to the waist, and showing a most Herculean torso. He did feats of weight lifting, and wound up by heaving the rigid bodies of four strong men into the air and slowly whirling them above his head. That any human could manage more than six hundred pounds of weight in this manner seemed to Reata a miracle, but the bulging, straining body of the cat-faced man gave explanation for the miracle.

The show had been brisk, but it had been short when the final number was brought on. First came a call of "Anton! Anton!" from Queen Maggie, and out from the shrubbery, as though from the wings of a great stage, dashed a fellow on a beautiful chestnut stallion, a flashing wizard of a horse with silk knotted into his mane and tail so that he fluttered and streamed with color. On his back sat as fine a picture of youth as Reata had ever seen.

The tribe had picked up circus tights in the course of its travels, and Anton wore them—blue, with a golden fluffing around his hips. His black hair flew behind his head. He laughed as he rode, not a stage laugh for the sake of an audience, but the mirth of one who is lost in the happiness of his work. He rode into the very soul of the music that now broke out into a wilder and more triumphant strain, and from all those indifferent gypsies came a murmur of profound pleasure. They were seeing the hope of their tribe, the idealization of it, as it were.

Anton, leaping from the stirrups, braced his feet before and behind the saddle, and, his body swaying sharply in to keep its weight against the racing circles that the stallion was drawing, snatched a heavy saber out of a sheath that hung by the saddle and gallantly slashed the air to either side of him.

He dropped into the saddle again. He picked handkerchiefs from the ground. He swung himself under the neck of his horse and came up on the other side. And he ended—while the horse went at a much slower gallop, to be sure—by standing on one leg and throwing the saber into the air and catching it again as it fell. But at the third trial of this the saber missed his hand and stuck in the sod.

The voice of Queen Maggie rose stridently in criticism, and she waved the iron spoon to send Anton away.

"Miriam!" she called.

No one appeared for a moment. Then a red-bay mare was led out, bare-backed, without reins, and sent off cantering on the beaten track that circled around the grass. Without varying the easy roll of her gallop, the mare stuck steadfastly to the trail which had been formed, as though an even fence contained it.

"Miriam! Miriam!" screeched Queen Maggie.

She added a torrent of angry words in the gypsy jargon. But it was not for a long moment, and after heads had begun to turn and bright eyes peer, while a hush fell over the tribe, that the girl came out. And, as she appeared, a universal cry of delight burst forth.

Reata himself started forward a step or two from the tree against which he was leaning.

CHAPTER 11

She had on a circus rider's costume, like Anton. She was all in pink and blue, with a fluff of skirts and soft slippers with lacings over the ankles. She did not mince like a girl, but she stepped like a boy, and Reata could imagine the muscle under the smoothness of her. She was not quite like the others. She was more finely made. Her hair was as dark, but her skin had been bronzed, not sun-blackened like the rest. She walked with one hand on her hip, slowly, with a vast insolence in her posture. When Queen Maggie barked a fierce rebuke at her, she dismissed the criticism with a careless gesture of the whip she carried. And as she walked into the circle marked out by the galloping of the bay mare, she was accompanied in every step by the approving murmur of the crowd.

Now, pausing, she watched the mare around the circle and yawned without attempting to cover the flash of her teeth. After that she went forward—one could hardly call it running—and leaped at the mare. The good bay rocked steadily along; the flying slippers patted against her shoulders, slipped on the smooth barrel, and then clung to the back of the horse.

Slanting with the slant of the mare as the bay made the circle, the girl feathered her weight on her toes and let the wind of the gallop blow her. Her sullen indifference was gone. She was smiling like a child.

That was the picture which remained in the mind of Reata afterward. He kept hearing the sweep of the jolly music and seeing the sway of the horse and the flash of the girl. The other things she did were not important to him. She was as much at home on the back of that pretty mare as though she were on a broad dancing floor, and dance she did in good rhythm with the music, and constantly seeming about to sway from her balance as she made the whirling steps, but never coming to a misadventure.

The gypsies followed this performance with greedy eyes and laughing lips, and the children fairly danced with joy, so that when the riding ended, they flooded out and swept around and around her like a flutter of leaves in a wind. But chiefly Anton greeted her, and took her hand, and they went off together, laughing at each other over their shoulders.

Queen Maggie, in the meantime, had remained silent throughout the latter part of the performance, merely wagging the long iron spoon from side to side in time with the music.

Reata lay under a tree and tried to think about Harry Quinn and the task of liberating him. There was no Harry Quinn in sight, but, of course, a dozen men could be hidden in those capacious wagons. But he could not think of Quinn. The gypsy show had ended, and the music was still. The men were gambling on blankets, or gossiping under the trees. The women were helping now with the last stages of the cookery, and Reata saw one of them get a resounding clip over the head from the iron spoon of Queen Maggie, which was immediately afterward plunged into one of the big iron pots.

But Reata merely smiled.

He looked up through the entangled green branches above him at the blue of the sky in which the sunset color was beginning, and it seemed to him that there was nothing in the world more delightful than to live as these rascals did, without a thought or a care.

Someone approached; suddenly feet stumbled over him. And there stood Anton, the rider, even gayer in his ordinary clothes than in his riding costume, raving and raging down at him. Why did he stretch himself like a log on the ground and leave no space for men to walk?

Reata sat up slowly, smiling a little. He saw an eager group of the gypsies watching. Even in the faces of the children there was a world of malice. And off to the side, contemptuous, but a little amused, stood Miriam. She was not nearly so gay in her dress as Anton. A red scarf twisted about her hips was all that she had to distinguish herself. But she did not need color. There was something about her that drew Reata with its difference; he wanted to get closer to see what the strangeness was.

Then he said to Anton: "You want trouble, Anton. Is that it?"

"All the trouble you could give me," said Anton, "would not make a taste on the back of my tongue!"

The gypsies laughed.

"You want to fight," said Reata. "But I don't like to fight."

"Hi!" cried a gypsy voice, and there was a sneering babble at once.

Miriam turned her back and strolled away from the shameful scene of that admission.

"I don't like to fight," said Reata, "but if you want to send me away from the camp, I'll ride my mare, over there, against your stallion. If you beat me, I go away."

"*If* I beat you?" said Anton. "I'm going to ride the chestnut all the way around you! And after you're beaten, maybe I'll follow you a way from the camp!"

Rags, sitting up on his master's knees, growled softly. But the gypsies kept on laughing. They were still rollicking in mirth as they watched Reata saddle Sue, and as he rubbed the velvet of her nose and she snuggled her head sleepily against him. As he mounted, Reata saw Anton already in the saddle on the chestnut, and drawing through his fingers, with a significant gesture, a long-lashed black snake. No doubt Anton did not expect to use that whip on the stallion.

Reata was shown the course. They would ride down the green at the bank of the stream, and so they would come to the white rock that projected above the grass. Afterward they would turn and swing back to the camp, and the first man across the line which Queen Maggie was drawing with her heel would be the winner.

To the queen Reata gave Rags.

"Keep him till I get back," said Reata. "He won't bite."

"He ought to bite his master for being a fool," said Maggie. "Go ride your race and get your whipping—and tell me afterward how much money you used to buy Sam."

Sam was the cat-faced strong man, of course.

"You may see in the race," said Reata, "how much money I spent on Sam!"

He laughed in his turn, very cheerfully. Then he brought Sue to the mark. Sam, the strong man, stood to one side, glowering at Reata, the revolver raised from which he would fire the starting shot. But Anton drew the lash of the black snake through his fingers once more, significantly, smiling askance at the stranger.

"Give him the gun!" shouted Queen Maggie suddenly. "And if he loses, the whole tribe can put the whip on him till he has something to remember us by!"

They gave a short, shrill yell at that. And then the gun barked.

The stallion knew what that gunshot meant as well as any man could do. He went off his mark like a trained sprinter and opened up lengths on Sue in no time. He was away so fast and she so slowly that the triumphant yells of the gypsies turned into a noisy mockery of the stranger. But by that time Sue was running at her top.

Even in a race there was a sort of mildness in her. Her pull on the bit was just enough to balance her stride a trifle; she was as much in hand at full speed as at a dog-trot! And yet she went like the wind. Those whipcord muscles which were inlaid endlong and athwart her body were showing their power now. The fine stallion began to appear like a hobby-horse, bobbing up and down on one spot, as that queer-looking thoroughbred mare swept up on him and caught him at the white rock.

The stallion whirled around the marker like a dodging dog. But Sue had her head opposite the saddle girth of Anton in half a dozen jumps.

It was too much for Anton. His amazement was so great that something like fear widened his eyes as he looked back at the ugly, reaching head of Sue. Then, deliberately, he struck her twice across the face with his whip!

And she did not falter!

Her ears did not even go back, in spite of that torment, but before a third stroke could fall, her head was in front of the stallion's.

Anton, quite mad with incredulous rage, raised his black snake to slash at Reata. That hand never fell. For the swift noose of the rope snared Anton and jerked him forward. He tried to save himself. He dropped his whip and jerked out a knife, but as the mare drew ahead, the stallion swerved to the side, and one more jerk on the lariat pitched Anton from the saddle.

He showed that he was a fine gymnast and athlete even then, for he landed on his running feet to break the shock of the fall. Yet, of course, he could not maintain that racing speed for an instant. His knees buckled, and, skidding on his back across the grass, with his knife flown away and the lariat snugly about him under the pits of his arms, he was brought swiftly toward the finish.

What a riot of noise there was at the finish line, beside which Queen Maggie stood with her iron scepter, puffing furiously on her long cigar! It seemed to Reata like the screeching of tortured cats as he dragged Anton across the heel mark on the grass, and then, freeing the noose of the lariat from the victim, dismounted.

The girl, Miriam, was the first to Anton, babbling shrilly, but when she dragged him to his feet, it was plain that it was not about his welfare that she was concerned—it was her demand that he should revenge himself for this disgrace.

Poor Anton could barely stagger, however. He had been bumped till his head was ringing and the breath had been crushed out of his lungs.

When she saw that, Miriam stopped her appeal. She simply snatched a knife from the belt of the nearest of the gypsies and went at Reata silently and with the speed of a hunting cat. He stood laughing to meet her. Not with the noose, but with a flying loop of the lariat, he caught both hands and jammed them helplessly together.

She tried to draw back then, but a strong pull on the rope dragged her straight up to him until the flat of the useless knife which was still in her grip was pressed against his chest. He saw now what it was that made her so very different from the others. It was her eyes, for they were a deep, dark blue, quite free from the night that darkened in the eyes of her fellows.

Reata kissed the lips that were snarling at him. Then he stepped back and let her go.

He saw her stamp. He saw her throw up her hands. She ran to one of the gypsy men after the other and caught them by the hands and tried to drag them forward into the fight in her behalf. But not one of them could be budged, and when she saw that, she threw her hands over her head again and fled into the brush, with a scream trailing like fire behind her.

CHAPTER 12

Sam, the giant, had sat at the right hand of Queen Maggie until that supper, which was eaten in a big circle around the fire. But on this night the queen had on her right the stranger. And she actually permitted him to help himself immediately after her majesty's plate had been filled. When she had eaten her fill, poured down a quart or more of scalding coffee, and lighted a fresh cigar, she drew back a little from the circle and made Reata sit down beside her.

She said at once: "Why did you come out here, Reata? You're too smart and too white to want to spend the rest of your life as a gypsy."

"I didn't come here to spend my life. I came here to have some fun," said Reata.

"Are you havin' it?" asked Queen Maggie.

"I've had a lot to do since I arrived," said he. "It's not quite dark yet, and the afternoon's been pretty well filled."

He stroked Rags, who lay between his feet, keeping his eyes constantly on the face of the huge woman.

"The afternoon's been pretty well filled," agreed Queen Maggie. "But the night may be a lot fuller."

"You mean Anton may help to fill it?" asked Reata.

"Why shouldn't he?" said Maggie. "Today he was the best rider and the best moneymaker in the tribe. The silver used to come out and shine like rain when the folks saw Anton prance around on his hoss. He had the best hoss, the best girl. Now his hoss has gone and got beaten, and he's been dragged like a calf on the ground with everybody to stand by and look on. That's the end of Anton. He's got to kill you, Reata, or he'll never be able to hold up his head again. You can't blame him for that?"

"No," said Reata readily enough. "I understand what's in his head, burning him up. But that won't keep me from sleeping tonight."

"You're a fool, then," said Maggie.

"No, I'll be guarded," he answered.

"By what?"

"Rags," he said, and pointed to the dog.

At this she leaned a little closer, so that she could make out his face more distinctly in the dim flicker of the firelight.

"I guess you mean it," said Maggie.

She added: "There's Miriam, too. She's not ended. She'll make all equal with you yet. It's the first time there's been a hand laid on her since she joined."

"How long ago did she join?" asked Reata.

"Too long ago to remember," said Queen Maggie, grinning.

The blood of Reata went suddenly cold. They had kidnaped her, then? He saw the picture of the child and the dark, reaching hands. But he said nothing.

"She was always a good moneymaker," said the queen. "She could only toddle, but she could toddle a dance. And folks liked to see a gypsy gal with blue eyes." She laughed broodingly and went on: "Then she grew up. And she's always made money. She and Anton, they mostly keep the tribe. And now they both want your blood. Why don't you leave, Reata?"

He thought of Harry Quinn. Tomorrow would be the last day of his life unless something were contrived in the meantime.

"I'm staying a few days to see how the life goes," he answered. "Miriam belongs to Anton, does she?"

"She belongs to herself," said Queen Maggie, "but she'd be married to Anton before long, I guess. Since you came and shamed him, I dunno. A gal like Miriam, she's gotta have the best. There's more pride in her, Reata, than in the whole rest of the tribe. Anton wouldn't come out to eat tonight because there was shame in him. She wouldn't come out for the same reason. Anton is settin' and gloomin' in the dark, but the gal is rollin' around in the dark, bitin' the ground and beatin' her head, and yearnin' for the taste of the blood in your heart. I know her pretty good. Hi! I know her! She's the one and the only one that I've never dared to put a hand on. But you—Reata, get out of the camp tonight. I'll see that you ain't follered."

"There may be luck for me here," he insisted. "Why not?"

"Luck for you?" she muttered. "Well, we'll take a look and see."

She pulled from her pocket a pack of cards and shuffled them, then dealt out rapid hands, which she picked up, glanced at, restored to the pack, and dealt again and again. A gloom came over her, and her face darkened. At last she jammed the cards back into her pocket.

"The cards say that there's luck for you in the camp— and bad luck for the rest of us!" she declared. "Luck for you and bad luck for us—and how could that be?"

"We'll be able to see when the time comes," said Reata.

"I ought to march you out of the camp," said Queen Maggie, "but dog-gone me if I got the heart. There's a part of a man about you, and I ain't seen a man since I started to wear black. But there's meanness in the air. And—hi, here it comes! Here comes Miriam with a flower in her hair, and a smile on her face, and a good hot bit of hell in her heart, I can tell you. I could easily warm my hands at the fire inside of her even from clear over here!"

Miriam, in fact, walked around the fire, went to the simmering pots where the stew which chiefly fed the camp was never cold, and helped herself to a great, heaping spoonful on a tin plate. She cut off a chunk of bread, poured a tin cup of coffee, and then, with her hands full, came straight to Reata and sat down at his feet.

Little Rags stood up and snarled at her. She put out her hand and offered a morsel of meat. Rags growled at the offer, trembling with angry suspicion. She coaxed him in a soft voice, and Rags cautiously tasted the gift. Then he sat down, and with his pricked ears made an attentive guard and barrier between his master and the girl.

She had not spoken except to the dog. She sat cross-legged and ate heartily, but not with the noisy, offensive, gluttonous manners of the tribe. She was as natural as a cat; she was as dainty, also. As she ate, she lifted her eyes continually to the face of Reata. She did not smile, but there was a brightness better than smiling.

"Now," said Queen Maggie, "she's putting out her hand on you. Don't be a fool, Reata. Be scary as a dog with a scratched nose when you're around a cat like her. She hunts wild and she hunts tame, and there ain't a minute when she ain't dangerous."

Reata said nothing.

The girl said nothing, but lifted her head and looked

long and steadily at him, as though asking him if he could believe such a thing.

"Well, you fool?" asked Maggie. "Have you got it?"

Reata still said nothing. His blood was working with a dizzy sweetness. Queen Maggie caught him suddenly by the hair of the head and leaned and stared closely into his face after she had jerked his head back.

"Bah!" she said, her wide lips snarling around the cigar. "You've got it already. They'll pull your head back like this to cut your throat before morning. And I hope they do. There's no fool better'n a dead fool!"

With that she immediately stood up and strode away with the swaying gait of a horseman.

The gypsy circle was breaking up. As they went off, they stole glances, almost as though in fear, at Reata and the girl. She had finished eating. She put the plate and the empty cup aside and stroked the head of Rags. But the little dog would not relent. He remained tense with watchfulness.

The moments went on until Reata was aware of the slow drifting of the stars to the west, and the universal sweep of the lighted universe seemed to be imparting movement to his own soul which carried the girl with him. She was perfectly silent. She was not staring at him, but simply watching. Now and then her head canted a bit to one side or the other, as though she saw him then from a new angle.

She stood up and held out her hand. There was only a red eye of light from the last embers of the fire, but that glow was enough to suffuse the face of Miriam slightly, and again he saw, or thought he saw, the blue of her eyes. So he rose in turn and took her hand. It was cool, gentle, but he felt the strength of it submitting to the clasp of his fingers.

She did not seem to guide him. It was as though a common volition led them forward, with little Rags at their heels.

They crossed the meadow. They walked down the bank of the stream, far along it where the green narrowed to a path with the shadows of the shrubbery rising up on either side of it. Now and again, off to the side, he saw the faces of the stars in patches of still water. Insects hummed faintly near them. And Reata moved through a dream of happiness with that quiet hand still in his.

He almost stumbled when Rags bolted suddenly between his moving feet and darted into a bush with a sharp snarling. A man's voice gasped. A shadow rose beyond the bush, and the girl's hand was gone from the hand of Reata as she leaped instantly to the side.

The treason went through him like the cruel pain of a knife. But his nerves were fitted for electric reactions, and his body moved on springs. So, as the girl sprang aside, he sprang, also, but not to the side, for he had seen the gleam of the gun in the hand of that rising shadow. And now there were two shadows—another looming beyond the first, armed, also. Low, as into water, Reata dived through the bush. A gun boomed just above his head. Then his shoulders struck hard against knees that buckled, and the weight of the first man crashed down on him.

That burden did not matter. It was the second man that counted, as he loomed big and leaning, probing into the dark with his gun to find the right target.

Reata writhed snakelike from under the first gypsy, and caught the barrel of the probing gun in his hand. The revolver spat fire twice, the bullets thudding into the ground, and as the fellow jerked back, he merely pulled Reata to his feet.

In the background, the girl was calling out in the gypsy jargon words which Reata could not understand. He was leaping in, pulling himself strongly by the gun. He tried for the face, but not with his fist. A futile and a foolish weapon is a fist, except when there is sufficient light to give fine direction to the blows. But he jammed the point of his elbow into the face of the big man.

He heard a gasp. The revolver came free in his fingers. Incredible hands grasped him and crushed him. At the first touch of them he knew that it was Sam, the cat-faced Hercules of the tribe.

And hastily, half blindly—for the grip of those hands seemed to be burning the flesh from his bones—he hammered the gun against the skull of the giant.

Yet the deadly grip of those hands did not relax. The head of Sam swayed to the side as though his neck was broken, but there was still sense in his hands, and they held Reata helpless for the stroke from behind which he felt coming as the first man gained his feet.

"Anton!" groaned Sam as the hammer stroke beat down on him.

And Reata bent his back in as he felt the knife of Anton coming.

Something stopped it. Something had checked Anton, and surely it was not the frightened yipping of Rags.

Anton was cursing, and the name of Miriam was mixed with his curses as Reata beat the gun once more on the head of Sam. The great bulk slid down before him into the dark of the ground, and Reata, turning, saw Anton fling away from the entangling grip of the girl and flee like a deer into the night.

CHAPTER 13

Rags came moaning and mourning to the feet of his master. Reata picked up the little dog whose warning had meant the difference of life and death and put him on his shoulder, and the trembling body of Rags pressed close against his face.

Reata could hear two sounds of breathing—from the hurt, stunned giant on the ground, and from the girl as she straightened her tousled clothes.

But when she spoke, she was immensely calm.

"So—the cowards!" said Miriam. "I thought it would be only Anton, but he was afraid—even with a gun, even when he could shoot you by surprise, the way a butcher would shoot a beef. Think of such a fool and a coward, and I was giving you to him so easily! Bah! He is gone. He is finished. He's as far from me as the other side of the world."

"Give me your hand," said Reata.

"What will you do? Beat me?" she asked.

"I don't know," said Reata. "Come along with me."

"Well, here's my hand," said the girl, and she walked on down the green path with Reata as quietly as though their stroll had never been interrupted.

He noticed that her other arm, away from him, was not swinging. It was held close to her side.

"Was your right arm hurt by that Anton?" he asked.

67

"No. I'm holding a knife," said the girl.

"You know about men, eh?" said Reata.

"A little," she answered.

They walked on silently. With every breath that little Rags drew, he uttered a faint snarl, for he was on the shoulder nearest to the girl. On a fallen tree trunk, Reata sat down and drew the girl down beside him.

"For that back there," he said, "you have to pay."

"Aye," she answered calmly.

"This is what you'll pay, beautiful," said Reata. "Your camp has been here for quite a time, eh?"

"Yes, too long. Already by one day too long—for me!"

"But there's been a real reason for the stop, eh? Tell me what the reason is."

"The horses are thin. You could see that," she told him. "And they had to be fattened a little."

"Ah?" said Reata.

"You see, when we go through a town, if the horses look very thin, people yell at us and call us cruel brutes."

"Gypsies are not really cruel, I guess?"

"Yes. But they're cruel gypsies, not cruel brutes. We can't help being what we are," said the girl.

"You talk better than most of your tribe," said he.

"I use two ears, and they only use one. So Maggie sends me to talk, if any of the men get drunk and into trouble. I've talked a dozen of them out of jail."

"And so the long halt at this camp is because the horses are so thin?"

"Yes, of course."

"That's a lie," said he.

There was a pause.

"Yes," she admitted, "that was a lie."

"What's the real reason you keep in this camp, then?"

"We want to go down to the big towns and try to make money. But there's been a real circus—a real one-ring circus going through the mountains, stopping at all the little villages. Queen Maggie wants us to wait here a while. Then we'll start when the people have forgotten about the circus a little."

"And that's the real reason you stay on here?"

"That's the real reason," she said.

"It's a lie," said Reata.

After a moment she murmured: "Yes, that's a lie."

"Tell me the true reason," he demanded.

"If you know when I lie, why do you want me to keep on talking?" she asked him without passion.

"Why do you lie so much?" he asked her.

"Because I like it," she answered. "I can be angry, or I can laugh, but the best is that I can cry, and that makes people believe me when I lie."

"The fact is," said Reata, "that you're camped up here because you're waiting for the ransom of a poor devil the tribe kidnaped."

He kept his touch on her hand light and sensitive, but he felt not the slightest betraying tremor.

"We haven't kidnaped anybody," she said.

"That's another lie," he told her.

"No, it's not a lie."

"All right," he answered. "I happen to know the truth. You have Harry Quinn somewhere near your camp under a guard."

"Well, if you know it, it must be true," she answered.

"Then it's a lie that you didn't kidnap him?"

"We didn't. He walked into the camp, drunk, and made trouble. That was all. If we kept him, that was his own fault, because he talked about money."

"If that money is not paid tomorrow, will Maggie have him murdered?"

"Yes, of course."

"Why do you say 'of course'?"

"Well, if she didn't keep her promises and her threats, the next time nobody would think of paying."

"How do you feel about it?" he asked her. "D'you think it's a good thing to do?"

"Why not?" she asked. "It's one way of making money."

Reata was utterly amazed.

"You kill grouse, deer, and things like that, and you eat 'em. Why do you talk?" asked the girl.

He saw that words were of no use.

"Where is Quinn?" he asked.

"An hour's walk from here."

"Where?"

"Up in the mountains—yonder." She pointed. "You see that gorge?" she explained. "There's a cave in the left side of it as you go up. There are two bushes, one on each side of the entrance, so that you can't see the hole in the rock. Harry Quinn is in there."

69

He looked up at the gorge. The mountains on each side were dim in the starlight.

"That's another of your lies, Miriam," he told her. "They wouldn't keep him so far away."

"Well," she replied, "the truth is that there's a cave under the bank of the creek a ways down. That's where they keep Harry Quinn."

"Come and show me the place."

"I have to go back. The women are talking already," she answered. "Even gypsy women talk about things, you know."

She shook her head, and the white flower trembled in her hair. He leaned over her and put his arm around her shoulder and tilted her head with the back of his hand. He kissed her.

"Ah-ha," breathed the girl. "That is quite good!"

She let her head rest on his shoulder passively, and he saw the glimmer of her eyes as they drifted casually over his face. He kissed her again. The fragrance of the flower seemed her own breathing.

"Now I can tell you the truth," she said.

"Yes, tell me the truth," said Reata.

"Well, there is a clearing back in the woods, and Harry Quinn is there."

"How many men are guarding him?"

"Only three," she said.

"Three?" he groaned.

"What are three—to you and your dog?" she asked.

"Where is the place?"

"I don't want to talk," she said. "Kiss me again."

He kissed her.

"I don't want to talk any more at all," she said. "Talking is no good."

"Then show me where the place is."

He stood up and drew her to her feet. She hung in his arms, swaying a little.

"They'll kill you if you go there. They'd have to kill you, because if they let Quinn get away, Maggie will have them strangled. They know that, both of them—both Ben and Frenchie."

"You said there were three."

"There's no use lying to you," said the girl. "There are only two. Ben and Frenchie—they have killed men before.

They'll kill you, Reata. I don't want to go. I don't want you to be killed."

"Show me where they are," said he.

"If you should be able to get him away—hi, how I would love you!" said the girl. "Ben and Frenchie are two cats. They never close their eyes. They can throw their knives and hit a line. They can shoot sparrows out of the air. Kiss me again, Reata, and tell me you'll stay here with me!"

"No," said Reata. "Show me the place."

"I'll never show it to you."

"You owe something to me," he reminded her.

"Well, here I am," said Miriam.

"I want Harry Quinn," said Reata.

"Ah, how it makes me love you when you say that!" breathed the girl. "It crushes my heart. I am happy enough to cry. Let me tell you a funny thing that happened. I opened my heart to hate you. It was a big hate, and my heart opened wide, and all at once love slipped inside, and my heart closed, and the love is in there—like whisky!"

"Show me the way to Harry Quinn," he insisted.

"Come with me, then. Keep the dog on your shoulder, because he couldn't squeeze through some of the underbrush. When it is found out that I've showed you the way, Maggie will beat me for the first time."

"Aye, but she won't strangle you," said he.

"Why should she strangle a purse of money, and that's what I am!" said the girl. "And when they beat me, I'll laugh. I shall think of you, Reata, and laugh. The burn of the whip will be nothing like the burning in my heart. Come, now. Don't even let your feet whisper. Ben and Frenchie can hear people think miles away. Are you going to kill Ben and Frenchie? Well, they have killed others. It's better for bulls to die young. Afterward they feed by themselves and get sway-backed, and their bellies are like the bellies of old cows. Put your arm around me and walk slowly. This is our last walk together, and every step of it shall stay in my mind forever."

71

CHAPTER 14

The moon came up, slanting its light obliquely through the woods, and by that light Miriam said good-by with silent gestures. She moved backward among the trees, and when she was gone, Reata turned to look once more at the scene in the clearing near which he stood.

There had been a spark of firelight, but the climbing moon drowned that eye of light and showed him Harry Quinn, with legs tied at the ankles, sitting on the ground and playing cards on a saddle blanket with a gypsy whose silken, black mustache was curled up at the tips. Moving stealthily around the edge of the clearing, generally among the trees, or leaning at a tree now and then to exchange a few words with the other pair, was the second guard. He was one of those tall men who have no more weight in their legs than has a crane. When the moon fell on his face, it was distinguished by a gigantic scar that ran down his cheek on the right side, pulling all his features in that direction so that he always seemed to be looking and talking askance.

He was Ben, as the observer soon discovered, and Frenchie was the card player with Quinn. As for Harry Quinn, he was perfectly like his picture, broad-faced, with rather a good-natured cast and plenty of brute in his expression. But he was much shorter than his big head and shoulders suggested. The short legs were bowed for greater strength and less length.

Reata, moving by inches, wormed closer and closer to this group. The game was seven-up. The shortness of the hands, in that game, invites conversation. Quinn was losing steadily. He lost his boots just as Reata got into a favorable position behind a big tree trunk, and at this Ben stepped out from the shadows and burst into a fluent torrent of the gypsy lingo.

"Hey, wait a minute, wait a minute!" called Harry Quinn. "Gimme a chance to know what you're sayin', brother. I ain't got much time to enjoy things, have I? Lemme have a chance to hear you gents yap at one another, will you?"

Frenchie laughed.

"Tell him, Ben, will you?" he demanded.

"Yeah, sure, I'll tell him," snarled Ben. "You wait till it's my turn on guard, Quinn, and then you up and gamble all your clothes away. What good are them boots to Frenchie? But they'd fit me real fine."

"That's too bad," said Quinn. "All I hope you get fitted with is a rope, Ben, you wolf!"

"Look how he likes you," said Frenchie. "He'd do everything for you, Ben, if he got a chance."

"Tomorrow *he* gets a chance, and maybe I can do something for *him*, then," said Ben. "How will Maggie have him killed?"

"So!" suggested Frenchie, pulling his forefinger suddenly across his throat.

"No, kill cattle with a tap on the head," said Ben, and moved softly away on his rounds.

Quinn was not horrified, but deeply impressed. He said: "Now you listen at that, Frenchie. That was kind of bright—what Ben said. 'Kill cattle with a tap on the bean,' he says. Well, I'm kind of a bull. I'm kind of heavy in the head and shoulders, like a bull. But you wouldn't expect a gent like Ben to have ideas like that up his sleeve."

"Ben, he can use his head a little." Frenchie yawned. "Deal, Quinn."

Quinn dealt.

"Bid," he said.

"Two," said Frenchie.

"Three," Quinn said. "Nope, I'll shoot the moon on clubs. I'm going to go the whole hog."

"What you betting?" asked Frenchie.

"I'll bet my shirt."

"It ain't worth a bet."

"My shirt and my belt," said Quinn.

"All right. Two and a half agin' that layout."

"Wait for me!" called Ben from the other side of the clearing. "I'll bet three dollars agin' that outfit, Quinn."

Frenchie leaped to his feet and turned loose the violence of his tongue. Ben leaped into the circle in an answering rage.

"Go on, boys!" called Quinn. "Pull out your knives.

73

Wouldn't I like to see you carve each other, though? Go on, Frenchie. Get at him, Ben!"

This urging quieted the gypsies at once. They glared at one another for a moment, and then Ben said: "Someday, Frenchie!"

"Aye, someday!" promised Frenchie, adding: "How I always hated your long legs!"

"Those long legs will stomp you down in the mud after I've choked you!" said Ben.

"Shut up, you," said Quinn. "You're spoilin' the game. Come back here while I shoot the moon on you, Frenchie."

Frenchie returned, and, after the draw, Quinn led. His card was immediately snapped up by Frenchie, who laughed loudly.

"There goes my jack for high," groaned Quinn. "I never have no luck in this here game—and you'd boost the bets on me, would you, when you was setting there holding an ace agin' the shooting of the moon?"

"Why shouldn't I boost the betting?" demanded Frenchie. "What I don't get, Ben'll clean you out of. You can't play cards, Quinn. You got no more head for card playing than any poor fool!"

Quinn pulled off his shirt and belt. He sat in red flannel, which he promptly rolled to the elbows. Frenchie picked up the shirt and looked it over carefully.

"You been and burned a hole in this here with a cigarette," he declared. "Here you spoiled a good shirt on me, except that it's got a lot of stains all over it."

"Those stains'll come out once it gets a good boiling," said Quinn. "You know how it is when you're out on the road. There ain't any chance to boil up, most of the time."

"The belt's all right," said Frenchie. "But why can't you walk straight? You got the heels all slanted over to the outside. How d'you expect me to walk bow-legged like you do?"

"One of my legs is worth ten of yours, you bum," answered Quinn with a good deal of heat. "Go on and play cards, or shut up and give Ben a chance."

"He can walk the beat till his time's up. I'll have you bare as the flat of my hand by that time," said Frenchie. "Deal, you dummy; deal!"

Ben stepped out four strides from the tree of Reata, and at that moment Reata made his throw. The whistle of the noose over his head made Ben shrink, but before he could wince down low enough or throw up his warding arms, the rope was tight around his throat and he was jerked to the ground with a crash.

A skillful, swift wriggle of the rope enabled Reata to set it free from the neck of the fallen man, who lay prone, turning rapidly from side to side, bubbling sounds pouring out of his throat, and his hands fumbling at his neck.

Frenchie, silently out of his place, springing up and running low-bent, gun in hand, gasped out: "What is it, Ben? Hi—a snake! A snake!"

For he heard and saw the ripple in the grass as Reata, unseen, drew the rope back into his hand. Frenchie fired twice into the grass, his eyes distending with horror. Then he screamed out with terror as a filmy line of shadow, a mere whisper in the air, darted out at him from behind the tree. He threw up one hand to ward it off, and tried to leap back. He merely succeeded in putting his weight back against that noose which jumped tight around his arms, and the first wrench pulled him flat on his face.

He was not ready to give up without a fight, though, and he was striving to struggle to his feet and regain his fallen gun when Reata ran out at him. Toward the scene came Harry Quinn, leaping like a vast, clumsy frog on his hands and his tied feet while he shouted: "Mind your back! Mind Ben! Mind Ben!"

Reata had reduced Frenchie to helplessness with two or three running loops of the rope; now he spun around in time to see that he was too late, for Ben, though half strangled by the first jerk of the rope, had managed to recover a bit of wind and had surged to his feet with a leveled gun in his hand.

Reata saw that, and then Ben was knocked flying, his legs sprawling wide apart like a jack-in-the-box. Harry Quinn had heaved himself at the tall man like a thrown log flung endlong, and had knocked Ben into a heap. In that heap the free hands of Quinn found the fallen revolver and shoved it into Ben's stomach.

"Lay still, you rat!" said Quinn. "Am I believin' my eyes? Have I got you down all at once? Lend me your knife. There—and now I got both hands and feet! Hey, partner—don't choke Frenchie. Leave me the job of doing that, brother!"

Quinn began to laugh in a hysteria of almost womanish

joy, and with every breath of laughter he jabbed the muzzle of the gun a little deeper and drew a groan from Ben.

CHAPTER 15

They made the two gypsies show them, in deadly silence, to the place where the two horses of the guards were tied, just away from the clearing in a grassy patch among the trees. Then they tied Ben and Frenchie face to face, but with the trunk of a tree between them.

"If they holler, they'll be heard, maybe. The camp ain't much more'n half a mile away, hardly," said Quinn.

"We'll gag 'em," said Reata.

"Aye, but why would you waste the time?" asked Quinn. "Leave me put a coupla ropes around their necks, and I'll hitch 'em to a hoss and give their necks such a stretchin' that they'll never be able to spit ag'in. The rats!"

The honest indignation of Quinn made Reata smile a little.

"We'll use gags. We're not murdering anyone, Harry," he said.

Quinn submitted with a groan.

"It's a waste of time, when we might use rope so good!" he declared.

But he helped in the work, and the pair were quickly gagged and left standing with their arms tied together, spanning the rough bark of the tree. After that the horses were saddled. Quinn wanted to linger a little in order to lay a quirt on the back of each of the men.

"Why make the noise and take chances?" asked Reata. "It's going to be hard enough to do my last part of this job."

"What part?" asked Quinn.

"I have to go back to the camp."

"Back to the what? Boy, you ain't nutty, are you?" asked Quinn. "I'd rather fool with rattlesnakes on the

76

ground and hornets in the air than with any more of them gypsies. Leave them be!"

"I've left a horse behind me. But she'll come to a whistle," said Reata. "Ride up to that ridge yonder, Harry, and wait for me half an hour. If I don't come, you hit the trail back to Pop Dickerman and tell him that I was—er—permanently delayed."

"No," sighed Harry Quinn. "I wish that I could leave you, kid. But dog-gone me if I ever seen a slicker job than you done with them two gypsies. Besides, the kind of a gent I am, I can't let down a partner in the middle of a mean deal. Come along and we'll go together."

However, well back from the camp, Reata left Quinn and went in with no more company than little Rags. From the edge of the tall brush, at last, he looked out on the clearing and saw the sleeping camp. From a few of the wagons came muttering sounds of voices, here and there; but the horses were grazing the grass, and in the very center, near the red, dying eye of the fire, he spotted the outline of Sue, with the slender silhouette of a girl standing beside her.

The heart of Reata swelled suddenly in the aching hollow of his throat. But already the past held Miriam.

He whistled, keying the note very low. At the second call the mare tossed her head and turned. He saw the arms of the girl restrain her for an instant. Then Miriam let the mare go, and Sue came straight as a string to the place where her rider waited.

By the mane he led Sue away. And she stepped as softly as a hunting cat, and made the brush trail almost noiselessly down her flanks. And there was not a sound, not a murmur of pursuit behind them. There was only, in the mind of Reata, the dim picture of the girl making a gesture of farewell as Sue had moved away.

He reached Harry Quinn.

"By thunder!" muttered Quinn. "You got it, eh? But what kind of a long-drawed-out dog-gone bit of rawhide is this? Hey, man, it ain't Sue, is it? It is! It's Sue! And how'd you ever get her out of Pop? How'd you ever know that she was *worth* gettin'?"

The saddle was placed on the mare, and, side by side, the two rode up the ridge, turned, and headed away for Rusty Gulch.

The night whitened around them. Said Harry Quinn: "It

was a good job that you done. And you ain't told me much about yourself except your name, Reata. And that was a name that I would 'a' guessed at myself if I'd once seen you work your rope, daubin' it on gypsies or what not!"

"There's not a whole lot to tell about myself," answered Reata. "The main thing is that you're on the loose. And that's one day's work done for Pop Dickerman."

"How many more days are you goin' to work for him?" asked Quinn curiously. "I was kind of thinkin' that the old hound had let me down, and that he'd see me rot sooner than pryin' himself loose from any hard cash on my account. But here he ponies up and sends you along, and I reckon that you're a lot better than gold. Are you with Pop Dickerman for good, like the rest of us?"

"I don't know," said Reata. "There are two more days of work for me to do. And then—well, then I'll go back and make a call on Queen Maggie, maybe!"

"Go back and call on her?" shouted Quinn. "Hey, what you mean by that, Reata? Go back and call on that old devil? Why, she'd throw you to the dogs. She'd laugh herself sick, she'd be so glad to feed you to the dogs!"

"You think so?" asked Reata thoughtfully.

"Think so? Sure, and I know so! There ain't nothing but poison in her."

"Maybe not," said Reata. "But I'll have to take the chance one day."

"Hey! But why?"

"Because she's got a claim on something that I want," said Reata. "She's got a claim on something that I've gotta have!"

It was not until they were in full sight of Rusty Gulch and saw all the windows of the town flashing in the morning sun that the heart of Reata failed him. He halted the mare suddenly and dismounted. The reins of Sue he handed to Harry Quinn.

"What's up?" asked Quinn as he took the reins.

Reata shook his head. Rags came and sat down at his feet, looking constantly up at the all-wise face of his master, on which a frown was to Rags like the sweeping of storm clouds across the heavens.

"I can't go on with you," said Reata, pointing to the town. "Now that I see the place, now that I think of Pop Dickerman a little more clearly—well, there's a smell of rats choking me, like an old attic. I can't go on. You tell Dickerman that I'm a liar, that I'm breaking my word to him, that I won't see him again. Tell him that, and give Sue back to him."

"You're going to break with Pop?" murmured Quinn breathlessly. "Yeah, but nobody breaks with him! It can't be done. If you bust with him, he'll get you, Reata. He'll smell out a way to you right through to China. You can't beat him!"

"Maybe not," said Reata. "But I'm going to try."

He rubbed the nose of Sue and stroked her neck. Rags had already turned and started back up the road.

"I'm sorry," said Harry Quinn, holding out his hand.

"You done a grand good job for me," went on Quinn, "and now lookat! Maybe the next time I see you I'll be lookin' at you down a gun! But I know how it is. You thinkin' you're thinkin' for yourself, but all it is is the curse on you from Queen Maggie. She's put the gypsy curse on you, and you've got to go back!"

Reata waved his hand and turned quickly, because he wanted to have the shining windows of Rusty Gulch out of his mind, together with all they suggested to him. He wanted to forget Harry Quinn, and perhaps a good, swinging stride up the trail would ease the longing to have the fleetness of Sue again under him.

So he turned a sharp corner of the trail and came in view of the far-distant mountains, and one jagged, white-headed peak which stood up, he knew, above the gypsy camp. Toward that goal he aimed himself grimly, and even little Rags slunk down-headed at his heels. Out of the distance behind him the good mare whinnied. It seemed to Reata like a call that summoned him back to his duty, but he put his head down and strode on. His feet went lightly and swiftly. He had a queer certainty that they would find their way blindly, because the devil was guiding them.

But after that he began to think of Miriam, and that thought started him singing up the trail.

Part Two

Part Two

CHAPTER 16

The scattered length of Rusty Gulch drew the whole heart of Harry Quinn. By the roofs of the houses he knew them. His brow puckered at the flat top of the jail, and his mouth watered when he identified the saloon. He could hear, merely through the power of the mind, the clicking of dice as they rattled and rolled, the whisper of shuffled cards, and the clinking of ice in the glass. As he looked across the town, he was biting his teeth into the fat of a good cigar and lifting one finger to tell the bartender to set them up all down the line.

There were not many elements in the heaven desired of Harry Quinn, and he could find them all in Rusty Gulch. But instead of riding straight into the arms of that paradise, he knew that it would be wisest for him to turn aside, in the outskirts of the town, to what looked like a barn from a distance, and only appeared as a dwelling when one came up close to it and saw the high wooden wall pierced by a few shuttered windows.

The gate to the yard was open, so Harry Quinn jogged his mustang inside and looked over the familiar heaps of junk which were ranged in ordered piles. It always seemed to him that Pop Dickerman's junk yard was a cemetery of the entire range.

Pop himself was now unloading a wagon in front of which stood two little down-headed skeletons of mules. He must have been out early to collect this load, the relics of some small shack among the hills, the sign that one more family had moved away.

Rubbing against the legs of Dickerman were a score of cats. A Maltese giant sat on the driver's seat and luxuriously licked a forepaw and washed his face with it. And

81

Harry Quinn thought of rats so strongly that he could almost sniff the odor out of the air.

He thought of rats, too, when he saw the long, grizzled face of Pop Dickerman, furred over with curling hair like the muzzle of an animal. Harry Quinn came up close and dismounted, calling out: "Hello, Pop. How's things?"

He began to untie the lead rope of the wiry roan mare he had brought in with him.

Pop Dickerman went straight past Harry Quinn as though his arrival were a matter not worthy of comment, as though he had not schemed day and night for the delivery of him from most imminent death. But Dickerman went by him and first greeted the mare, stroking her ewe neck with his grimy hand.

"How are you, Sue, old gal?" he asked. "How they been treatin' you, honey?"

She pricked one ear and looked at him with lazy eyes.

"And where's him that was ridin' Sue?" asked Dickerman.

"He's gone," said Harry Quinn.

"Dead?" asked Dickerman.

"He ain't dead. But he's gone. He brought me all the way along the trail until we come in sight of Rusty Gulch, and when he seen the roof of your house, he looked like he was smellin' rats under the roof of it. He hopped off Sue and throwed me the reins. He ain't dead, but he's gone for good."

"If he ain't dead, he'll come back," said Dickerman. "He's swore to me, and he's got a conscience. Maybe he thinks now that he won't come back, but a conscience is a funny thing. You dunno nothin' about it, Harry, because you never had one, but when the night starts and the world gets dark, a gent's conscience will come out with the stars. Yeah, we'll have Reata back here with us not long after dark. Here—gimme a hand unloadin' this stuff, will you?"

"I ain't hired out to handle junk," protested Harry Quinn. "I'm goin' to put up the hosses and go have a snack of sleep. I stopped sleepin' when the hangin' day got closer."

Pop Dickerman did not argue. He merely stood there with a rusty bale of plowshares in his hands and watched Quinn lead the horses away.

Afterward Quinn entered the barn. He so hated the

sight of the piles of junk on the floor of the old mow that he half squinted his eyes and hurried on to the little rooms at the end of the building. There he found the kitchen, found the five-gallon jug behind the door, helped himself to a large slug of good whisky, and then went up to a room where bunks were built in two tiers against the wall. Those bunks were heaped with disordered, secondhand blankets of all colors, but the taste of Harry Quinn was not at all fine.

"In jail again," was all he said, and, pulling off his tight boots, he lay down and rolled himself in one blanket. He stared for a moment at the window, dusted over with cobwebs, and then went to sleep.

When he wakened, it was near the end of the day. He went down and discovered Pop Dickerman cooking supper. On the oilcloth covering of the kitchen table, three places were laid out.

"Who's goin' to chow with us?" asked Harry Quinn.

"Reata. He'll be back," said Dickerman.

"Yeah? And the devil he will!" answered Quinn. "That hombre was so fed up when he just seen the roof of your barn, Pop, that he looked sick at the stomach. He couldn't come no nearer."

He went to the stove and lifted the lids from the pots. He found boiling potatoes, stewing chicken which gave out a rich mist of savor, and a great pot of coffee. Inevitable bacon simmered in another pan.

He opened the oven door; a hot breath of smoky air boiled out at him, but he saw a deep pot of baking beans, brown-black and bubbling at the top, and two wide pans of baking-powder biscuits which were just coming to the right golden brown.

"You feed a man," admitted Harry Quinn, slamming the door shut. "I gotta say that the chuck is all right here. Dog-gone my heart, though, but it must nigh kill you to part yourself from so much good grub."

"A good man has gotta have good grub," said Dickerman. And he lifted one eyebrow at Harry Quinn.

"Meaning that I ain't so good, eh?" said Quinn. "That's all right by me. But hop to it, Pop. It's sundown, and I get a regular appetite at the regular hour."

In fact, food was presently on the table, and Harry Quinn sat down to it with a capacious grin on his bulldog face. He leaned forward, and with sweeping gestures of a broad-bladed knife, conveyed quantities to his mouth.

Opposite him, at the other end of the little table, Pop Dickerman ate some stale pone he had found in the breadbox, and drank small sips of some milk that had just gone sour. He seemed half revolted, and one could not tell whether it was the taste of his own portion or the vast appetite of Quinn that disgusted him.

"This kid—this here Reata," said Quinn when his mouth was only occasionally filled, "there's something kind of clean about him, and he wouldn't stand the dirt around here!"

Said Pop Dickerman, with irritating assurance: "Conscience, it comes out with the stars. I'll get some of this food back into the stove."

He set about it as Quinn said: "Leave me another slab of them biscuits, and I'll mop up some syrup with 'em. Gimme some more coffee, too. You think Reata is goin' to come back here, do you, and keep on with you till he's got Dave Bates and Salvio both loose?"

"He'll try," said Pop Dickerman.

A shrill sound of barking came stabbing through the night, small and thin.

"There!" said Dickerman, his little eyes glistening. "There he is now, with his dog, Rags, tellin' him not to come back inside here, and Reata comin' along just the same. You'd think that a smart feller like him would have sense enough to listen to a dog, wouldn't you?"

A moment later the back door opened, and Reata stood on the threshold. The little dog, Rags, crouched whimpering at his heels.

The welcome for Reata was very effusive, Quinn calling out: "Hey, Reata—dog-gone me if I ain't glad to see you! Dog-gone me, old boy, but it's good to see your mug ag'in."

And Dickerman kept grinning and pointing to the third place at the table. "I knew that you'd be along," he declared. "Set down there and feed."

Reata pulled up his belt a notch.

"I'm not hungry," he declared.

Two or three of the cats began to stalk little Rags. He backed against the feet of his master and looked up. Reata held down his hand and caught the slender body as it jumped. Rags, with great dexterity, ran up the crooked arm of his master and perched himself on the broad shoulder.

"Not hungry?" gasped Harry Quinn. "Hey, you *gotta* be hungry when you take a look at chuck like this here. This is food, old son."

Reata pulled back the waiting third chair and sat down. It's a bad job when most of us sit down, bending our bodies, slumping our weight suddenly off the legs. But Reata sat down as a dog might sit—when it is waiting for the start of the race. When he leaned back, no one would be deceived into thinking that this was a lasting inertia. The sleeping wolf is only a second away from the naked fangs and bristling mane of full consciousness; Reata, reclining in the chair, making a cigarette with an idle twist of his fingers, made one think of the same static power. One touch of need could discharge all the danger that was in him.

"Lookat here, Reata," urged Dickerman, "I'm goin' to take it pretty hard if you don't pull up a chair and join us. These baked beans, they're prime. Ain't they, Harry?"

"Yeah, they'll grow hair on the palm of your hand," stated Quinn, grinning with much kindness at his rescuer. "How's every old thing, kid? Dog-gone me, but it's good to see you again. Pop, here, he said that you'd come along, all right. Pull up the old chair and have a shot at this here chicken stew. It's the goods!"

Reata pulled from his pocket the snaky handful of his rope, and his unthinking fingers made swift designs with it in the air.

"I'm not hungry," he insisted. "But I want to know something, Dickerman. I don't think I would have come back, but all at once I remembered that I'd finished one third of the job, and it seemed a shame not to finish the trip. Tell me the next item on the list, and I'll start again. There were three men. Well, here's Harry Quinn back with you. What's the next one?"

"Dave Bates—he hangs next month for murder," said Dickerman.

"Yeah," murmured Quinn, "and the funny thing is that he didn't do that job. Am I wrong, Pop?"

"He sure didn't do the job," answered Dickerman. "It's like this, Reata." He looked into the gray eyes and the brown face of Reata for a moment, gathering his thoughts. "It's like this. My big man—Gene Salvio—he's in a terrible jam. I send out Dave Bates to get him. Dave starts, all right. The next thing I know, Dave is bein' tried for murder. Charge is that he got drunk and killed a rancher by name of Durant. They find Durant dead, Dave asleep and drunk in his chair, and on the floor is Dave's gun with two bullets fired out of it. Looks like a good case, and they sock Dave. He hangs next month, and he's in the pen, waiting for the noose."

"The funny thing," said Harry Quinn, "is that Dave never gets drunk."

"I'm to break open the penitentiary and bring Dave Bates out with me. Is that all?" asked Reata ironically.

"No, no. I'm not such a fool," said Dickerman. "All you do is to get up there and find out who really *did* kill that rancher. You see? Hang it on the right man so clear and heavy that the law is goin' to turn poor Dave loose. That was what Quinn was ridin' north for when he snagged himself on those gypsies!"

The eyes of Dickerman burned as he stared at Quinn.

Reata stood up and threw the butt of his cigarette out the window.

"I'll start now," he said.

"Wait for the morning. Harry'll go along with you and show you the way, and tell you everything we know," suggested Dickerman.

"I'll go now," insisted Reata. Suddenly his lip curled a little. "I'd rather sleep in the open," he added.

"Yeah, and I told you," remarked Harry Quinn—"I told you that he had the smell of the rats up his nose."

"Take Sue, then, and get started," said Dickerman.

"All right," said Reata. "One more thing. What price do you put on Sue?"

Dickerman frowned.

"He'll never sell Sue," said Quinn.

"You'll sell her at a price," said Reata. Suddenly scorn welled up into his voice. "You'll sell your own hide—for a price. What do you want for Sue, Dickerman?"

The contempt of Reata made very slight impact upon Dickerman. He kept squinting his little eyes for a moment and stroking his hairy face. Then he said: "When all three of 'em are back here—Harry, and Dave, and Gene Salvio—then I'm goin' to throw in a bonus for you, Reata. I'm goin' to throw in Sue and let you have her free!"

A little glint of yellow light came into the gray eyes of Reata as he nodded.

"If you're coming with me, build your pack," Reata told Quinn. "I'm starting now."

He walked out into the open night, leaving Quinn and Dickerman to stare at one another for a long moment.

"Don't seem so dog-gone good-natured as he was on the road," said Quinn regretfully.

"Any sharp knife is goin' to give you a nick now and then," said Pop Dickerman. "But he wouldn't eat none at my table. You notice that?"

"Hey, and how could I help notice it? And him pinched in the gills, too. And he pulls up his belt when he tells you that he ain't hungry. There's a kind of a pride about Reata, all right."

"Pride's the grindstone that rubs the knife sharp," said Dickerman.

"Maybe he's steel," admitted Quinn, "but how's he goin' to cut into that big cheese up there at Boyden Lake? How's he goin' to have a chance to cut in and find out who really done the murder? There ain't a chance in a million, Pop. You oughta know that there ain't a chance in a million."

"Sure I know it," said the junkman. "It ain't an easy job, and I ain't offering low pay. Sue—if he gets out all the three of you—Sue is what he gets from me. Go on now and get your pack!"

Harry Quinn rose with a sigh. He went to the stove, picked the iron spoon out of the pot, and loaded a large heap of dripping beans into his mouth thoughtfully. He was still munching these as he left the room.

When he came downstairs again, carrying a roll over his shoulder, he said to Dickerman: "I'm takin' the big gray."

"You wanta advertise that you're a real man, do you?" Dickerman sneered. "You take the same hoss that you rode down here. It's plenty good enough for you. And it won't draw no attention."

Harry Quinn looked sullenly at his chief for a moment.

"Aw, all right, then," he said.

That was the only farewell.

CHAPTER 17

By the time, two days later, that Reata and Harry Quinn had come close to the Durant ranch, Reata knew very little more about the killing of Cleve Durant than Pop Dickerman had told him.

All that Quinn knew in addition was the testimony of Dave Bates at the trial. Bates had said that he had asked hospitality at the ranch while he was traveling through the country, and that during the evening he had taken a drink of the whisky that was offered to him after dinner. When he had drunk the stuff, he began to get very sleepy. He was about to go to bed when sleep overwhelmed him in his chair. He awakened to find the deputy sheriff shaking him by the shoulder. On the opposite side of the room lay Cleveland Durant, dead; and on the floor beside his chair was the gun of Bates, with two chambers of the revolver empty.

Quinn's comment on the story was characteristic.

"Think of the poor sucker tellin' a yarn like that!" he said. "Long as he was goin' to tell a lie, why didn't he cook up a good one? Dog-gone me, but I was surprised when I read that yarn in the paper. Dave Bates ain't a fool. He's a pretty bright hombre. But a lot of gents, when the law gets hold of 'em, it sort of freezes up their brains, and they can't think none."

"Maybe it was the truth?" suggested Reata.

Quinn stared as he answered: "You mean that Dave was doped? They couldn't dope Dave. He's a bright hombre—he's real bright, is the facts of the case."

It was a broad, flat-bottomed valley in which the Durant ranch lay. The naked hills surrounded the district with walls of cliffs. Little trails like chalk marks, and a few narrow white streaks that were roads, wound through the country and focused on the town of Boyden Lake, which got its name from the little blue patch of water beside it.

So the scene appeared to Reata from the top of the southern hills. It was a bare land, without a tree.

"It's a tough spot," said Harry Quinn as he surveyed the broad map. "Yonder—that oughta be the ranch house. We'll go down there and take a look. The word is that old Sam Durant will pay high for the right kind of a cowhand, but the right kind for him is hard to find."

They got a cross trail that swung onto a road which ran between fences of barbed wire. Harry Quinn was indignant when he saw the fences.

"Look at a free country," he said, "that's said to be free, and all the gents in it equal, and along comes a lot of bums and checks off the free range with fences. Is it free? Look for yourself. Suppose that you had to make a quick break across country, with maybe a deputy sheriff or something behind you; why, what chance would you have? You'd be jammed agin' a wire fence in no time, and they'd have you. And what kind of a life is that?"

Reata gave no answer. He had a way of keeping up his end of a conversation merely by smiling and nodding, assuming at the same time a look of such interest that the other fellow was sure to be drawn out. He had had plenty of chance to estimate Harry Quinn on the trip north, and he did not think very highly of his traveling companion. Harry was a good hand with a gun, and probably his nerve was excellent. Otherwise he was a brawler, a noise maker, and gifted with a very loose mouth.

For what important affairs could Pop Dickerman use a man of this sort except actual fighting? And why should Pop Dickerman need fighting men around him?

He asked Harry Quinn bluntly: "What did you and Bates and Gene Salvio do for Dickerman when you were all together?"

Quinn simply answered: "Hey? And what didn't we do?" And he laughed, but did not offer any more details. It had been crooked work of some sort—that was fairly apparent. Certainly Pop Dickerman was far more than a mere collector of rags and junk.

A sudden lane opened from the battered road, and at the mouth of the lane there was a board tacked across a post, and on the board, roughed in with red paint, were these words:

This sign moved Harry Quinn very much.

"A hundred bucks!" he said. "Why, dog-gone me, that had oughta raise every cow-puncher on the whole country-side! How can a sign like that keep stayin' up?"

In fact, they had hardly gone down the long lane a quarter of a mile before they saw, coming toward them, a big man on a tough little mustang. He was gripping the pommel of the saddle with both hands. His body slouched low. When he came nearer, it was seen that his clothes were badly torn, dust-covered, and that his face was decorated with a greatly swollen eye already discoloring from red to black.

Harry Quinn ventured to halt him.

"Are you from the Durant ranch?" he asked.

The big man did not stop his mustang. He allowed it to jog along as he slued himself around in the saddle and shouted: "It ain't a ranch. It's an Injun massacre. I'm goin' to come back with friends and wipe that place up. I'm goin' to take it apart! I'm goin' to—"

Here his rage overcame his vocabulary, and he could merely curse. He began to talk and wave from a distance, but his words could not be made out.

"I'd say that gent was kind of peeved," suggested Harry Quinn. "Looks like he's been in some kind of a ruction. But if that's what they want on the Durant ranch, you and me oughta get on pretty good there. Gun, or knife, or hands, I don't mind a fight—and when they bump into you, Reata, they're certainly goin' to find themselves tied!"

He laughed very cheerfully at this idea, but Reata shook his head a little. Rags, riding over the withers of Sue, the roan mare, he now put down on the stirrup leather, and Rags jumped to the ground and ran happily on ahead.

"Rags might smell out the trouble," said Reata. "And here's Sue cocking her ears. We'll see what we see."

"That Rags, now," said Harry Quinn, "you mind tellin' me what that dog-gone mongrel pup is good for?"

"He's not a worker," answered Reata, chuckling. "He's a thinker. He's like me."

They came out of the lane to the ranch house itself. There was nothing much to it. It was long and low, with an open shed between the kitchen and the rest of the house. This being close to midday, two men were idling in the shade of the house, waiting for the cook's call. One of them, tall, lean, middle-aged, grizzled, was whittling a stick. The other sat on the ground with his back against the wall of the house. He was a red-headed fellow with a fat, round, good-natured face.

"Howdy, boys," said the older man as Quinn and Reata swung down to the ground.

"Howdy," they answered. And Quinn added: "We're lookin' for the boss. We seen that sign on the board down the road."

"I'm Sam Durant," said the tall man, "and when I put the sign out there I wanted to get me a real man for the place. How about you?" He looked at Quinn.

"Aw, I can daub a rope on a cow now and then," said Quinn, "and I guess that I could stretch wire, too, if I have to."

The rancher smiled a little, as though in sympathy. And the red-headed fat fellow sat up and nodded violently.

"We got a lot of snakes and coyotes and what not around here," said Sam Durant. "How would you be with a gun?"

"Fair. Pretty fair," said Quinn, brightening.

"There's a chicken over there that we might use for supper," said Sam Durant. "Suppose you take a whack at that?"

There were a dozen or so chickens scratching holes here and there, and now Durant had indicated a speckled Plymouth Rock twenty yards away.

"We'll sure eat him, then," said Harry Quinn, and in a flash he had pulled a gun and fired from the hip. The first bullet kicked a spray of dust into that bird. As it rose into the air with a flop and a squawk, beating its wings as it jumped, the second big bullet smashed into it and through it. It was hurled along the ground, scattering feathers and blood, and lay still, without kicking. All the other chickens fled, squawking loudly.

"Hi! That was a good shot!" called the red-headed lad. "That was sure a beauty. You can do it, stranger!"

He began to laugh, rather too loudly, and walked over and picked up the dead rooster.

"Give it to the cook," directed Sam Durant. "Tell him to stew it for supper, Porky. And thanks," he added to Harry Quinn. "That was a good shot, all right. A fellow

91

who can shoot as straight as that wouldn't ever go hungry, eh? No, sir, you'd never have to look around very far before you ate. No use in tyin' you down to life on a ranch, and drudgin' all day long for the sake of three squares. I'll have to keep the place here open for a gent that ain't so sure with his Colt."

Harry Quinn, who saw that he had overshot his real mark, took in a quick breath in order to make a hot answer, but the hard, cold eye of Reata stopped him.

Sam Durant said to Reata: "Now, maybe you're the man that I'm goin' to use, but I'll have to try you first. It's a kind of a mean job, too. You see that bay gelding out there in the corral?"

He pointed out a well-made mustang in the corner of the corral, now with dropped head and a pointed rear hoof, taking a noonday nap in the sun.

"That gelding looked so dog-gone good to me," said Sam Durant, "that I bought it from Bill Chester for a hundred and fifty dollars. But after I got it over here I decided that I didn't like it, and I been meaning to return that mustang to the Chester place and get my money back. Somehow I ain't got around to it. Suppose you just saddle up that hoss and take it over to the Chesters for me. Tell 'em I'm dog-gone sorry to send the hoss back, and that I'd like to have my money."

"All right," agreed Reata. "Why shouldn't I lead him over, though, instead of riding him?"

"Well, son," said the rancher, "it's just an idea that I had—that Chester would be a lot more pleased, sort of, if you rode that hoss over there today. I think he'd be a pile more likely to take the mustang back and gimme the money that I spent."

Reata nodded. Something, of course, was in the air. But he obediently pulled the saddle and bridle off Sue, leaving her with only a lead rope, which he tied up around her neck. She would follow, unguided, even as she followed her master now to the gate of the corral.

Porky had come out of the house and stood by with a brightly cheerful smile to watch the proceedings, while Reata, leaving his saddle near the gate, took the rope which he carried from his pocket and crossed the corral. There were a dozen other horses in the big enclosure. They herded up around the big bay colt, which watched

92

impassively until Reata was near. Then, as the other horses spilled to either side, the bay flashed to the right.

He ran fast, head down, as though he knew what might be the target, but the thin, heavy line of Reata's rope shot like a bullet from his hand. A small noose opened in the head of the rope and snagged the mustang fairly and squarely. He came up gently on the rope, far too trained to risk a burn.

Moreover, he stood with perfect calm while Reata saddled him. Even when the leg of Reata swung over the saddle, the gelding stood with pricking ears, as though delighted. But at the last instant he shifted with a catlike spring to the side and let Reata drop in the dust of the corral.

CHAPTER 18

A loud, howling cry of glee came from Porky, who now sat on top of the corral fence. Reata, on one knee as he had fallen, watched the bay colt fly into a fine frenzy, racing around that corral and pitching in every style Reata could remember. A fine, free-hand improviser was the bay, from fence rowing to sunfishing, and his object was to buck that saddle off his back! In fact, the saddle presently was loosened and began to twist to the side. At this point Reata intervened with another perfect cast of his rope. The forty feet of that lithe and sinewy lariat went out like a shadowy extension of Reata's will, and at the touch of it around his neck the bay was instantly still again.

He stood with head up, and the red blaze of deviltry in his eye, the perfect picture of the untamable outlaw. From the fence boomed the loud, loon laughter of Porky, the red-headed cow-puncher. Harry Quinn was grinning by the fence, also, but the rancher remained seated on the chopping block near the kitchen door, whittling his stick, and apparently indifferent to what was happening in the corral.

The mouth of Reata jerked a little to one side as he came up to the bay. This time when he loosened the rope

93

from the neck of the horse the mustang stood as still as before, and now Reata tied the slender thong under the fetlock joint of the off foreleg, and passed it with a single half hitch over the horn of the saddle. He tightened the cinches once more and mounted. It was not the leisurely effort he had made before. This time it was the spring of a cat that clapped him on the back of the bay, and his two feet instantly slammed into the stirrups.

The mustang, at the same instant, shot up into the air. As he rose, Reata pulled up by a few inches the length of the rope that was fastened to the leg of the horse, and secured the slack with a jerk on the half hitch. The result was that the bay landed on three feet instead of four, staggered, and almost fell.

He tried to buck; he could only hobble with the right forefoot lifted. And presently he stopped and crouched a little, shuddering, unable to realize what had happened to paralyze his strength.

Reata, at this, let out the rope once more, until the gelding had four feet on the ground. The bucking started again; again it was stopped after the first flourish.

Here, deliberately, slowly, the bay put down his head and sniffed at the rope that imprisoned his foot. After that, lifting his head, he calmly submitted to the bridle, and was content to jog quietly to the corral gate!

Porky, standing up on the fence, whooped with amazement, holding up both hands in a rather feminine gesture of astonishment.

"That's a good one, kid," said Harry Quinn, opening the gate for his companion. He added in a low voice: "But where do I get in on this show?"

"You don't get in," answered Reata. "Ride down the road with me. We can talk there."

He guided the bay across to the rancher, whose head was still bowed over his work.

The gelding went on calmly and smoothly, except that there was a slight limp in his right foreleg, where the reata flapped and snapped tight with every stride, just measuring the length of that limb.

"You tell me where the Chester place is," said Reata, "and I'll take this broncho over there. But why d'you want to send him back? He looks like a right good one to me."

"You don't see anything wrong with him?" asked Sam Durant gravely.

"No. Got four good legs under him, and he's sound in wind and body. He can jump like a wild cat, and he looks as tough as rawhide."

"He's got a good eye, too," said Durant. "Now that I notice it, he's got a nice red eye. I never seen a redder. But what I don't like is the color of the rest of him. I dunno why. You take him down the road east, and turn off on the first north trail. It'll take you bang into the Chester place. Just leave the colt there, and when you come back here with the hundred and fifty bucks, you'll find some hot lunch waitin' for you."

"Thanks," said Reata. "I can see you're the sort of a boss that does everything for your cowhands. See you later, Durant."

He jogged the bay gelding down the lane, with Sue, the roan mare, following, and Rags running out in front. And every minute or two a start ran through the bay, and his whole steel spring of a body flexed and trembled a little. He was not tamed; he would never be tamed. The instant the viselike grip of the reata on his leg was relaxed, he would be at his deviltry once more. That was the comment of Harry Quinn as he rode at the side of Reata.

"He's all one grain, and it's bad all the way through," said Quinn. "But how you goin' to get a hundred and fifty bucks out of this here Chester hombre?"

"I'll know when I see him," answered Reata. "Maybe I can talk him out of it."

"And what about me in the rest of this game at the ranch?" asked Quinn.

"You lie low, off the place," said Reata. "You can come in at night, and I'll tell you what's happening. There's going to be plenty for you to do from the outside, I think. It's a queer layout, Quinn. What do you think about it?"

"The gent called Porky is a kind of a loud-mouthed half-wit," said Harry Quinn. "And this here Sam Durant is as sour as they make 'em. I wouldn't blame anybody for socking a dose of lead into him. He needs it for softening!"

"There's a lot more in the air than I can make out," said Reata. "I'll have to see this place by day and night. There's a lot you can see by night that never shows in the daylight."

"Like what?" Harry Quinn frowned.

"Ghosts and things." Reata smiled. "Here's the north

trail, and I'll follow it. You cut off wherever you please and come in after dark. I might have something more to tell you by that time."

"You know what I think, Reata?" declared Quinn. "I think there's goin' to be hell poppin' around that place before the finish."

"I think that there's hell popping now," answered Reata. "So long, Harry."

He kept the gelding at a jog. He loosened the rope so that the horse could gallop freely. And it was at a gallop that he came up to the Chester house. Here, too, the hands were in for lunch, and as Reata drew near, he saw the cook come to the kitchen door and howl through cupped hands—though the men were not five steps away: "Come and get it! Hi! Come and get it!"

The men did not troop instantly in for their food, however. They began to stare and point at the bay gelding, and at the mare which cantered softly in the rear, stretching out in a long and perfect stride that made her standing ugliness disappear. Little Rags, running at his best, fell well behind those long legs.

Reata, as he came up, decided to trust the bay for the last few strides. Therefore he shook loose the noose that bound the gelding under the fetlock and jerked the lariat up into his hand. The mustang ran on, unheeding. Perhaps for a moment he could not tell that the pressure was gone. At any rate, he allowed Reata to bring him up in fine style to a sliding halt in front of the hitch rack.

There Reata dismounted, tied the gelding to the rack, and shifted saddle and bridle onto the roan mare. The whole group of six men crowded about him.

"Hey, brother," said one, "you ain't found this bay a spooky devil, have you?"

"Me? Not a bit," said Reata. "He just takes a little handling."

"Aye," said the man, rubbing his right shoulder absently. "He takes a little handling, all right. A fifth chain is all that he needs to be handled with."

"Bill Chester here?" asked Reata.

"Yeah, he's inside the house somewhere. He'll be comin' out to lunch in a minute. Here he is now."

Bill Chester came out of the house with a mighty stride, slamming the door heavily behind him. He was not a tall man, and his legs were too long. They seemed to hitch onto the bulge of his chest and leave no space for a stomach. On this singular underpinning there was mounted such a pair of shoulders as one seldom sees in this world. He had the brute look of one who has used nothing but strength all the way through life.

He came up to the bay gelding and called out: "Is that there a saddle mark that I see on the bronc?"

"This hombre rode him over as easy as you please," said two or three men at once. "They've gone and busted him, all right. He runs right along like a dog on a lead!"

"They never busted him. Nothin' ever busted him," said Bill Chester. "Who's been lyin' to you about it, eh?"

He strode up to Reata.

"You been sayin' that you broke that gelding?" he demanded.

"I rode him over," said Reata modestly.

"You don't look to me like you could break nothing," declared Bill Chester.

"No," said Reata, smiling on him, "but sometimes I can bend things a little."

"What could you bend?" asked Chester.

"Something worthwhile," answered Reata.

"You could, could you? Well, unbend the rope that's holding that gelding to that hitch rack, and take him off of this place, will you?" He added: "What does that mossy old fool of a Durant mean by sendin' back the gelding?"

"What would you guess, partner?" asked Reata.

"Guess? I don't want to guess. It ain't any business of mine to guess," said the rancher. "Get the hoss off my place, and get him off quick. You hear me talk?"

"The fact is," said Reata, lowering his eyes so that the little yellow light might not be seen usurping the place of the gray, "the fact is that Mr. Durant wants to make a deal with you, and he thinks it would be to the advantage of both of you. Can I talk to you inside the house?"

"Deal with me?" said Bill Chester. "I'll deal with anybody. And I ain't seen the man yet that's ever got the best of me in a hoss trade. Come in here with me!"

CHAPTER 19

He led the way into a bunk room, long, low-ceilinged, with two rows of bunks built into the walls on two sides, and windows and a door at either end.

"Now," said the rancher, turning sharply around and planting his huge fists on his hips, "now, what you want, kid? What's Durant's idea? Make it quick, because I got a hot lunch waitin' for me!"

"Mr. Durant," said Reata, "had in mind making another exchange with you."

"What kind of an exchange?"

"He thought that he'd give you the bay gelding back and take a hundred and fifty dollars in exchange."

"Hey? He what? He thought what?" demanded Bill Chester. "He thought he'd make another exchange, did he? The moldy old fool, I took and trimmed him good and proper, and he thinks he can talk me out of the bargain now? He can rot first!"

"Or," said Reata, "seeing that he's had a lot of trouble gentling the mustang, he thinks that you might be glad to throw in an extra ten dollars or so for the work he's done on the horse, and call the bargain price a hundred and sixty dollars."

"A hundred and— Say, kid, are you tryin' to make me laugh or cry? Or are you just wastin' my time? Get out of here before I throw you out!"

"The more you argue, Chester," said Reata, "the higher the price goes. You'll have to pay twenty dollars to boot to take that horse back now."

"Who'll make me?" asked Chester.

"I'll make you," said Reata.

"You? You make me?" shouted Chester.

He opened his mouth, his eyes, his hands, and then he charged, speechless with rage, hitting out with his mighty right hand.

Reata staggered, or seemed to stagger. The huge fist

missed him. Chester, checking himself with both hands against the wall, thrust around and charged again at that reeling, unbalanced form which seemed to have been unsteadied by the very wind of Chester's passing. A savage glow of joy worked into Chester's eyes. He was a man who loved fighting; and, more than fighting, he loved punishing. The biggest Spanish curb was not too big for his use; the longest Spanish rowels were just right for his spurs; and when he had a chance to manhandle a human victim, it was the supreme moment of his life.

So he raced at full speed at that staggering, retreating, helpless Reata. With the full reach of his arm, all his weight behind it, all the thrust of his massive charge, he struck at the head of the smaller man. But Reata had swayed—bowed with fear, as it were—under the drive of the blow. He had dropped almost to one knee. It seemed the sheerest accident that, when the weight of Chester hurled against him, the lean, rubbery arms of Reata locked around the legs of the big man just above the knees. But the truth was that as Reata straightened, lifting with all his might, Bill Chester hurtled on through the empty air, making vain passes at nothingness, and crashed head and shoulders against the wall of the building.

He fell in a heap.

Reata took a pair of revolvers from him and hung the guns on two pegs against the wall. Then he sat down on the central table, all littered with the carved initials of cow-punchers, and made a cigarette. He was smoking it at leisure when Bill Chester got to his feet with one hand clasped against his bruised head.

Vaguely he saw the slim figure of Reata seated on the edge of the table, with feet crossed; only by degrees the truth dawned on Chester. He made a vague, moaning sound deep in his throat, like the first noise a bull utters before it begins to bellow. Then he started forward to resume the fight.

Something checked him. It was the negligent attitude of Reata, in part, and in part it was the little yellow point of fire which had turned the eyes of Reata from pale gray to hazel. So Bill Chester paused—and reached for his guns.

His hands came away empty. His face, at the same time, emptied of all meaning, also. Gradually, very gradually, fear began to occupy the big void.

"Now that we've had a chance to talk things over," said

Reata, "you can realize that the bargain's made. But the price is a little higher. Mr. Durant is a little queer about that. The longer people bargain with him, the more the price goes up. He'll have to have two hundred dollars for that first-rate gelding, Chester."

Such anger raged in Bill Chester that he balled his fists and started to bellow an answer. The bellow turned into a groan.

He stood swaying from head to foot, wanting to lay his grasp on this will-o'-the-wisp, but checked by a mystery. He had confronted at last, he dimly knew, a being of an order superior to his, and more dangerous by far.

"I'll go—and I'll get some cash," said he. "It's—I'll go and get some money."

"You don't need to go," said Reata. "You'll forget about it. I know how a fellow is when his mind is all full of cows and horses and business, the way yours is, Chester. But now, if you'll feel in your upper left-hand vest pocket, you'll find a little roll of bills that ought to have all the money I want in it."

Chester stared. His glance gradually fell to the little dog, Rags, who sat in front of the feet of his master, looking up with bright eyes, and canting his head to one side.

Even to kill the dog—even to wring the head off that small neck—would have been a delightful consummation to Bill Chester. But instead, his huge brown hand pulled out the money.

He could not believe the thing that he found himself doing as he counted out the money and threw it on the table.

Two hundred honest dollars—or more or less honest— he had abandoned to this slender wildcat of a man!

"There's law—there's a law for robbery!" said Bill Chester.

"And there's a laugh for bullies and fools," answered Reata. "So long, Chester. Treat that gelding well. He's worth a lot of treatment. And when you want the sheriff to arrest me, he can find me at the Durant place. I'll tell him exactly how I got this money."

He left Chester swaying from foot to foot, stunned, and went out to the mare. Little Rags bounded up to the stirrup, and under the steadying hand of his master gained the pommel of the saddle. So, in a moment, the roan mare was stretching in her long canter down the trail that led back to the main road. Seven pairs of eyes followed him agape.

For strange sounds had been heard issuing from the bunk house—and if there were any bruises, it seemed plain that the stranger was not wearing them.

He went straight back to Durant's and found that tall, lean rider in the act of mounting a mustang for the afternoon's riding of the range. Durant pulled his foot out of the stirrup, hooked the reins over his arm, and turned with his hands on his hips.

"You left that colt—and then you got out, eh?" he demanded.

"That's what I did," said Reata, nodding.

"It won't do, son," said Durant, shaking his head. "You got a brain in your head, and I know it. But I gotta have more than brains workin' on this ranch just now. I gotta have *men*. I told you to bring back a hundred and fifty dollars in trade for the colt."

"Bill Chester wouldn't have it that way," said Reata.

"Sure he wouldn't," said Durant. "I kind of had an idea when you started over that he wouldn't have it that way!"

"He wouldn't have it that way," repeated Reata. "He thought that, considering all the time you'd put in taming that bay, he ought to add something to the price. A hundred and fifty wasn't enough. He gave me two hundred, and here it is."

He held out the money.

Durant counted it, one bill at a time. When he reached a hundred and fifty dollars, he handed the rest back to Reata.

"What's this for anyway?" asked Reata.

"Why," said Durant, looking earnestly at Reata, "when I hire a good man, I like to give him a bonus to start with. It's something that makes him want to keep living up to his reputation."

"Am I hired?" asked Reata.

"You knew that before, son," said Durant. "Go pile your pack on a bunk and come out here again."

CHAPTER 20

In the kitchen, Reata found Porky seated at one end of the long table, still consuming food with the waning of an enormous appetite. The cook was also at the table. He was an old man, so old that the wrinkles on the back of his neck were crisscrossed by deep, vertical incisions which looked as though they must give pain. But his face was ennobled and lengthened by a pointed white beard. It was a severe face, full of dignity and repose, with a magnificent forehead. One could not help wondering how such a man came to be cramped in by the labors of a ranch cook.

Porky, when he saw Reata standing in the doorway, gaped at him widely enough to show the mouthful of beans he was eating. Then he ran his hand over his head and made his red hair stand up in confusion.

"Look, Doc. He's got back! He must 'a' collected the coin from Bill Chester."

"Nobody collects nothing from Bill Chester," said the cook. He turned aside toward Reata.

"Durant sent me here to eat," said Reata.

He had washed his face and hands at the pump outside the house. Now he took the place which Doc indicated.

"Set down here," said the cook. "I'm going to feed you fine if you got anything out of Bill Chester except kicks."

Porky stopped eating, and, picking up his coffee cup, he moved over opposite Reata and sat down.

"I ain't met you proper," he said. "I'm Sam Durant's nephew. Porky's my name."

He held out his hand. It was damp and soft to the grip of Reata's lean fingers.

"I'm Reata," he said.

"Dog-gone glad to know you, Reata," said Porky. "This here is Doc. He's a bang-up cook, too."

Reata stood up and shook hands with the cook. No head boss or straw boss is so dreaded a tyrant as the cook at a ranch. Doc accepted the hand of Reata with dignity and composure. He began to heap a large portion on a plate.

"You tell us what you done to Bill Chester to collect that hundred and fifty!" said Porky. "I wish I'd been there! That's what I wish!"

Porky leaned back in his chair and laughed till his eyes wrinkled almost shut. He was not an altogether displeasing sight; there seemed to be so much brute simplicity in him. Now he was choking his laughter for fear of losing a word of the narrative to come. The cook, also, having put the liberal plateful in front of Reata, came to the end of the table and rested his knuckles on the board, all attention.

"Well, there was an argument," said Reata. "You see, Bill Chester seems to be the sort of a fellow who likes to argue a little."

"Yeah. With his fists he likes to argue, or with a gun," said Porky. "Go on."

"And he took a run at me," went on Reata, "when I said that Durant wanted the money back. He scared me so that I dodged, and he sort of tripped over me and slammed his head against the wall. And after he came to, he seemed to be thinking about everything in a different way. He seemed to think that he owed not only a hundred and fifty bucks, but a bonus, too. So he gave me fifty more for a bonus, and Durant, who seems to be a pretty big-handed sort of a boss, handed that fifty dollars on to me. It's a lucky day for me, I should say."

Even if he had had more to say, which he did not, he would have been drowned out by Porky, who was howling with delight.

"Listen to him!" shouted Porky. "Ain't he a wonder, Doc? Bill Chester tripped over him, eh? I bet he picked Chester up and slammed him. I bet he knows *how* to slam. Look at him, Doc. He ain't so big all over, but he's got it in the shoulders, ain't he? By Jiminy, Reata, I'm glad you're on the place. We're goin' to have some larks now!"

The cook continued, all during this speech, to rest his knuckles on the board and look steadily at Reata. Now, as though he had made up his mind about something, he turned away to his duties of cleaning up the dishes.

Porky remained at the table, drinking coffee, spreading his elbows wide, admiring Reata, and talking busily. He wanted to know all about everything. Every man who has been long in the West knows that personal questions are rarely advisable. But Porky, with the license of one who never can know better, poured a shower on Reata.

"Where you from, Reata?" he asked. "And where you been that we ain't heard about you a whole long time before this? You been around wearin' another name? Because I bet you been in the newspapers a lot before this!"

"Maybe I have been," said Reata, "but I never recognized my name. They must have spelled it differently."

The cook began to chuckle. "Shut up, Porky," he said. "He's just kidding you, and you don't know enough to see through it all!"

Porky stopped his happy chuckling and looked sad.

"Aw, are you makin' fun of me?" he asked, with his eyes big.

"No, no," answered Reata. "You just don't want to judge a man by his lucky day. That's all."

When he had finished a small meal, he asked for food for Rags before he carried the dog to Sue, mounted the saddle, and joined Sam Durant, who appeared suddenly, riding around from behind a feed shed.

"I'll show you the layout," said Durant, and led the way straight up a big swale of ground that was almost a hill, to the charred and brush-grown ruins of a building which must have been very large when it was standing.

"This is the old house," said Durant. "The folks used to live up here when I was a kid. You see the stumps of them trees? They were the only stumps anywheres around Boyden Lake. You could see 'em on the hill here for miles and miles, and the roof of the house stickin' up over them all."

"What happened? Accident?" asked Reata.

"I suppose so. One day it caught fire and burned up. There's the grave of my father. You see back there in that berry tangle? My mother's there beside him, and my brother Cleve, too. That's where I'll be planted."

"Your brother Cleve? I've heard something about a Cleve Durant," said Reata.

"Yeah, he got into the papers by being murdered," stated Sam Durant. "That's the only way that he could 'a' got up to headlines. He was a simple sort of an hombre, was Cleve, and never done much harm and never done much good. What for would they take and kill old Cleve for? Unless they were just tryin' to keep their hands in."

"I heard it was a stranger that came along to the ranch," said Reata.

"Maybe it was him. A fellow with half a face, twisted a little. Dave Bates, he's called, and they're goin' to hang him for that job. But I dunno, Reata. It wasn't Dave Bates that killed Big Ben. He's planted back there in the berry patch, too."

"Who was Big Ben?" asked Reata.

He could not help feeling that there was a distinct though obscure point about the manner in which Sam Durant was opening up and talking with such frankness.

"Big Ben was my dog," said Durant. "Kind of a cross between a greyhound and a mastiff and a bull moose, if you know what I mean. He wasn't handsome, but he had a brain and a big lot of teeth in his head. And one day, not long after Cleve was killed, we were all out on the range, even the cook, and we'd cooked up some coffee and I'd just finished pouring a lot of canned milk into my cup. And a mountain grouse busted out of some brush near us, and we all took a shot and missed.

"Well, when I turned around, I saw that Big Ben had lapped up my coffee for the sake of the milk that was loaded into it. I swore at him and washed out the cup, and we were all settling down again when Big Ben began to act sort of queer. He pretty quick was acting queerer and queerer, until it looked to us like the best thing we could do was to try to find out what was wrong. But there was nothing we could do. He died right there, pronto."

"Poison?" asked Reata, feeling his flesh crawl at the thought.

"We gave some of that tinned milk to a chicken afterward," said Sam Durant, "and the chicken died pronto, too."

"But how could they get the poison into a can of milk?"

"Stick a needle into it and work a drop of solder into the hole afterward."

"You think that they did that?"

"I don't think. I know. We had to do some looking, but we found the place, all right."

"Poison?" said Reata breathlessly.

"Poison enough in that can of milk to kill a team of horses. They would 'a' wiped us all out—the cook and poor Porky and me."

"But who's after you?" urged Reata.

"How would I know? I'm just telling you things so maybe you'll see why I want a real man on the place."

"A man good enough to drink poison?"

"Yeah, and it might come down to pretty nigh that, for all that I know!"

He led the way, afterward, all around the ranch. The soil was not very good, the stand of grass small, but the dimensions of that place were surprising, and the number of cattle. Two creeks crossed its boundaries. The ranch was so big that, as Sam Durant pointed out, some of the cows had to trot for the greater part of a day to get from their outermost posts to the nearest of the creeks. This was wealth spread out very thin, but, gathered into one heap, it would make a very big pile indeed.

"Now you know the lay of the land," said Sam Durant, "tell me just how good you are with a gun."

"Give me plenty of time and a rifle, and I can knock over a deer now and then," said Reata.

"Give you a Colt and no time at all and you can knock over a man?" asked Durant.

"I never shot at one," answered Reata.

Durant jerked up his head, a grim glittering in his eyes.

"You didn't pull a gun on Bill Chester?"

"No," said Reata.

"You used your hands on him, eh?" asked Sam Durant.

"Yes," said Reata.

At this reiteration, Durant stared more keenly than ever at his new man.

"What else do you use?" he asked. "Just brains?"

Reata shrugged his shoulders.

"All right, all right," muttered Durant. "If you don't want to tell me about yourself, you don't have to. I've got to be thankful for a small blessing, it seems. I thought I might be getting a man that I could lean on. But— Well, have *you* any questions to ask?"

"You're convinced that Dave Bates didn't kill your brother?"

"I'm not convinced. I'm only convinced that there was something behind Bates. That was what put poison into the milk later on."

"There's nobody on the ranch you could suspect?"

"My honest nephew," said Sam Durant, "he ain't much better than a half-wit. Nobody would try to buy that kind of a fool for any sort of a real job. And the cook's too old to be taking chances. These things have been done by people from the outside. It's not an inside job!"

They started riding home. Durant said: "You take your blankets out of the bunk house. Bring them up and bed down in the room next to mine. Even if you can't use a gun, you're going to be better than nothing, I suppose."

"If you wanted a good man with a gun, why didn't you take that fellow who showed up along with me?" asked Reata.

"Because he's a crook. He's got the face of a crook," said the rancher. "And if he shoots straight, he'll be bought up by the others behind the scenes to use his gun on me. Nobody can help me except an honest man. That's all I know about it."

"That's all you know, but how much do you guess?" asked Reata.

"I guess," said the rancher, "that I'll be dead inside of forty-eight hours."

CHAPTER 21

The limited section of the house which was given up to the family was two stories high, and the bedrooms were not a great improvement over the comforts of the bunk house. They gave a bit of privacy, to be sure, but not a great deal, because the partitions everywhere were paper-thin, and a footfall in any part of the place was sufficient to send a squeaky tremor to the farthermost limits of the building. Reata rather regretted that he had been put into the room next to that of his employer; yet it gave him a chance to sit down and think things over undisturbed.

He was by no means certain that he could accomplish anything in this case. He put Rags on the table that stood in the center of his bedroom and sat down to consider the problem, because the bright little eyes of Rags encouraged optimism and seemed to suggest that light was about to fall upon the most obscure details of the mystery. He stroked the fuzzy head and the strange, sleek body of the little dog, and added up what he knew.

The mere knowledge was not much. But there is a feeling about things that should give to the strong mind the extra sense that leads to far-cast hints and guesses at a buried truth.

Sam Durant, by leading him up to the ruins of the old house, had seemed to suggest a number of things. One was that he, Durant, was the last of his family except the half-witted Porky; another was that the same source of malice which had caused the death of Cleve Durant might be that which had destroyed the dog, Big Ben, and burned the old house in the first place.

The idea seemed to be, simply, that the Durants would be wiped off the face of the earth, and then the total possession of the property would pass—to whom?

That was a point to be discovered.

Inside the house, the agents that could have been employed to murder Cleve Durant and poison the dog were the cook, who seemed less trustworthy to Reata than Sam Durant considered him; Porky, whose extreme simplicity ought to remove him from all shadow of a doubt, and finally Sam Durant himself.

Brothers have murdered brothers in this world. Yes, and they have afterward gone many years undetected, suspicion diverted by the very enormity of the crime and the ghastly unnaturalness of it. Sam Durant might be the man for such a job. His sour dryness might cover the most honest of hearts. It might also be the face of a fiend. As for the poison story—perhaps that poison was directed at poor Porky, who, rubbed off the slate, would limit the inheritance to the hands of Sam Durant alone. The dog's part in the affair would have been equally inopportune in any case.

As for suspicions, therefore, Reata was inclined to place them against Sam Durant, unless there proved to be some other relative in the world. He determined to ask that question as soon as possible.

So when he saw Sam Durant that evening, after they had all come in from the range, he took the first chance of saying to him: "Got many relatives anywhere?"

"No," said Durant. "So far's I know, there ain't a soul outside of my sister's boy, Porky. There ain't even so much as the first cousin of an uncle's sister's aunt. I don't know of anybody in the world that would ever have a claim to this here place except me and Porky, if that's what you're driving at." And his keen eyes held fixedly upon the face of Reata, obviously reading his mind with ease.

"All right," said Reata cheerfully. "We'll have to tackle a different angle, then."

But in spite of the keen, steady glance which Sam Durant had given him, Reata determined that Sam himself must be the guilty man.

He carried that conviction with him through supper. He held it while he was smoking his after-supper cigarette in the gloom of the evening. Then, putting out the cigarette, he looked up at the house and saw that Durant already had gone to bed and put out his light. Porky still manipulated a mouth organ, wheezing out foolish tunes with a great lustiness, until the cook thrust out a head from the bunk house and shouted for silence.

Porky's music was instantly still. That was the amiable quality of the poor fellow. He might be simple, but he was willing to be checked and rated into his proper place by anyone.

Now that the house was black and silent, Reata went out for a walk. He did not go very far from the house, and his course led him from one patch of brush to another. At each one he paused and whistled softly. He had come to the fourth of those small clusters before a stocky form rose up to meet him.

"Back up, Harry," he said. "You're up here on the top of a hill where you'd show as clear as a light against the stars if anybody looked at you from the house!"

"Yeah, and I didn't think about that," said Harry Quinn, hurrying back into the shallow hollow behind the swale. Rags followed him, sniffing suspiciously at his heels, and Reata joined him.

They sat on the ground. Quinn would have smoked, but Reata would not permit it. The scent of the smoke might reach to any passer-by, he said.

"Who'd be passing?" asked Quinn. "Ain't everybody else in the house asleep?"

"They may all be asleep, and they may all be awake," answered Reata. "You never can tell in a house where there's been a murder."

"Hey," muttered Harry Quinn, "are you trying to give me a chill up the spine?"

"I'm not trying to give you a chill up the spine," answered Reata. "I couldn't give you that unless you caught it from me, and I've had gooseflesh right in the middle of the afternoon."

"What's the matter?" asked Quinn.

"An old cook they all trust, with an eye that might do murder as soon as look at a sheep. And a half-wit that could be a tool, but never a good one, and Sam Durant himself, who could be anything you want."

"Him!" said Harry Quinn. "I been thinkin' all day, while I was roasted back there in the brush. I been thinkin' all the day that it might be Sam Durant himself. I ain't seen him much, but I hate the heart of him already."

"Because he gave you a run," answered Reata. "But there's something else for you to pay attention to. I want you to do the rounds about the house tonight, Harry."

"Keep a long watch, you mean?"

"Yes, till the sky gets a little gray. If there's outside work taking a hand in this, it may show up this same night, the first night a new man comes on the job. If there's a murderer inside the house, and a tool outside of it, or vice versa, it may be that they'll get together tonight and talk things over. They may want me out of the way, and choose tonight to talk it over. They can't find a time any sooner than this."

"So I'm to walk the rounds?" groaned Harry Quinn. He broke off, lamenting: "Why do I stick with Pop Dickerman? I never get a real easy job from him, and even if I get good pay now and then, I sweat blood for it in the long run. Why do I stick with him?"

"Because you're afraid to leave," suggested Reata.

"You know that much, do you?" said Quinn. "Then you know a whole lot."

"You start the rounds," said Reata. "My job is to be there in the house, asleep in my bed, not suspecting anything. They may want to try their hands on me this same night."

"Great thunder, man," said Quinn, "are you goin' to go in there and lie like the bait in a trap and sleep?"

"I'll lie there. I may not sleep," said Reata. "Keep out at a distance. Stop and squat and look along the ground now and then. That's the way to spot things at night."

"I know it, and I'll do it. When do I see you again?"

"I don't know. Maybe not till tomorrow night. If I want you, I'll make a cross at my window with a lighted lamp. You see? Like this."

"Which is your window?"

"The second one from this end. Up there in the second story. I'm moved in to be bodyguard."

"And him you guard is the one that may stick a knife in you, eh?"

"That's the idea exactly."

"Well," said Quinn, "so long. It's a rotten job. I never had a worse one. Good luck to you, Reata. I hope you're goin' to be alive to throw me the flash tomorrow night, but—I got the chill out of the air, now. You've passed it to me. Maybe you'll be so cold you'll be stiff by tomorrow night!"

Harry Quinn got up and moved away through the night, disappearing at the next cluster of shrubs.

Reata remained for a moment, looking away from the blackness of the earth to the white and scattered fields of the stars overhead.

Little Rags gave him the alarm at last. The dog jumped from the knee of his master, ran to the top of the little swale that sheltered Reata from spying eyes, and then whisked quickly back to the man.

It was too plain a signal to be overlooked. Reata, crouching to keep his body from outlining against the stars on the horizon, went cautiously up the little slope and instantly saw a shadowy figure coming toward him from the direction of the house!

The cook, half-witted Porky, or Sam Durant himself? All three of them had pretended to be silent in sleep a long time ago; and if he could catch one of them, the result might be the solution of the mystery.

Crouched almost flat on the ground, he stared at the advancing figure.

It was not Porky. There were too many inches to him for that.

It was not the cook, unless Doc had been able to put strange suppleness into his knees and step out like a youth and an athlete.

Was it Sam Durant? Even he could hardly have a step like that, swift, and rising lightly on the toes. No, the whole outline of the head and shoulders was different from

111

that of Durant. It was, in fact, a man who had not been seen at the house during the day!

Had he been hidden there, then?

Had he come in from the outer night long before this, and was just now departing?

The latter alternative did not seem very plausible. It had not been long after twilight when Reata himself began his vigil; and if the man were leaving in this direction, he probably had approached the house in the same line. Instinct would make him do that.

At any rate, it was certainly an unnamed stranger. If he had been at the house in this manner, perhaps it was he who was responsible for the murder of poor Cleve Durant?

The stranger went by, stepping lightly, easily still, his feet almost soundless on the ground, for the very good reason that he was carrying his boots in his hand! Reata could see them, now that the man had gone by.

He half rose, shook out the noose of his reata, and cast it with that sudden, subtle movement which he had learned south of the Rio Grande.

The thin coil opened in the air with the softest of whispers. It fell true, and with one jerk Reata had pinioned the arms of the stranger to his hips. The pull on the line made the fellow stagger backward, but he uttered not a sound.

And that, strange to say, completely convinced Reata of the guilt of his prisoner. He advanced, throwing over the other two rapid coils of the lariat that secured him as well as ever the sticky silk of a spider secured an insect in its web.

"Who are you?" asked Reata.

He got no answer.

So he scratched a match on his trousers and moved the dim blue light of it across the face of the other. What he saw was the handsome features of Anton, the gypsy!

CHAPTER 22

Reata dropped the match to the ground. It made only a dim streak of light, and a glowing spot, on which he stepped.

"Do you know me, Anton?" he asked softly.

Anton hissed like an angry cat. But he spoke the gypsy dialect, and his words were unintelligible to Reata.

"Say it in English, Anton," he suggested.

"Sure, I'll say it in English," went on Anton, getting easily into range vernacular. "I'm sent here to find you, Reata. And when I get to you, you throw a rope on me. Well?"

"Ah, you're sent here to find me? By whom?"

"By Queen Maggie."

"What does she want with me?"

"She says that she wants to see the fellow who made a fool of her and walked off with Harry Quinn. But that's not the main reason."

"Tell me the whole thing, Anton."

"Maggie wants you to come back because Miriam is no good since you left. She sits and moons. We went to a town two days ago, and Miriam couldn't do her tricks on the horse. She slipped and fell, and wouldn't try again. Maggie came sashayin' into her tent. Maggie had a quirt in her hand, and she swore that she'd give Miriam a beating, and Miriam, she pulled out a knife and waited for the fun to start. Hi," breathed the gypsy softly. "That was a thing worth seeing, Reata! But Maggie wants you back, and Miriam wants you back."

"And so do you, I suppose?" said Reata. "The whole tribe of you want me back, eh?"

"Why should I want you?" asked Anton. "But I come on the errands when Maggie sends me."

"Why should she have picked you out unless she wanted to have a knife dug into my back?" asked Reata.

"Because if I came to you, you'd know that the whole

tribe really wants you. I hated you more'n the rest of 'em. If I came to ask you back, it'd show that we all wanted you to come."

"You think that I should come, Anton?"

"Why not?" asked Anton. "There ain't a better job in the world than doin' nothin' and eatin' fat, is there? You can lay in the shade all day if you want to. Miriam'll be there to keep you happy. She gets plenty of dollars throwed at her when she rides bareback at the shows. And you can do your rope tricks if you want."

"How did you know you'd find me here?" asked Reata.

"That I can't tell. Maggie knows pretty nigh everything. She's always got her ear close to the ground."

"What room did I have in the house?"

"The one next to Durant's."

Reata was amazed.

"Did you go in?"

"Yes."

"Through the window?"

"I picked the lock of the door. A gypsy in Maggie's outfit—well, we gotta know how to do all kinds of things."

"Anton," said Reata, "you've told a good few lies, standing here. A lot of 'em, and good ones, too. Maggie didn't send you at all. Miriam didn't send you. If you came for me, you'd only come with a knife in your hand."

"All right, all right," said Anton. "You tell me why I came, then, eh?"

"For the sort of work a gypsy would be hired for. Murder, Anton, or stealing!"

"Murder? Hi!" cried the gypsy softly.

"We'll go back to the house and have some light on you," said Reata.

"All right," said Anton. Reata was amazed again by the calm of the gypsy. He could see his shoulders shrug up. "Nobody knows me there," said Anton. "And you won't believe me. I go back to Maggie and tell her. Well, she'll see that it's better to keep to the pure gypsy blood, eh? Or if she takes another man in, swear him in blood first. Come on, Reata. We'll go back to the house."

Reata was of half a mind not to fulfill his threat, but he knew that gypsy tongues can lie faster than a clock ticks, so he marched Anton back to the front of the house and then called out, under the windows: "Hey, Durant!"

There was an answer so instant that it proved Sam Durant had not been asleep so far during the night.

"Who's there?" he called a moment later, leaning shadowy from the window.

"Reata and a friend of his on a rope. Come downstairs and light a lamp, and we'll come in for a chat."

Suppose, thought Reata, that Sam Durant had actually worked with this handsome scoundrel in planning the death of his brother, and then shifting the blame for that act upon the innocent shoulders of Dave Bates?

Well, if that were the case, it would be strange if he failed to surprise some flash of a glance as it passed between the two allies.

As he waited, he could hear the rancher's steps as the latter moved about his room, dressing, no doubt. A light had bloomed behind the window of Sam Durant. Now his footfalls came down the stairs, and their squeaking was accompanied by the deep, bass snore of Porky.

The light entered the lower part of the house. It shone through the windows of the kitchen.

"All right," said Durant, opening the kitchen door.

"Walk in," Reata invited Anton, and, again to his surprise, Anton walked jauntily forward, as though there were not a care in the world on his mind.

As he passed through the doorway, Sam Durant drew back, his eyes working keenly, deeply on the handsome face of the young gypsy. Reality like this could hardly be counterfeited. Reata was instantly sure that the eyes of Durant had never rested on the gypsy before this moment!

CHAPTER 23

When they were in the kitchen, the young gypsy showed perfect unconcern. He even seemed to be enjoying his position in the center of the stage.

"Where'd you get this?" asked Sam Durant, sleeking his long face with one hand.

"He was coming out of the house. He's somewhere in

the game that we want to find out about," answered Reata. "Name is Anton. He belongs to a gang of gypsies that drifts around under a woman called Queen Maggie."

"I've seen 'em do their show," said Durant.

"This is the fellow who rides the horse and swings the sword," explained Reata.

"Have you frisked him?"

"I'll go through him now," said Reata.

He got from Anton one compact little .32-caliber revolver and a slim bit of a knife, a stiletto with a weighted handle, evidently meant more for throwing than for stabbing. Reata took it across the palm of his hand and smiled down at it.

"You see this?" he said to Durant. "He can hit a patch as big as your hand at ten steps with this knife. It's better than a gun, in some ways. There's no sound except a whisper in the air, and then you're dead with a needle jabbed right through your heart, so to speak."

"He's got a good, sleek look about him," said Durant. "I sort of remember him from that show. A fine bit of riding was what he done. Anton, what brought you here?"

"I come along for Reata," said Anton. "He was in our band, and Queen Maggie wants him back. I came here. I looked in his room. He was gone. So I left to go away, and he stood up out of the ground and roped me like this."

"Queen Maggie wants me? She wants me dead," said Reata. "The point is—how did he know which room was mine? He says that he got up there and picked the lock and looked in. But I was away. If I'd been asleep there, he would have slid that knife through my back, I suppose."

"Who told you which was Reata's room?" asked Durant.

"Maggie told me."

"Where did she find out?"

"I don't know. Maggie finds out anything she wants to know."

"You were goin' to bring back Reata to your gang, were you?" said the rancher. "How were you goin' to bring him?"

"By telling him that a girl in the tribe, she is waiting for him. You have seen the show, Mr. Durant. Maybe you remember the bareback rider? She told me to talk to him."

"That's a loud lie," answered Reata. "She's a wild little

116

devil, Durant. But she's a proud little devil, too. She wouldn't send for any man and ask him to come back."

"I kind of remember her, all right," said Durant. "She danced on a gallopin' hoss like she was on a big floor. I can remember the sleek and the slim of her, all right. If she called a man, he'd foller."

"She sent for Reata," insisted Anton.

"She'd never do it in the world. She'd rather choke first," declared Reata.

"Reach into the inside pocket of my coat," said Anton. "There's something to see, Reata."

Reata dipped his swift fingers inside the coat and drew out a small brown envelope; from the envelope he took a picture of Miriam, the bareback rider. There was only the face and the slender round of the throat smiling at him. Under the picture, written in a small, swift hand, like that of a man who uses his pen a great deal, had been scribbled:

Reata, it's a long, long time.

He stared at the snapshot for a while, and then passed the picture into his pocket.

"You see him?" said Anton to Durant. "You see how she put her hand on him from a long ways off? Now—is it true that I came from Queen Maggie to call in Reata?"

"I dunno," remarked Durant. "What good would a fellow like Reata be to your gang?"

"If they can pull me away from this house, they'll have a freer hand to tackle you, Durant," suggested Reata.

"Aye, that's straight," agreed Durant. "But would that tribe really get anything out of Reata, Anton?"

"More cash than for anything except Miriam's riding. He can do rope tricks. He can snatch the hat off your head and the gun out of your hand. Well, people like to see such things. Besides, he's a very good pickpocket. He could take your watch and your wallet while you watch his rope jump like a snake in the air. Gypsies need people with quick fingers."

He laughed, not without malice, as he said this. Reata merely shrugged his shoulders.

"Well," said Durant, "it looks as though he might be telling part of the truth. Not that I care a crack what you can do with your fingers, Reata. Hadn't we better turn this hombre loose?"

"No," said Reata. "We'll keep him here. He hasn't told the whole truth. Before morning, maybe I'll be able to make him talk. Maybe he'll say something that'll interest us a whole lot. Maybe it'll even interest the sheriff, eh?"

"You think that he's in it?"

"I know that he's in it. Maybe he was hidden away in the house all day, and that's why he knows about my room. But wait a minute. What did you find on the table in my room?"

"Matches, a sack of tobacco, and an old magazine," said Anton.

"That's right," agreed Reata, shaking his head.

"Let him go," urged Durant. "I believe what he's said, mostly. He came to take you back to the gypsies."

"I'll try working on him tonight," said Reata. "I may not get anything out of him, but I'll try. Anton, you're going up to my room with me."

Anton chuckled. "You want to know more about Miriam, is that it?"

"It's no good," insisted Durant. "You ain't goin' to get a thing out of him. He don't know a thing about what's happened here."

"Because you haven't seen him, that doesn't mean that he hasn't been around. You'll see, Durant. Up this way, Anton."

He made the gypsy climb the stairs in front of him to the room on the second floor. There Reata, in fact, found that the door was unlocked. He pushed it open, entered, and kept taut the rope which held Anton while he lighted the lamp on the little center table. After that he set Anton free, and shut the hall door and locked it.

The gypsy sat down by the table and picked up makings of a cigarette, which he manufactured with quick, skillful fingers. He had an air of suppressed smiling about him, and it was plain that in some way he considered that he held powerful cards up his sleeve. Reata walked the floor with an irregular step, trying to think his way to a conclusion.

His hand in his coat pocket presently found the picture of the girl, and that suggested something to him. However, he would try other measures first.

He paused and leaned against the wall, partly facing Anton. The gypsy was a bigger man and a dangerous fighter, but he had tried conclusions once before with

118

Reata, and he would not attempt to fight him again. Of that Reata was certain, and for this reason he had taken the rope from the arms of his prisoner.

"Anton," he said, "the fact is that I've got you, and you know it."

"So?" said Anton, smiling and blowing a cloud of cigarette smoke toward the open window which he faced.

"But it's going to be better to talk to me than to talk to a sheriff. Durant is slow in the head. He don't fully understand what you're up against."

"You tell me." Anton grinned with the utmost insolence.

"There's a burglary charge," said Reata. "You've broken into a house and picked a lock. That's burglary, Anton, and they send 'em up for a long time for that. Eight or ten years for you."

Anton shook his head. "I took nothing. There ain't a way to railroad a man for taking nothing. It's too far West for that, Reata." Then, still grinning, he added: "Try another way to scare me."

"I've got a mind to beat it out of you," said Reata.

Anton shook his head in silence, as though to indicate that he knew perfectly well that there was not enough brute in his captor to permit Reata to use cruel measures.

Reata took a deep breath and controlled himself.

"There's another way to look at it," he said. "There's money, Anton. You could make a good bit of hard cash out of talking to us."

"So?" said Anton again. "What do you want me to say?"

"Who killed Cleve Durant?"

"That other Durant? How could I know that?"

"You could know it if you thought for a minute."

"Well, I can't think."

Reata wanted to smash a fist into that smiling face. But he held himself in check.

"You could make enough, Anton, to buy yourself the finest horse ever seen in the tribe."

"I have the finest horse already," said Anton.

"You could have a gold watch, jewels in your ears, diamonds on the hilt of your knife. You could have a thousand dollars, Anton, for telling what I want to know."

Anton shook his head.

"Let Bates hang," he said.

At this sneering remark, which proved how completely Anton understood the reason for the presence of Reata on the place, the latter felt like giving up the task on the spot. However, he persisted grimly. There was one last chance for him.

"Anton," he said, putting the picture of Miriam on the table, "suppose that you knew I'd never come back to the tribe?"

Anton sat straight, suddenly interested. His bright eyes narrowed.

"To stay away," he said huskily, rapidly, "all the time? *Never* to come back?"

"Never," said Reata.

"Aye, but she'd come to you," sand Anton. "She says that she belongs to you."

"She'll forget me quick enough," said Reata. "She's not meant for me. I never could marry her. My trail hasn't stopped winding uphill. And—suppose I say that I'll never come back even so much as to see her? You understand that, Anton. Would there be any other man in the tribe for her except you?"

"No," said Anton, leaning forward from his chair. "But if you promise never to see her again—then how could I trust your promise?"

"Because you know I'd stick to it," said Reata.

Anton, staring at him with feverish eyes, at length nodded.

"Yes," he said, "I could believe you."

"Then talk," said Reata. "You'll have to say enough to make it worth my while. I want to know who killed Cleve Durant, and I want to be able to hang it on him. Can you tell me enough for that?"

"Yes!" said Anton.

Reata sighed. "All right," he said. "It wasn't Dave Bates, to start with?"

"No, no. It was the last man you would think of!"

Anton began to chuckle a little. Then he leaned forward.

"I'll whisper it, Reata," he said. "His name was—"

Something flashed in the air; there was a soft, thudding sound as a weapon penetrated the throat of Anton.

He leaped up, trying to scream, but only able to bubble blood, and, tearing the knife from his throat, he dropped on the floor the weighted hilt and the slender blade of that same knife which Reata had taken from him only a few minutes before.

CHAPTER 24

Reata got to the window in a single leap, the lariat in his hand, but only to hear the thud of feet on the ground beneath; and as he leaned out, he saw a dark form scud around the corner of the building.

He slithered over the sill of the window, hung a second by the tips of his fingers, and dropped catlike. In his turn he sprinted around the corner of the house, scanning, all the while, the ground beyond. But he completed the entire circle of the house without seeing the fugitive.

He dropped to one knee, controlled his breathing, listening either for the beating hoofs of a horse or for the pounding feet of a running man. But it seemed that the fugitive had dissolved into nothingness.

There was no use in hurrying back to Anton in that bedroom. He was dead before this, stifled by his own blood. So Reata stepped out into the night and whistled until he heard a faint response. And Harry Quinn came quickly up to him.

"You saw somebody come out of the house. Why didn't you stop him?" demanded Reata.

"Because I didn't see nobody," said Quinn.

"Harry, you were asleep. Tell me the truth. It's important."

"Nobody left that house, and I certainly wasn't asleep," vowed Quinn. "That's the straight of it."

Reata was stunned. For the only other explanation was that the murderer had simply circled the corner of the house and run back into the dwelling.

He merely said: "There's a lot of queer stuff in the air, Harry. Stay out here. I'm going to see if I can call you in tonight, and tell Durant that you're on the job. But I have to go easy with him, because he's a hard man."

"Aye, and maybe he'll be softened before a long time!" said Harry Quinn.

Reata returned to the house straightway. He moved slowly. In that house, he felt sure, was the murderer of Anton. In that house, as far as he knew, there were only three people—Sam Durant, Doc, and Porky Durant. Perhaps the cook was not too old to have clambered up the side of the house and dropped again to the ground. Porky had probably been asleep through the whole affair. In fact, now that Reata listened, he could hear the deep, soft snoring of Porky, making a mournful sound through the house. And as for Sam Durant—well, of course, if it were he, then the murderer of Cleve had been found!

It was Sam Durant, also, who had been present to see the knife and the other things taken from the clothes of the gypsy. It was Sam who had heard the remark about the excellence of that knife as a missile weapon. And still it would be very strange if the big, horny, labor-hardened hands of Sam Durant were able to use a knife in this fashion, for knife throwing is an art which can only be mastered by indefatigable practice.

In the door of the house, Reata paused. The obvious answer was that the crime had not been committed by any of the three inhabitants of the place; it had been done by another man who might still be lurking inside the premises. If that were true, then he could search the place in the morning, when daylight shrank the dimensions and dismissed the mysteries of the house.

He went to Porky's room, and, standing outside the door, listened for a moment to the snoring. He felt equal parts of disgust and reassurance as he heard that deep, regular sound. Then he went to his own room and set his teeth hard before he entered.

He hated blood, and there was plenty of it. It was streaked and smeared on the floor in a great circle where Anton had writhed around and around. Now he lay face down, his head doubled under his shoulder. One hand was still fixed in his hair. The other arm was thrown out to the side.

And, leaning against the wall with folded arms, calmly looking down at this spectacle, was Durant!

The rancher lifted his eyes grimly from that picture on the floor and stared at Reata. He said nothing. He simply kept watching and waiting for some sort of an explanation.

Driven inches deep into the floor was the small stiletto which Anton, in his last agony, had drawn from his throat and plunged into the wood as he stifled in his own blood.

"I was talking to him," explained Reata curtly. "Someone threw that knife from the window and caught him in the throat. I dropped out the window and chased the fellow. I saw him dodge around the corner of the house, but I didn't come up with him. Whoever threw that knife is now in the house. He must have run back into the house. The reason the knife was thrown was that Anton was about to give me the name of the man who killed Cleve Durant."

He brought out these facts slowly, dryly, watching Sam Durant with a merciless eye, ready, in fact, to see the rancher pull a gun. But Durant was moveless.

"He didn't get out no part of the name?" asked Durant.

"No part of it," said Reata.

"It was somebody from the outside," said Sam Durant. "He managed to sneak away across the open ground. You missed him, was all!"

"I wasn't very far behind his heels. Besides, I've got another man out there watching the open," confessed Reata. And again he narrowed his eyes at the rancher. This time he saw the big man start.

"You've got a side kicker out there?" said Sam Durant.

"Yes," said Reata.

"The gent that rode up to the house with you today?" asked the rancher.

"That's the one."

"What's your game, you two?"

"Dave Bates is going to hang for a job he didn't do," said Reata. "I'm here to discover the real crook."

He rather wondered to find himself speaking so frankly to the rancher. But as he looked at the big fellow, it seemed certain to him that Sam Durant could not have killed this man, dropped from the window, circled the house, and then, stealing back, come to the very room of the murder to look silently down at his handiwork.

Besides, trying to remember how the shadowy fugitive had seemed as he ran around the corner of the house, it appeared to the memory of Reata that the figure had been rather shorter and stockier. However, that would be hard to make sure of, since he had been looking down at an angle that foreshortened the outline of the silhouette very considerably.

"You know that Bates didn't do the job?" queried Durant harshly.

"Dave Bates never got drunk," said Reata, equally terse.

"Turn your friend over and we'll have a look at his face," said Durant.

Reata nodded, and leaned to lift Anton's outthrown arm, and by that leverage twist the body over.

As he raised that arm, he saw red letters scrawled on the floor beneath the shelter of it. Hastily he moved his foot in and obliterated the writing, making a red smudge of it, but what he had seen written on the floor by Anton as the gypsy choked was the name of the murderer whose face at the window had been glimpsed while the knife, perhaps, was still in the air.

And, as he lay gasping, Anton, had written on the boards: "Durant."

CHAPTER 25

Durant had, after all, killed the man; Durant had dropped from the window; Durant, on soundless feet, had stolen back into the house and come to stand and look at his victim. The rancher had on socks, and no boots. That would explain the silence with which he was able to move. Durant it must have been who, in the first place, had bought the help of the gypsies; he had used them while he planned the murder of his brother, determined finally to have the whole property of the ranch in his own hands.

No doubt Anton had returned to the place to extract another cash payment, or to levy a little additional blackmail.

The story began to straighten out in the mind of Reata, and he felt a powerful physical sense of loathing and repulsion. It was hard for him to remain in the same room with this perfect hypocrite.

So great was his mental preoccupation with the rancher that he hardly was aware of the face of the gypsy as he turned the body on its back. However, gradually he saw it clearly. The handsomeness of Anton had departed in the agony of his death, and the mask that last looked on life contained all the vicious facts about the gypsy's nature. A sleek and evil fellow he had been, and like a contorted snake he looked now.

Perhaps out of the murder of the gypsy more events would follow than big Sam Durant bargained for. Queen Maggie would strike for her band. She would battle to avenge her fallen man.

Reata straightened the limbs of the dead man. He closed the staring eyes. He tried to smooth and compose the features, but they kept pulling back faintly into the lines of the death agony.

"A lot of people might do some talking about you and this job," said the rancher. "Reata, there's a lot of gents that might think that maybe *you* jammed the knife into him, and then dropped out the window and run around the house."

"A lot of people might think that," said Reata.

"You didn't make no holler. You just jumped through the window, according to what you say!"

"That's what I did," said Reata. He kept looking down at the dead body. If he looked up, the rancher would plainly see the yellow devil in his eyes.

"Or, leavin' you out of it, suppose that your friend outside the house— What's his name?"

"Harry Quinn."

"Suppose that Quinn crossed you all up and done this murder, partner?"

Reata started a little. The thing was not totally impossible. If there was enough money to buy gypsy help, there was enough money to bribe Harry Quinn, of course. The flaw in this argument was that Harry Quinn certainly had been too far away to take part in the first crime—the destruction of Cleve Durant. The second and greater flaw was that the name written on the floor by Anton was "Durant"!

The rancher was saying: "Go saddle a hoss and ride to Boyden Lake. Get the sheriff up. Bring him out here so's he can see things. Maybe we shouldn't 'a' turned this feller on his back."

"I don't want him lying on his face—on the floor," said Reata.

"His face is dead."

"Aye, but I don't want it."

The rancher snarled something. Then he said aloud: "Go get on your way. Call in your friend Quinn, first. As long as he's here, we'll have to try to use him."

They went down the stairs. The snoring of Porky Durant followed them, and at one point Sam Durant actually paused and growled: "Fat, half-witted fool!"

He went on. The heart of Reata suddenly warmed toward the fat fellow and the round, soft, good-natured face. Far better a half-wit than the iron cruelty of the rancher.

From the front door he whistled in Harry Quinn, who came out of the darkness quickly.

"Here you are, eh?" said Sam Durant. "Quinn, your partner thinks that the killer of the gypsy is still somewhere in this house. We've got to pull out away from the place and keep a guard over it. Reata is going to ride into town and get Sheriff Greely. He'll be out here about sunrise or before, and when it's daylight, we'll search the house. Meantime, you and I'll keep a close watch. Reata, get going!"

Reata nodded. He went by Quinn and muttered rapidly, softly: "Watch Durant!"

Then he went to the corral, snagged a mustang, and saddled the horse and rode up the lane. The low, black silhouette of the house pointed after him like the barrel of a clumsy gun. He was glad to get on the main road and start the mustang away toward Boyden Lake.

There was no weariness in him. He possessed one of those bodies which can defy fatigue as long as there remains a well of nervous strength to draw upon.

Now he walked, now he trotted, now he loped the tough little horse. And all the way, until he had sight of the dark smudge of the town rising against the dim sparkling of the water of the lake, he kept thinking of Harry Quinn left alone on the ranch with the grim rancher. Poor Harry Quinn! In many ways he was as low a fellow as one could find, but, after all, he was above murdering Sam Durant.

He remembered, also, the total silence in which the crime had been committed and the quiet that had followed it. Fat-faced Porky Durant had continued to snore; the cook had not been roused. And this soft-footed quiet made the death of Anton even more strange and horrible.

When he came into the town of Boyden Lake, it was dead, silent. He had to rouse a household to learn where he could find Sheriff Greely's house, and down by the starlit lake he was presently tapping at a door. A window pulled up with a groan humanly deep.

"Who's there?" asked a man's gruff voice.

"News from the Durant ranch. A gypsy's been stabbed. He's lying dead out there. Want to have a look?"

There was an answering, wordless growl. He heard the man moving about inside the house. Lamplight glistened across a couple of windows. Then the door was opened, and he looked in on a half-dressed man of thirty-five, a range type, wind-burned and sun-blackened, fleshless, tough as rawhide. He had pale-blue eyes, very bright and steady, and always taking aim with a slight puckering of the lids.

Reata took a chair. He told, very briefly, the facts as they had happened. Then he slid out of the chair and stretched himself on the floor.

"When you're saddling up, saddle two broncs instead of one," he said. "I've got a spent horse out there. And I'm tuckered out. I'm going to rest here for a minute."

The sheriff said nothing. He rolled a cigarette, lighted it, and went silently out of the house. In the distance, Reata presently heard the racing of hoofs on the hard-beaten ground of a corral. He closed his eyes and drew in deep, regular breaths. The weariness began to flow out of his body into the coolness of the floor. He was almost unconscious when he heard the bumping of hoofs and the squeaking of saddle leather coming around the side of the house. Then he got up and went out to change the saddle from his tired mustang to a new mount. Instead, he discovered that the sheriff already had made the change and put the spent horse in the corral.

They were off together, the sheriff keeping to a continual, sharp trot. He was a man of iron in the saddle, and Reata accommodated himself quickly to this most trying of gaits. They rattled out of Boyden Lake onto the long road.

Only when the horses were pulled back to a walk, as they went up a very sharp, steep ditch, did Reata speak.

"What sort of a fellow was Cleve Durant?"

"Best you ever seen," said the sheriff. "Always smilin'. The kind of a man it was good to hunt with, work with, drink with. You knew where he'd be all the while. Him and Sam was two different cuts. They was always wranglin'. Sam's a great worker, but Cleve was mighty fine."

After a moment he added: "Why d'you ask?"

"Because Sam killed the gypsy; that means he killed his brother."

"That's a bit of news," said the sheriff.

"Maybe I'm wrong," said Reata. "But it's my guess. When I lifted that gypsy's arm, I saw 'Durant' scrawled out in his blood. He'd written that while he lay there, choking."

The sheriff whistled.

"What did you do?"

"I rubbed the letters out with my foot."

"You fool," said the sheriff, "that spoils the case for us!"

"Maybe not," said Reata, "and maybe so. But how could you hang a man just because his name's been written on the floor, even if it was written in blood? All that would have happened, if Sam Durant had seen that writing, would have been to put him on his guard. You can't catch a smart man when he's on his guard."

"That's right," admitted the sheriff. "But you sure thought fast when you were turning that body."

"I thought fast, all right," said Reata. "I thought just fast enough, I guess. He thinks that I think that somebody else did the job."

"We'll lay our heads together," answered the sheriff. "If Sam killed his brother Cleve, he's the meanest skunk that ever rode a hoss. What's your name?"

"Reata."

"Reata, you're a bright feller. We're goin' to do something together out of this here case."

They jogged on into the gray of the morning before they saw the house looming; the dawn was brightening when they came up and found Sam Durant on one side of the building with a rifle across his knees as he sat on a rock, and Harry Quinn walking up and down on the other side of the building. They had kept to their posts all the night.

"He's keeping up the bluff—that Durant," said Reata.

128

"You've got to do your part now. Don't let him think that you suspect him. Give him an extra hard handshake."

"I'd like to shake him into a hangman's rope!" snarled the sheriff.

He went straight up to the rancher, however, and grasped his hand.

"Reata's told me everything," said the sheriff. "You two fellows stay out here, will you? And Reata and me, we'll go inside and search the place."

That was the program. They went into the narrow, low cellar. There were only two small, empty rooms in it. Not even a rat could have hidden away from the first glance.

They climbed up to Doc's room. He sat up suddenly and blinked at them, his old face wrinkling with surprise as he stared at the lantern light.

They went through every room in the house, and finally into Porky's.

Porky rolled over in bed.

"All right," he groaned. "I'm goin' to get up—in a minute I'll be up."

And he relaxed and began to snore again. He had slept all night with his window closed; the room smelled like a kennel.

"Bah!" said the sheriff as he stepped back into the hall with Reata. "There ought to be a way to get rid of the half-wits. They oughta be put off somewhere in an asylum where they can't do no harm."

"Get the murderers first and the half-wits will take care of themselves," said Reata.

They went up at last to Reata's own room.

He had left Rags behind him. The little dog jumped down from his master's bed and bounded across the dead man. He began to whine and leap around the knees of Reata until he was picked up and put on the shoulder of his master. From that vantage point he looked down on all that happened.

The sheriff said to Reata when he had completed his examination: "There's nothing to it. If you saw that name written on the floor, then it's a fact that Sam Durant killed the gypsy, and that makes it ten to one that he murdered poor old Cleve. Ah, Reata, there was a man for you! One of the best in the world! And that sour-faced devil murdered his own brother! There's going to be some way of grabbing him and pinning it on him. If we can't prove it by the law, maybe a lynching mob is goin' to turn out to be a right thing for once in a lifetime!"

Reata nodded.

"What'll we do with the body?" asked the sheriff.

"Leave it here," said Reata. "The gypsies'll come for it, likely."

"Shall we send word to 'em?"

"Why send word to 'em? They'll know. They know when one of their kind dies, almost the way a buzzard knows and comes a hundred miles to have a whack at a dead rabbit. The gypsies are the same way. They always seem to know!"

"You've been a lot with 'em?"

"I was with 'em a day, but it was a lot," answered Reata.

At that the sheriff smiled. He took out a bandanna, unfolded it, and laid it across the face of the dead man.

"If Anton was hired by Sam Durant, then what Anton knows is dead with him. Would any of the other gypsies know anything?"

"Queen Maggie knows everything, of course."

"Can you make her talk?"

"Sure. String her up by the thumbs and light a fire under her feet. She may say something before her feet burn off—but it's not likely to be what you want to know."

The sheriff considered for some time. "What d'you think we ought to do?" he asked.

"Pretend that you think it was an outside job; go back to town; but be ready to come pelting out here the minute you get word. Something is going to break around here before long. I feel it in my bones. Aye, and in my throat, too, just where the knife sank into Anton."

CHAPTER 26

The sheriff left. He told Sam Durant that he had to get back to Boyden Lake, but that he would not let the case drop. There might be some connection, he remarked, between this murder and the unfortunate death of Cleve Durant. With a perfectly calm face, the sheriff shook hands with Sam Durant, begged him to keep looking for clues, and to send the first word of any importance to him at once. Then he rode away.

Reata saw him go, entered the bunk house, and promptly stretched himself on a bunk and fell asleep. Rags, curled up at his feet, would be his guard. There Reata remained until noon, when Porky Durant came in and shook him by the shoulder to wake him up.

"Hey, wake up, Reata!" Porky said. "Y'oughta see what's out here to see you!"

Reata wakened, and saw Porky slapping his thigh and doubling over with mirth. The mouth of Porky was opened wide by laughter, but the cheeks of Porky were so fat that his mouth could not stretch very far. In that it was actually like the mouth of a pig. He seemed one who would have to take small bites.

"There's a man out there in a covered wagon," said Porky, "and he's askin' for you; and he's got that dead gypsy loaded into his wagon already. And you'd laugh to see the mules that are pullin' the wagon, and the way he rolled his cigar in his mouth. And the funny part is that he ain't a man at all. He's a woman! Come on and see, Reata!"

Reata knew well enough that it must be Queen Maggie who had come for the dead. He went out at once and found her sitting slued around in the driver's seat, resting one booted foot on the top of the right wheel. She had on her man's sombrero and coat, as usual, and the long, fat Havana stuck up at an angle in a corner of her great mouth. It always seemed to Reata as though coffee and tobacco, working together, had dyed her complexion to its present color. It looked like the sort of skin that would keep water out for a long time. The oil of the good tobacco seemed to have soaked through and through her body. And now she rolled the cigar across her huge mouth with a motion of her lips and said: "Hello, Reata. How's things?"

"Pretty good," he answered. "How's things with you?"

"Fair," she replied. "Pretty fair, I'd say. Except this fool goes and gets himself bumped off. He used to bring in a good pile of money to the tribe when we put on a show. You seen him ride. You know how good he was."

"Yeah, he was good on a horse," said Reata.

"You're right," said Queen Maggie. "He wasn't no good noplace else. He was a lyin', sneakin', thievin', worthless hound."

This frankness of hers did not surprise Reata. Nothing about her ever surprised him since their first meeting not so very long before.

"Well, I got him laid out in the wagon here and lashed down," she said. "And that makes me remember that things would be pretty good for you if you wanted to join up with us now, Reata."

"You want me back?" he asked her curiously.

"Aye, we want you back bad," she stated.

"I'll bet you do," agreed Reata. "Every knife in the tribe would be good and sharp for me."

She shook her head, and the long ash at the end of her cigar broke off and rolled down into the wrinkles of her coat.

"You don't understand," she answered. "We know when we lose a man; we know when we want a man to take his place. Your rope tricks, they'd make a lot of money for you and for us. It's an easy life, Reata. Besides, I need you. I ain't as young as I used to be, and I need a gent that I can kind of lean on. I could lean on you. Because you're a right man."

"Thanks," said Reata. "But I'm pretty busy."

"Where's Miriam in that hard head of yours?" asked Queen Maggie. "Ain't she got a place in it?"

"Sure she has," agreed Reata. "You don't forget a girl that's brought you as close to murder as she brought me."

"Now, now, now!" murmured Maggie. "You wouldn't go and hold that agin' her, would you? And there she is,

132

yearnin' and mournin' for you. There'll never be no man for her except you, Reata!"

"No?" said Reata.

He tried to smile, but a sigh was rising in his throat as he remembered.

"Chuck this ranch job and hop up here with me," said Queen Maggie. "We sure need you, and we sure want you! There won't be any knives out for you. Now that Anton's dead, there ain't anybody that hates you enough to count."

"No, you wouldn't use knives. Guns would do just as well," said Reata. "And the tribe has plenty of guns."

"Is that the way you figger us?" asked Queen Maggie.

"That's the way," said Reata.

"So long, then, and the devil with you!" answered Maggie, and whacked the mules with a long stick.

The mules lurched ahead. At a little dogtrot that carried them hardly faster than a walk, they pulled the wagon bumping over the irregularities of the lane, and so drew off onto the main road.

Porky was standing beside Reata, shading his eyes with his plump hand as he stared after the wagon.

"She wanted you to come back, eh? You been with 'em, Reata? I guess you been pretty nigh every place in the world. That's the way you look. Like you been around a lot of places. Who's Miriam?"

"She's a gal the gypsies stole—I don't know where. And they're taking her—I don't know where. To hell, I suppose."

He went back into the bunk house and stretched himself on the same bunk, for he was still very tired. And Rags, as before, sat up at the feet of his master and guarded him. It was the whining of Rags that wakened Reata from a doze. Big Sam Durant stood beside him, his keen, hard eyes drilling into the younger man.

"Are you all petered out, or up to riding range with me?" asked Durant.

"Petered out," said Reata.

"Me and Quinn and Porky are goin' to do some work down the line. There's a stretch of fence that needs some work on it. Reata, I wanta know how long you'll keep on here at the ranch?"

"D'you want me to go?" asked Reata.

"You've brought me no luck," said the rancher bluntly.

"I'll go tomorrow, if you want me out of the way."

"I'll pay you for your full month," said Sam Durant. "But I'd rather have you gone. Tomorrow will be all right."

"Thanks," said Reata tersely. And he closed his eyes again and heard the boots of the rancher thumping noisily out of the bunk house.

It was a little too patent, this speech of the rancher's, thought Reata. He might have waited a few days before trying to elbow Reata off the place. If, in fact, he was to pretend that the gypsy had been murdered by outside agencies, then he ought to pretend that he needed more protection than ever before. But even in the best criminal mind there are bound to be flaws. It was clear that the removal of the gypsy had been a great gain for Sam Durant. Perhaps he had now removed the one man who could intimately witness to the process by which Cleve Durant had been destroyed.

So Reata closed his eyes tighter and summoned sleep from a distance. It came gradually closer. Finally unconsciousness came.

His dreams were not good. He thought that he lay in a powerful furnace, scorched by the heat, and that Miriam sat by the open door of the furnace, laughing, throwing in bits of fuel to increase the blaze. The heat was not actually burning his flesh, but he was stifling for the lack of air to breathe.

Finally he heard the whining of Rags, and he wakened.

The brilliance of a burning furnace was around him. The sun was far in the west, and the slant tide of its golden light washed through the room and painted and gilded the wall at the farther end. Rags stood on the chest of his master, and with his ratlike tail straight and one little paw lifted, he was pointing like a hunting dog toward the doorway.

A shadow now fell obscurely on the end wall of the room, and Reata, turning and lifting on one elbow, saw that Miriam was there on the threshold.

She was not as he had seen her last. There was not a single slash of color in her outfit. She was all olive-drab in her loose riding clothes. There were fringed gloves on her hands; a quirt hung from her wrist by its loop. She might have stood as the regular image of the typical range girl out on a long ride, but the roughest of clothes could not diminish the grace of her carriage. Under the deep shadow

of her Stetson he probed for the blue of her eyes and
found it.

She waved to him, saying: "Am I coming in or staying
out?"

"Staying out," said he.

CHAPTER 27

He lay down again quickly. He wanted to wink her out of
his memory and clear his eyes of her, because far down in
his heart there was a region of pain and dizzy joy which
she occupied. He had to forget her. He had to cut her out
of his thoughts. Because even if her blood was white, her
life and soul were gypsy.

"All right," said her voice from the doorway. "I'm coming."

Rags began to wag his tail and whine an eager welcome.
Her heels tapped on the floor.

"I told you to stay out," said Reata brutally.

She came up to the bunk and looked down at him.

"You only said it twice," said she. "Three times would
have made it true."

He could smell the dust on her clothes and see it in the
wrinkles. He could smell the horse sweat, but also he
found in the air a thin scent of lavender. It reminded
Reata of riding over a white summer road at the end of a
day, and having the first breeze of the evening carry down
from the uplands a breath of coolness and of sweetness.

"Move over there a little," said Miriam.

He closed his eyes and waved his hand.

"You ought not to be here," he said.

Although he kept his eyes closed, he could see her, and
more clearly. He decided that it would be better to look at
the reality than at the thought. So he opened his eyes
again.

She sat down on the mere edge of the bunk.

"It's no use our talking to each other," said Reata.
"You'd better go away."

She pulled off her gloves, folded her arms, and held her chin between a thumb and a forefinger.

"How does it feel," she said, "all at once having a girl that you like so close to you?"

He stroked the head of Rags and said nothing.

"I thought you were bigger," went on the girl. "But you're not such a big fellow, after all."

In spite of himself, he found that he was taking a big breath.

"When you're on your feet, then you're big enough," she said.

He kept patting Rags. He wanted to smile, so he made himself frown.

"It's pretty good to be like this, isn't it?" said Miriam. "The other things stop."

He did not see, but he could feel the shadow of her gesture.

"The gypsies just turn into shadows," she told him. "All the years of my life flicker and go out. It's so nice to be here, Reata, that I even like this rotten old bunk house. What do you say? Isn't it pretty good to have me here?"

"Quit it," said he.

"Sit up and talk, will you?" she pleaded.

He sat up.

After that, rising, he walked over to the long table and sat down on the end of it, swinging one leg and watching her.

"It's no good, Miriam," he said.

"Why isn't it any good?"

"We know each other too well to be silly about the old game."

She stood up in her turn and smiled at him. In the slouchy clothes she was more exquisitely feminine than gypsy finery could ever make her.

"All right," admitted Reata. "I feel trapped when I see you, but believe me, I'm going to get out of the trap."

She kept her silence. He felt her eyes travel on him, half amused and half contented.

"You say that if a fellow struggles against the trap, he just tears himself up," he went on.

She shook her head. "I'm not saying anything," she answered. The fact was, he thought, that she did not have to say very much, because to look at her was enough, and to keep waiting and listening for her to speak again.

"What sort of a sap do you think I am, Miriam?" he asked her. "I can see the facts, can't I? I can see you, can't I?"

"I hope so," she answered.

"What would it turn out? Suppose we marry—there's Miriam and Reata. Reata, the pickpocket, with his rope tricks; and Miriam, the bareback rider and gypsy. Would it be a bust? Of course it would be a bust. You want your own sweet way, and I simply wouldn't have it."

"Of course you wouldn't," said she.

"There'd have to be a master in my house," he declared.

"I've always wanted to find a master," said she.

"The fact is that it wouldn't work. There's something fine about you; there's something in you that the right sort of a man could bring out. By Jove, Miriam, how clearly I can see you fixed up in a fine place with everything that a woman could want, from servants to blood horses. You could be happy like that, with nothing but velvet ever to come under your hands. But the way you'd have to live with me, starting at nothing, in a shack, eating beans twice a day, roughening up your hands on a scrubbing board, wearing calico, getting down at the heels, would that be a life? No, you'd hate it. I'd hate it, too, when I saw you begin to change. You see how it is?"

She said nothing, but watched him, and he felt the gentle traveling of her eyes.

"Well, say what you think," he finally snapped.

"I'm not thinking," said Miriam.

"I mean, about what I was just telling you. Don't you admit that it's all true?"

"I don't know."

"Now, you look here, Miriam," exclaimed Reata. "I want to tell you one thing."

"I want you to tell me," she said gravely.

He snapped his fingers in the air, scowling.

She snapped her fingers in the air, smiling.

"Quit it, will you?" exclaimed Reata.

"All right," she said.

He started to stride around the room, taking bigger and bigger steps.

"I'm making a fool of myself," said Reata.

"Yes, but it's sort of nice," said the girl.

At that he walked straight up to her and stood so close

that he could look down into her face, which, in fact, she made easy by tilting back her head.

"You make me so mad that I'd like to put my hands on you," he told her.

"I wish you would," said she.

He did throw out his arms at that, until they almost closed on her, but by degrees he fought himself away from that tip-toe attitude of expectancy and got back on his heels, and forced his arms away and clasped his hands behind his back.

"You'd better go on home," said Reata.

"I'll go if you'll go part of the way," she replied.

"What's the idea of that?"

"I've got what you want. I've got the answer to all of this riddle."

"What riddle? This one here on the ranch, you mean? About Anton—and Sam Durant, you mean?"

"I don't care about Anton. But I've got the answer to the rest of it."

"Go ahead and tell me, then."

"I'm going to do better than tell you. I'm going to show you."

"Show me, then. Where?"

"Up in the hills."

"What sort of bunk is this?" he demanded.

"It isn't bunk. When Maggie admitted that she couldn't get you any other way, I begged her to let you in on the inside about all of this. I don't know what it is, but *she* knows, all right. She told me that if I could get you up into the hills, then she'd let you in on the inside."

He was frozen with amazement, with excitement, too.

"Wait a minute. What would Maggie get out of this?"

"She hopes that she can get you back into the tribe for good and all."

This chimed so perfectly with the way that Maggie had talked to him that noon that he could not help being impressed. For a long moment he kept in a balance, tempted, striving against temptation, wondering if he would not be acting the part of a fool unless he accepted this invitation to learn the heart of the mystery.

At last he said: "All right. That goes with me. I'll saddle Sue and go along."

She had been under such a strain, in spite of her

smiling, that the breath of relief she exhaled had a faint moan in it.

Reata went out to the corral, saddled Sue, and tossed Rags up before him. Then he rode out and joined the girl. She was on one of those half dozen little silken stallions, little gems of the range, that the gypsies always had in their string. With glaring red eyes and nostrils showing their crimson lining, he could do nothing but dance and prance while the long, low-geared mare traveled smoothly over the trail. Reata wondered at the ability of the girl to keep the steady pull which the little stallion needed. But her slender arm seemed tireless.

It was sunset before they came to the rim of the foothills; it was dark before they had been long among them, and then a moon came up and showed them the rolling hill forms around them, and the dark solemnity of the pines as the woods began.

She took off her hat and tied it behind the saddle. He knew that that was because she wanted him to see her, and he was glad. Their horses had learned to travel side by side, nose to nose, while Rags scurried up the trail ahead of them, hunting here and there, always busy, whipping his tail from side to side so fast that it disappeared from the eye. And he could see her leaving the watching of the trail to him, while she kept her head turned up to him, smiling. And he was smiling, too. They spoke hardly at all.

Once he said: "It ought to be always like this."

She answered: "It's *going* to be always like this."

It was long after sunset now, and the moon was well up when they came to a narrowing of the trail among big rocks, the trail passing in a straight line uphill.

"How much farther?" he asked.

"Do you care?"

"No, I don't care."

They laughed together; but all at once he heard Rags's shrill yipping of fear and anger, and saw the little dog come streaking down the trail toward him. The clang of a rifle and the waspish hum of a bullet past his ear followed instantly. He saw figures leaping up among the rocks and heard the outlandish voices of the gypsies crying out to one another.

This was the way Queen Maggie intended to let him into the mystery. Aye, into the greatest of all mysteries!

He was done—he was finished. He had hardly the sense

to pull the mare around, and automatically he caught up Rags as the little dog leaped for him. Had the girl known? Had it been all acting on the part of Miriam?

No, he saw her ride straight forward up the trail above him, throwing out her arms to either side as though that empty embrace of hers would shield her lover better from the bullets. He heard her crying out in the gypsy lingo, her voice like a shrill, mournful song.

Well, they would not risk putting bullets into the jewel of their tribe. They would spread out to either side to shoot past her into their chosen target.

He had loosed the good mare; she was running down the hillside like a bounding stone with terrible, unmatchable speed.

CHAPTER 28

When the three came in that evening and found that the cook had seen Reata ride away with a girl just before sunset time, the rancher said nothing, merely shrugging his shoulders. But when Harry Quinn swore that Reata was not the sort of a fellow to leave in the middle of a job, the cook said: "He ain't comin' back. I seen the girl."

"What did she look like?" asked Harry Quinn.

"I didn't see her face. I just seen the back of her, and that was enough. Reata, he ain't comin' back till that girl wants to let him go."

Harry Quinn argued, but rather vaguely. He wondered at the emphatic way in which the rancher exclaimed: "What would a girl have to do with this here?"

Then the loud mouth of Porky Durant was saying: "Hi! I heard the gypsy woman this noon talkin' about Miriam, that wanted Reata back. I heard her talkin'. Maybe it was Miriam that got Reata!"

"Miriam?" cried Harry Quinn.

Then he was silent in his turn.

"Who is Miriam?" asked Durant.

"Miriam? She's poison; that's all," said Harry Quinn.

140

For he remembered her from the time he had been held prisoner by the tribe. He felt her name as one feels the scar of a vital wound.

Afterward they had supper in a silence imposed on them by the scowling face of Sam Durant. When Porky Durant started to carry on with rambling words about the gypsy woman and her cigar, his uncle said to him briefly: "If you can't talk sense like a man, shut up and give us a few minutes of peace, will you?"

At that Porky hung his head, sulking, and it seemed to Quinn that there were tears in the eyes of the young fellow. He got out of the way quickly after supper, and could be heard moving about in his room, and there was the sound of the squeaking bedsprings as he turned in. The uncle, hearing this, merely muttered: "A swine from the day he was born to the day he'll go into his grave. So much pork. Bah!"

Having expressed himself in this manner, Sam Durant rose. He said good night, and then added at the door of the room: "Reata's leaving tomorrow. I won't be needing you after that, Quinn."

Then he went up the stairs, which creaked steadily beneath him.

Quinn was so angered by that curt dismissal that he stamped across the room and threw open the door leading to the stairs. However, the sound of the squeaking, mounting steps checked his shout in some manner.

He closed the door with a slam and listened to the echo go walking through the place. He turned about, growling in his throat that the place was a tomb, where everybody went to bed at the end of the day. No talk. No sitting around. Nothing to drink.

When he had said that to himself he remembered the jug which stood behind the kitchen door. Therefore he went to it, got himself a glass—a big one—and carried the jug and the glass to the side of the kitchen, where he poured out his drink and set down the glass on the sill of the window.

Here he settled down in some comfort. A good breeze came through the window and cooled his body. He rolled a cigarette, postponing the first taste of the whisky until he should have finished half his smoke. That was the best way, in the opinion of Harry Quinn, to get the full relish out of whisky.

It was while he was rolling the cigarette that a hand advanced in a swift gesture out of the outer darkness, dropped into the whisky glass some drops of colorless liquid, and withdrew again.

The last shadow of that gesture, in fact, streaked across the corner of the eye of Harry Quinn. He turned his head and frowned at the glass. However, the wind was rapidly rising, and he felt that trembling sparkle of the liquid in the glass was caused by the wind. In the distance, thunder began to speak in a full, solemn voice. Quinn lighted his cigarette and drew two or three strong whiffs of the smoke into his lungs. Then, still breathing out smoke, he slowly lifted the glass.

At the good aroma of the whisky, the dry griping of a mighty thirst passed through him. He felt that he could drink the whole contents of that jug easily without ever reaching the roots of dusty dryness at the base of his throat. He lifted the glass, tasted one small swallow, and felt that the stuff was extraordinarily bitter.

However, one meets all sorts of acrid stuff among the bar whiskies of the West. He merely shrugged his shoulders a little and then tossed off the dram.

Bitter? Yes, it was so decidedly bitter that he hastily poured out another drink to wash from his mouth the memory of the first. True enough, that second three fingers of whisky quite removed the taste of the first. Perhaps, thought Harry Quinn, something had gathered at the top of the jug of whisky. Something alkaline, puckering the tongue and the inside of the mouth.

He took another sip of the whisky, found that the bitterness was indeed gone, and then settled back in his chair to enjoy a good evening.

In fact, he did not require a great deal of company, for on occasion he was able to let his memory wander through the dim forest of the past and find many a pleasant spot. He began to daydream, puffing leisurely at his second cigarette, when he found himself nodding, almost overcome by a great sleepiness.

It was such a surprise that he jerked up his head, wondering. Only the moment before he had been feeling fresh, ready to put in a good time. Now he was dull, drowsy, full of yawning. He shook his head again, but that gesture did not serve to clear his wits. Instead, there was a gripping numbness that settled across his eyes like the pressure of a hot hand.

He regarded this sensation with bewilderment until something hot prickled between his fingers. He looked down and saw that his cigarette had burned up to the skin. He dropped it. Between his fingers there was a large white blister, and he had actually been almost insensible to the pain!

Sleep was charging over him. The soft beating of many feet was trampling over his brain, and in his ears, more and more audible, he heard the loud roaring of his pulse.

Thunder rolled outside the house, but it was dim and befogged.

Harry Quinn had come to his feet, and there reeled back and forth like a hopeless drunkard. But the terror that was springing ice-cold in his breast helped to give to his mind an instant of clearness.

This was the way the thing had been done before.

The entire testimony that Dave Bates had given to the jury now swept back over the mind of Harry Quinn. Dave had said that he had sat down and had a drink—one drink. And then he had grown sleepy—very sleepy. It was strange that a single drink could overcome the steel nerves and the hard, grim mind of Dave Bates. But, then, perhaps there had been in that first drink—if only Dave had remembered to speak about that!—a strange bitterness?

The terror ran wild in Harry Quinn.

He knew that a criminal is likely to use the same method in successive crimes. If a man kills with a knife once, he'll use the same tool again; if he kills with a hammer, he'll murder with a hammer the next time.

And now the murderer of the Durant ranch was commencing his work again.

Quinn had to get out of the place. But as he turned toward the door, he realized that he would not be able to take more than a few steps. He would be found and dragged back and put into position by the murderer, and his gun would be found, the next day, with at least one chamber discharged—and a dead man would be sitting in the chair opposite him!

What man would that be?

He had to get rid of his gun, then. He pulled it out of the holster and tried to throw it through the window, but it merely struck the sill and fell heavily to the floor.

It was strange. There was no force in his arm. It was limp.

He leaned and picked up the weapon. He raised it as high as the window sill, when it fell from his nerveless fingers.

He tried to pick it up again, but his body collapsed to the floor. He could not lift the revolver now. It was as impossible as though the little Colt weighed a ton.

He might cry out, though who could hear him except Porky Durant? The good-natured, foolish Porky seemed to Harry Quinn the one base and resting point of his salvation. He parted his lips. His own voice sounded like the roar of a sea lion on a rock, a noise submerged by the noise of the sea. Then all at once the body of Harry Quinn went limp along the floor.

CHAPTER 29

The sleep of Sam Durant was generally very sound, but since the death of his brother, there had been a tension on his nerves which rarely would relax. Because of that tension, the mere whistling of a draft through his room caused him to waken on this night.

He listened for a moment, and then heard the dull booming of thunder in the distance and the murmur of the wind around the edges of the house. A storm was coming up, and that would explain the whistling draft through his window.

Suddenly the draft ceased almost entirely. This was a trifle strange, he thought, for the wind was still murmuring around the corners of the building. It was as though the door of his room had been shut softly.

Gradually he relaxed, thinking again about that which had occupied his mind before he fell asleep—the disappearance of Reata. The man was too dangerous to be entirely safe. The manner in which he had handled formidable Bill Chester was proof enough of that. Above all, it was strange that Chester had not tried to retaliate in some manner, but perhaps the explanation was not only in the things that Reata had done to Chester, but also in the faint yellow gleam that came into Reata's eyes when he was excited. A fellow who had seen that light once might not care to see it again.

Just as the body of the rancher grew slack again, and his thoughts were growing obscure, he distinctly heard the fall of some metal body in the lower part of the house, from the direction of the kitchen. This puzzled him, since the cook was already in bed. But perhaps Harry Quinn was rummaging around in the kitchen for food, though he had eaten plenty for supper.

A moment later the sound came again. The same pan, perhaps, had slipped from the hand of the clumsy forager! The rancher frowned, but while he was still frowning he heard a cry so bestial, yet so human, so filled with despair and with horror, so unlike anything that he had ever heard before in his life, that Durant sprang out of his bed.

So doing, it seemed to him that he saw, very vaguely outlined near the door, the form of another man.

"Who's there?" he demanded.

But the form was not near the door. That was an illusion caused by the faintness of the light. Something rushed in the air. A crushing blow fell on the side of Sam Durant's head and knocked him to his knees. He was still stunned and helpless as the noose of a rope was tightened around his wrists. Then a gag was crammed between his teeth.

A whispering voice said at his ear: "Stand up, Durant!"

He rose.

"It's your turn!" said the whispering voice. "You remember Cleve? You're going to sit in the same kind of a chair, dead as hell. You'll like that, Durant. You're going to be wiped out. There's going to be nobody left but the fat-faced half-wit, Porky. He'll have the Durant ranch and the Durant money. Understand what I say?"

He nodded.

The thing was clear to him. Reata had been the outside agent who had killed Cleve Durant. Reata was also the fellow who came looking for a job in order that he might find his chance to destroy Cleve's brother. This shadowy form was about the height of Reata, and must, in fact, be he.

What devilish malevolence was behind the thing? Perhaps the desire was simply to wipe out the two older Durants, knowing that Porky could easily be handled in whatever way shrewd, hard men desired.

This explanation was enough. The only strange thing was that he, Sam Durant, with all his experience of men in this world, had not realized that in his new hired hand he had a man too dangerous to be used on a ranch.

Well, he would pay for that blindness now, and he would pay in full.

The whisper at his ear said: "Come on now, Durant. Walk straight through the door. Don't try to bolt. Don't even try to stomp, to make a noise, or I'll bash your brains out here. Besides, noise won't help you. Poor Porky's snoring, I suppose, and Doc is half deaf. That's why I didn't have to get rid of Doc—because he's half deaf."

Durant obeyed orders. As beaten men will do, he moved steadily on according to command. The door was opened for him from behind. He went down the stairs toward the kitchen, and the rope was kept taut about his wrists from behind.

"Wait a minute," said the whisper at his ear.

He paused, and a bit of cloth was wrapped about his head. When he was so blinded, the door in front of him was pushed open, and he knew that he was entering into the presence of light.

He was guided across the room, both his elbows being held in a powerful grasp. Then he was made to sit in a chair, and at once a long length of rope was wound around him. A man cannot be more helpless than he is when he's tied into a chair. There is nothing that he can do, no way in which he can move.

But Sam Durant was tired of this life, anyway, he told himself. It was far, far better to relax and let the thing be ended for him by the hand of another man.

The whisper at his ear was saying: "Now you see the idea, Durant? Harry Quinn is lying on the floor by the window. He's been drugged with stuff in his whisky. The fool! A hand dropped the stuff into his glass while it stood on the window sill. That was my hand, Durant. I drugged him. As the drug began to take hold, he realized what was happening. He tried to throw his gun away. That's what you heard fall on the floor twice, but you lay there in your bed like a swine. You had no brain to work with.

"Then Quinn tried again to throw out the gun, so that

you couldn't be shot with his Colt. But he failed again. The dope was working in him. He couldn't do it. Then he yelled, and that yell was what got you out of bed and in position to get a sock on the side of the head. You see!"

The whisperer chuckled. Durant sat rigid, waiting.

"Now," said the whisperer, "I've got you sitting pretty, and all I have to do is to cross the floor and get hold of that gun. Understand? And after I have it, I come up close to you and shoot. And where would you rather have it, Durant? In the head? Or in the heart? Nod once for the head and twice for the heart. I'm a kind fellow, Durant, and I give dead men anything they ask for!"

He chuckled again.

Durant nodded his head once.

"You want it quick and sweet, eh?" said the whisper. "All right. I'll aim the slug right at your mouth. I've wanted to smash a bullet through that mug of yours many a time before this. Because I know you, Durant, and you know me! You know me, but not as well as you think! Are you ready to die, Durant?"

Durant nodded. For it seemed to him just then that there was nothing in the world he wanted so much as the cessation of that frightful whispering. He heard the footfall cross the floor. The thunder was rolling loudly again, but he heard the rasping of metal against wood as the fallen gun was picked up.

As they had found Cleve, so in the morning they would find his body sitting freely in the chair, the ropes removed, a bullet through his head!

CHAPTER 30

Reata, as the mare fled like a falling stone down the slope, was brought to safety by a sweep of the trail to the side, so that a crowd of vast boulders projected between him and his pursuers. He heard their frantic voices screeching behind him, tearing through the air, and then the pelting hoofs of horses.

Well, Sue had traveled a good distance this day, but she would travel still farther, and at a rate that would make the best horses among the gypsies dizzy before long.

The way flattened out, running in a shallow valley with hills to either side, and behind him he heard the tumult of the horses, and the shrill cries of the gypsies to one another. He could see the dark of their faces and the brightness of their eyes without turning his head to look. They saw him, and a few bullets rattled among the rocks, but now he was around a farther bend, and every stride of the racing mare would put a safer distance between him and his hunters.

And the girl?

They would curse her and rage against her, no doubt, but they would not touch her. She meant too much for them. It was savagely in his mind to suspect that she had known the trap into which she was leading him, but in his heart he knew that she had been innocent. And never would he see, in all his days, a braver thing than that picture of her riding before him toward the guns to cover his retreat, her arms thrown out wide.

In the white of the moon or the thick black shadow of the hills, he wove a way out of the highlands and into the flat of the valley of Boyden Lake below. For half a mile he kept waiting for the pursuit to appear. Then he realized that they had surrendered their chase. They knew Sue of old, and that they could not keep pace with her long, easy stride.

So he rated her back to an easy lope which she could continue forever, it seemed, without fatigue, flowing smoothly along over the ground. She was still at that gait, with hardly a break, when he came to the Durant ranch. Half the sky was now adrift with thunderheads, and the noise of the storm was blowing up louder and louder out of the west. Still, he had moonlight to guide him, but that moon was almost hidden by clouds as he approached the ranch house.

He pulled off the saddle and bridle and turned the mare into the shed, where he fed her. He was barely through giving her grain when he heard, or thought he heard, a strange cry from the direction of the house.

No doubt it was an error of his mind. For the wind, when it is howling, can make strange sounds. And yet, as he finished giving the mare hay, and then rubbed her down with some twists of hay, he was seriously troubled, he hardly knew by what, and he had to turn back the pages of his memory for a few moments before striking again on the voice that he thought he had heard.

At once he gave up his work on Sue and strode from the barn without so much as closing the door behind him.

There was a light in the kitchen, which he had noticed as he came in, and attributed to Doc doing some late work—making bread, perhaps.

But when he came closer, he saw even from the near distance a man bending down behind the window to the floor, lifting at something, and against the opposite wall, lashed firmly into a chair, was a masked man. The rope went around and around his body and limbs, so that he could not stir.

Now the burden which was being raised behind the window appeared as Reata drew near, and he saw it was Quinn, looking like a dead man. His head was hanging; his arms flopped down; his mouth hung senselessly open.

He who lifted that burden could not be seen for a moment. And Reata exclaimed, not loudly, but in intense horror and surprise. Harry Quinn was dropped like a sack to the floor, and now, staring out the window, his red hair bristling, it seemed, and his face working like the face of a beast, young Porky Durant glared from the yellow lamp-light into the dull white of the moonshine in which Reata stood.

A gun flashed in Porky's hand; Reata was already racing, not away—distance would do him no good—but straight for the wall of the house.

As he ran, the subtle coils of his lariat were in his hand, and he cast full for the window. The noose gripped at the flash of the gun. Reata jerked back. He heard a yell. The gun exploded. He saw the Colt fall outside the window, and the lessening noose come off the extended hand of Porky.

Instead of running to the side, Reata dashed straight on at the window itself.

Porky had sprung aside; as Reata came up, he saw the chunky fellow standing with legs spread out, as though to receive a shock and withstand it—but he was facing, now, the open door, instead of the window. It had not occurred to him that any man would choose to enter the room by the window. There he stood, braced, and with another Colt balanced in his hand.

The whole thing was perfectly clear.

As Cleve Durant had died, so was Sam to go. "Durant" was the name that Anton had written as he died. "Durant," with Porky in mind.

It was Porky who had planned, so simply, to wipe out his two uncles and possess himself of the entire property without loss of time. It was Porky, again, who had made the bargain with the gypsies when he first needed help. It was Porky who, on this day, had twice tried to get Reata away from the ranch as a man too dangerous to have around when he was working out the last half of his schemes.

These things Reata saw clearly as he rushed for the window. He could not get through it before Porky had a chance to turn and fire into him. He could not enter the guarded door. And he carried no gun!

It was not the first time in his life that he had had occasion to curse his fixed resolution never to wear a gun. But he had that agent which could enter the room for him.

It was not easy. He had to build a noose so small that it would pass through the narrowness of the window, so broad that it would drop over the shoulders of Porky.

One gesture made that noose. One gesture threw it through the window, making a soft, slithering whisper through the air. And Porky, crouched a little, wavering a bit from side to side in the animal intensity of his hunger to kill, heard that whisper in the air.

He seemed to know what it meant, and that it was too late for him to sidestep. Instead, he twisted about as the rope descended above him, and with a bullet from his gun, held hardly more than hip-high, knocked the sombrero from Reata's head. It was good shooting. It was excellent shooting. But the next moment a powerful tug on the lariat had jerked Porky forward.

Reata went through that window like a cat. The gun was still in Porky's hand. He tried to twist around and use it, till Reata stamped on his wrist.

The bones crunched softly inside the fat of the flesh, and Porky lay still. A few twists of the little reata tied the fat fellow hand and foot. Then Reata stepped to the rancher and made him free.

Big Sam Durant leaned from his chair, staring, staring.

Reata, working busily over the inert body of Harry Quinn, would never forget how Durant said slowly: "I only thought he was a pig. I forgot—that swine eat meat!"

But Porky said nothing. He did not even nurse his crushed wrist. All the life of his body and of his soul was concentrated in the red stain of fire in his eyes.

It seemed to Reata afterward that there was no regret in Porky for what he had done. He had saved himself all his life, realizing his own vicious capacities, masking them under his affectation of simplicity which gave him idle days, saving himself for the great moment when he could strike to kill. There was only one real folly in his plan, and that was the exactitude with which he had copied the first crime in preparing for the second.

"When I seen you the first time," said Porky to Reata, later on, "I knew that you might make things go wrong. I knew it by the damn cool look of you. I seen the yaller in your eyes the first shot out of the box. How I wish that I'd cut your throat while you were asleep!"

That was all he would say.

They could not make him speak even at his trial. In silence he was to go to the end of his life, as far as legal answers went. But the proof that was gathered about him was too complete and too exact for him to wriggle out of the net.

Harry Quinn went to the penitentiary to get Dave Bates. He wanted Reata to do it because, as he said, Dave would think a lot of the first friend he saw when he was freed from prison.

But Reata wanted to go back to Rusty Gulch alone, slowly. He wanted to pass under long leagues of the blue of the western sky, and to let the honest sun burn out of him some of the memories of the Durant ranch.

Sam Durant did not beg him to stay. He did not insist even when Reata refused the thick sheaf of banknotes which he offered to his rescuer.

Durant said: "I know what it means to you. It's been like a lot of bad weather. On top of timber line. No sun to see. You wanta forget. Well, you'll never forget, Reata. No more'n we'll ever forget you!"

Then Reata rode south, leisurely. He had Rags for company. In that company he felt more than secure, because for the second time the little scrap of a dog had given him the warning that enabled him to save his life. And there was only one shadow on the soul of Reata all the way, and that was the thought of the girl.

But it was better that he should not try to find her. There was too much gypsy in her soul. She would be irreclaimable to the last moment of her life. One could not be in her company without finding the bright face of danger too often at hand. And yet the thought of her was always near him like a presence on the farther side of a door.

When he came down into Rusty Gulch, he came by twilight, ten days after he had left the house of Durant, and after he had put up Sue in the box stall which was her special place in the establishment of Pop Dickerman, Reata knew, as he patted her head, that she was two-thirds his own.

From the house, as he approached it, he heard only one voice sounding, loudly, and that was the voice of Harry Quinn. So Reata came up stealthily and peered through the window.

What he saw was Pop Dickerman waiting on his two men at supper, filling their plates and their coffee cups, stepping here and there in soundless slippers, with a cat curled securely on his shoulder, a scrawny, yellow-eyed tomcat.

Harry Quinn was enlarging himself over a glass of whisky, which stood beside his plate of food. But his words had no meaning to the mind of Reata, who was staring fixedly at the little man who sat at the table. The face of Dave Bates was so thin that, in fact, it looked like only half of a normal face. It was twisted and crooked. The brow alone was noble and wide, and the eyes were as cold as stones. Never in his life had Reata seen a thing so evil.

And it was for this that he had rubbed elbows with that whispering death on the Durant ranch.

Part Three

CHAPTER 31

Through the window, Pop Dickerman could see Reata reclining in the shade of the horse shed. It was the last place he should have been, because at any moment people from Rusty Gulch were likely to walk into the junk yard and rummage around through the assorted piles. Too many citizens knew Reata's face perfectly well, and too many kept remembering how he had sawed his way out of the jail; but Reata preferred the open air, even if it meant peril to his life, and Dickerman knew, by the increasing restlessness of that brown-faced young man, that he could not hold him very much longer at the junk yard.

The little dog, Rags, walked up and down on guard, scanning every bird in the air, canting his head at every sound near and far, but his master seemed totally indifferent to the world around him. He had in his hands that lithe little lariat which was his one weapon and his principal diversion, and now he made it rise like a running snake, now coil like a snake about to strike. Seen from such a distance, the reata seemed no thicker than a piece of twine, even though Dickerman knew that it was strong enough to hold a horse.

Reata threw his knife on the ground and began to strike at it with the noose of his rope. The noose flicked in and out like a striking snake, and at the third try the knife was caught by the handle and snatched into the air, where Reata caught it.

A very neat little trick, Dickerman thought, not particularly showy, but useful in many a pinch.

He continued to stare for some moments at Reata, his long, furry face wrinkling with intense distaste. Just now Reata was useful to him—very useful. But he felt that in the long run nothing but evil could come of his connection with Reata.

He had got as far as the kitchen when he heard a beating at his front door. He paused a moment before going to answer that knock. Any summons from the street always gave him pause, for an instant, and made his heart rise in guilty fear while he surveyed his actions of recent days. But always he was able to tell himself that, if he was a fence, he was such a subtle and secret receiver of stolen goods that the law would never get its hands on him. Even Reata, who now had worked for him during some time, did not yet know the actual profession of his employer, no matter what he might suspect.

These were the thoughts that streamed through his mind as he passed through his junk store; now he pulled open the street door and found a rider dust-covered, sun-reddened.

"Are you Dickerman? Aye, you've got the look of him. This letter's for you."

Dickerman took the envelope, opened it, read the message. At the first words, he wanted to draw back into the shadow. He peered up in suspicion at this stranger who had in his possession news so precious.

"They paid you, eh?" said Dickerman.

"They paid me half," said the messenger. "I got ten dollars more coming."

"Here," said Dickerman. And he put a five-dollar bill in the hand of the stranger. There was a shout of rage. Dickerman slammed the door shut, and the voice was partly stifled by the stout partition. In the dimness, he was reading:

We can't find Bill Champion, but we've found his horse. He's left it in a safe place, and a place that keeps traveling. A gang of gypsies has that horse in charge. We don't know how to get at it. Gypsies can steal, but they can't be stolen from. Reata won't be any help, because it's the same gang that knows him and hates him—Queen Maggie's outfit. We'll keep trying to snag the gray. BATES.

Reata would not be of any help? That was what Dave Bates thought, but Bates had not had time enough to learn the qualities of Reata in detail.

There was heavy beating at the back door of the house. Someone was shaking the door violently, then giving it the

154

weight of his shoulder. That would be the big, red-faced messenger, of course. He wanted his other five-dollar bill. But Dickerman preferred to part with blood rather than to give up dollars. Give a man half the price he asks, and in time he will be contented.

He went to the kitchen, and heard the voice of Reata call out: "Hey! Stop that racket, will you? I'm trying to sleep."

"*You're* trying to sleep?" shouted the big messenger. "Why, who are *you*, anyway?"

"I'm a sleepy man. Go on away and don't make such a noise, will you?" said Reata.

"What'll you do about it?" asked the big man. He went striding toward Reata, with his fists clenched so hard that his elbows cocked out to the sides. "I wanta know what you'll do about it."

Reata rose slowly. He seemed to be weak, and leaned a hand against the wall of the shed. But Dickerman laughed and then smoothed his furry face with his hand, still smiling.

"Go away and don't bother me," said Reata wearily. "I don't want to do you any harm. You haven't given me much cause—yet."

"How's this for cause then?" shouted the messenger, and struck with the flat of his hand for that brown, yawning face. The hand beat against the empty air. Reata stepped forward and to the side. He made a little jerking movement with one foot and caught the arm of the other in a twist. It was done so leisurely that only the eye of a Dickerman could have estimated the real speed. And the husky messenger fell flat in the dust. Reata sat on his chest. He had the two hands of the messenger lashed together with a couple of turns of his inevitable lariat. With the pinch of two fingers he could keep the big fellow helpless now.

"You don't want to make so much noise," said Reata, yawning.

"Dickerman," shouted the prostrate man, writhing. "The robber, he—"

"I don't care about Dickerman. I was just getting settled for a sleep," said Reata. "You want to remember that. You certainly ought to give a fellow a chance to have his sleep."

He stood up and turned the other loose. For an instant,

Dickerman hoped that the messenger would attempt to strike again, but the fellow moved away, head down, dusting off his clothes as he went.

CHAPTER 32

Dickerman went out into the junk yard, that outdoor domain of his wealth, and sat down beside Reata. Rags kept a space between them, growling softly. Nothing could make the little dog give up an instinctive hatred of the junkdealer.

Dickerman said: "Read this!" and gave the message to Reata. When it was read, Reata yawned again.

"Who's Bill Champion?" he asked.

"He's the thing that keeps Gene Salvio on the road," said Dickerman. "And Salvio's the third man you're going to bring back to me. You ain't forgot that, Reata?"

"No, I haven't forgotten. I thought he must be in jail somewhere."

"You got Quinn away from the gypsies. You got Bates out of the pen. It's goin' to be harder to get Salvio away from Champion's trail, so he'll be free to come back to me."

"What keeps Salvio on Champion's trail then?"

"You don't know Salvio," said Dickerman. "There's a gent that's all pride and fire."

"I saw his picture," said Reata. "He looked proud enough to rob a bank, all right. What's his pride got to do with Champion?"

"Gene was in a saloon one day," said Dickerman, "and he didn't like the looks of Champion. Nobody likes the looks of Champion, because he ain't got any. But Gene started to get more room, and Champion don't like to be elbowed. He elbowed back and knocked Gene flat, and then when Gene pulled a gun, Champion kicked the gun out of his hand and threw Gene into the street."

"He's hard, is he?" said Reata. "I mean Champion—he's a hard hombre, is he?"

"He's as hard as they come. When Gene got a broken collarbone healed up, he went after Champion and finally met him again. And it's hard to meet Champion, because he's a crook that works all alone. He does his jobs in the West, but he lives other places mostly. He does a clean job; he does it all alone, and then he travels a thousand miles. He's got no cronies. He's got nothing behind him that the sheriff can lay hands on. The only thing folks know is that Champion always rides a gray hoss with four black stockings and a big white blaze between the eyes. Understand?"

"I follow that," said Reata. "He sounds like a sensible sort of a fellow, except that he's always got to ride one horse."

"Maybe he thinks that hoss is his luck," suggested Dickerman. "Well, I was saying that Gene Salvio met up with Champion again, and they had a fair break, and went for their guns, and Salvio's bullet took off the top of Champion's ear, and Champion's slug hit Salvio through the hip and laid him flat. And he stood over Salvio then, and beat him up with a quirt, and some of the scars are still on Salvio's face. Understand?"

"Sounds like a fairly mean man," agreed Reata.

"That job spoiled everything for me," said Dickerman. "I had Gene Salvio so's I could use him whenever I had a hard job to do. I could pull him out like an ace, and win any hand I wanted to win. There's a man, Reata, you wouldn't believe how useful he is. He can pick a pocket or a lock. He can fan a gun with both hands. He can ride anything that wears hair and some that don't. He can smell out a trail like a hunting dog and he ain't afraid of the devil in the dark. But he's got one big fault. He's proud. And that's a devil of a fault, Reata. I'll tell you what it done to Gene Salvio.

"After he got out of the hospital the second time, when Champion had shot him up, I paid his hospital bill and I fixed him up with a fine outfit, and I gave him a little job that was right up his street. But he wouldn't listen to me. He wouldn't do nothing. There wasn't nothing in the world for him, except a third chance at Bill Champion. He said that him or Bill Champion had to die the next meeting. And nothing I could offer would turn him off of that trail.

"I sent out Bates and Quinn, when I seen how things

were, to snag Bill Champion and get him out of the way, so's business could commence again. But Quinn and Bates both got snagged. And then you come along, and you got the pair of them out for me. You've done two parts of your job for me, Reata. There's only one part of it left, and then you can forget about the way I pulled you out of jail, that night. You'll be your own free man, and you'll have Sue to ride away on, wherever you please to go. Besides, I'll heel you with a stake in hard cash."

"All I have to do is to find Champion and kill him, eh?" said Reata.

"That's all you have to do," answered Dickerman.

"And I never carry a gun. You know that."

"You've got the reata and you've got the brain. Brains can kill farther than bullets can. Don't say no to me, Reata."

"I'm a fool if I don't, but I won't."

"Good boy! Good boy!" murmured Dickerman. He stretched out his hand to pat the shoulder of Reata: the shrill snarl of Rags made the hand jump away to safety again. "They've spotted the horse, at last. They've located Champion's horse, and sooner or later, Champion is goin' to come for that horse."

"And the gypsies give it to him, and he rides away. What does that buy for you, Dickerman?"

"The gypsies have the horse now, but they won't have it long. You're going up there to steal that horse, son. And when you got it, you and Quinn and Bates are goin' to go somewhere and sit tight, and wait for Mr. Champion to come and find you."

"How will he find us?"

"He finds anything that he wants to find," answered Dickerman. "There ain't any way of pulling the wool over the eyes of Champion. He'd follow the scent of a hawk in the air, and he'd jump high enough to catch the hawk by the foot, if he had to."

"It's a kind of a ring around the rosy," said Reata. "There's Gene Salvio hunting down the trail of Champion, and Champion not giving a damn about Salvio. but getting ready to pull another crooked job, and coming back to get his lucky horse when he rides to work. And we slide in and catch the horse and use it for bait in the mantrap. That's the way of it, isn't it, Dickerman?"

"You understand me perfect," said Dickerman. "And

when Champion's dead, Salvio will sure come back to me. I been a good chief to him, old son. I'm a good chief to all of them that puts some trust in me. Don't you forget that!"

"Sure," said Reata. "The king of rats ought to be good to his tribe."

This remark stunned Dickerman.

"Reata," he said mournfully, "you don't like me much."

"Not much," agreed Reata cheerfully. "Now go on and tell me about Champion. How will I know him? What does he look like?"

"He don't look like nothing," answered Dickerman, instantly forgetting his personal feelings in the pressure of business. "When he looks down, there ain't even eyes in his face. He had smallpox, or vitriol throwed at him young, or something like that. There ain't much face. There's only a slab, and when he looks down, it's just flat. There ain't no eyebrows. There ain't no eyes. There's only a squash of a nose. But when he looks up, it's like something watching you from behind a mask. A bad mask, mind you. A mask like a kid could make with its thumbs out of wet clay—white clay—soft clay. Maybe you sort of foller me?"

"I sort of follow you," said Reata calmly. "I can see that this is going to be the rattiest job of the three."

"It's a lot the rattiest," agreed Dickerman.

"All right," said Reata. "I'll go and try to catch the bait that'll catch the man without a face. This fellow Champion, is he as mean with guns as you make him out?"

"So mean," said Dickerman, "that you'll never be able to beat him with a Colt. You'll have to use brains on him! Go on, Reata. Do this last thing for me, and I'll make you glad the rest of your life."

CHAPTER 33

Far north of Rusty Gulch and Pop Dickerman's, Reata sat in a front bedroom of Glosson's Hotel in the town of Orchard Creek. Through the window he commanded a view of the central square of the town. As a matter of fact, Orchard Creek had hardly progressed beyond that central square. It managed to have houses and shops all around the plaza and a scattering of shacks along the irregular trails that wound into the town, but that was all. He could see the orchard, also, which had given the place its name—a wretched half dozen of crooked little apple trees which stood in the center of the square. Rags, from the feet of his master, watched the mindless gyrations of the reata which kept bobbing and twisting into strange formations out of the hands of the juggler.

Harry Quinn, walking restlessly up and down the room, also watched the gyrations of the lithe rope, and so did Dave Bates, who was crumpled up in a chair. He appeared to have no backbone. Even when he stood, he was small, and when he sat down, he was no bigger than a child. He seemed deformed, though there was no visible malformation.

Quinn said: "Out there, they're goin' to give their show. You'll see Queen Maggie and the rest of the gypsy cutthroats yonder. And to wind up the show, you'll spot Miriam doing her bareback trick with a big gray stallion that has four black stockings and a big white blaze between his eyes."

"You mean that she's given up the old gelding? You mean that she's trained the horse of Bill Champion for her tricks?" asked Reata sharply.

"Yeah, that's what she's gone and done."

"Doesn't anybody recognize the horse?" asked Reata. "Or is that part of the show—to let folks see Bill Champion's own horse?"

"Of course it ain't any part of the show," said Dave

Bates. "Champion's idea was like this—he don't want to keep coming back to the same place for his hoss. So he leaves it with the gypsies, and they're always wandering around, because that's the way gypsies are. They're not hard to spot. He finds them, and then he can get his hoss. And there you are!"

"But I've heard somewhere that Bill Champion's horse couldn't be handled by any other man," said Reata.

"Sure it can't," said Quinn. "But Miriam ain't a man." He chuckled, and added: "She's got that big hellion eatin' right out of her hand. She's got him so's he'll canter in the circle, and she can do her tricks on him like he was a circus hoss. It sure sets her off, though, the size and the looks of that gray."

"And nobody recognizes the gray?" repeated Reata.

"How would they?" asked Dave Bates acridly. "They've all heard about Champion's stallion. They figure on seein' him jump across the mountains, from peak to peak, you might say, and here they up and find a hoss that jogs around like an old lady's pet. They wouldn't believe their eyes. Not if you was to tell them."

"But are you *sure* it's the right horse?" asked Reata.

"I seen Bill Champion once and I seen his gray," said Dave Bates, "and what I see, I never forget. Will you stop playin' with that rope, Reata, and get down to business?"

Reata did not seem to hear this last portion of the remark and the lariat ceaselessly wove and unwove patterns in the air. He had a dreamy look as he stared out over the square, where people were already beginning to gather.

Harry Quinn said: "That rope *is* his business, Dave. It's likely to see us through."

"What way will it see us through?" asked Bates grimly.

"I dunno," said Harry Quinn. "It got you out of the pen, Dave. It got me away from the gypsies. That's something, I guess."

"Well," said Reata, "if we can fetch the gray away from the gypsies and take it off somewhere, Bill Champion is sure to find the gray and us along with it. Isn't that straight?"

"Champion would find things on the bottom of the sea," answered Bates, "if he wanted to."

"We steal the horse from the gypsies, and we take it off into some faraway corner. And then we sit around and

161

wait for trouble and Bill Champion to show up. Is that right?" asked Reata.

"Listen," exclaimed Dave Bates impatiently, "you know well that you can't steal from gypsies. You can't steal from thieves!"

"We'll have to try," said Reata.

"He stole *me* from the same gang," remarked Harry Quinn.

"Forget it," growled Bates. "He had one whale of a shot of luck. But now let's see what he can do. Reata, you get the big brain workin', and tell us what to do. Here comes the parade right now!"

They could hear the shrilling of the flute and the thin whistling of the violins in the distance, and then the shouting of happy children. Leaning out the window, Reata saw the procession come around the corner into the square.

All in all, it was not a big affair, because the gypsy crowd was not a large band, but it was enough of a sight to fill the eye of Orchard Creek. They were all on horseback, even the fiddlers; and riders and horses blazed with color. The music jigged into common tunes, or went wailing and whooping into strange interludes that brought sudden choruses of yelling from the gypsies.

Queen Maggie passed, with big green glass jewels dropping from her ears and banging against her broad jaws. She had a crimson turban wound about her head and a sword at her side which her big hand looked perfectly capable of wielding.

And in the last group of the procession, with the entire swarm of Orchard Creek children yelling around her, came Miriam, the bareback rider. She was standing upon the back of a quiet gray gelding, a sheen of blue silk tights with a golden fluff of skirts around her middle. Her bare throat and arms were as bronzed as dull gilt. Reata looked at her laughter and tried to find the blue of her eyes, but failed. She seemed all gypsy just then.

She led along, dancing at her side, as fine a stallion as Reata had ever seen, seventeen hands of might and speed, stockinged in black velvet to the knees and hocks, with a broad, white blaze between the eyes. He was girt with a surcingle; the reins of his bridle dripped from the hand of the girl, and he never drew them taut but, in spite of all his restless prancing, seemed to be ruled and checked by all her will more than her hand.

The whole of Orchard Creek, pouring out around the square, applauded this picture. The hair of Miriam was done in a chignon; there was a gilt crown of brightness on her head; and every twist and shining of that crown seemed to bring out fresh shouting, and clapping of hands, and whooping from the cow-punchers.

"That gal is pretty enough to make a pile of trouble," said Dave.

"She's walked Reata into guns a couple of times," answered Harry Quinn. "Look at him now. You could kick him in the face, and he wouldn't know that you'd touched him."

"The fool's crazy about the gypsy, eh?" Bates sneered.

"I wouldn't talk too loud," answered Harry Quinn, a grin on his broad face. "You've only seen her. You ain't talked to her, the way I've done. It ain't her looks that poison you most; it's her voice."

Winding into the square, the gypsies formed a wide circle. The music fell into different airs, and the entertainment began. There was jigging, sword dancing, and that performance of the grizzled old man who did the Cossack dance as though there were steel springs instead of muscles in his legs. Reata had admired it before. He admired it again, but dimly, always waiting.

The cat-faced strong man, smiling his prop smile until his eyes wrinkled almost shut, took the center and lifted weights and then balanced men in the air, with his mighty muscles standing out as though painted.

"But Reata paralyzed that hombre," said Harry Quinn to Bates. "Reata tied him up in knots. The same way that he can tie up anybody, if he gets close enough."

"The fool don't carry no guns," said Dave Bates. "That lets him out."

"He stalks till he's close," said Harry Quinn, "because he's the king of cats, old son. And don't you ever forget it."

Dave Bates made an involuntary, swift gesture beneath his coat and grinned a sour smile as he drew out his hand again.

"Yeah, maybe," he growled. "There goes the girl. Lemme see how good she is!"

At the close of the show—it had not been very long, but

it had brought repeated cheers from the spectators—the gray stallion of Bill Champion was brought out by Miriam with his bridle reins tied back into the surcingle. He began to canter softly, but with a dangerous sweep to his stride, around and around in a circle.

The girl ran at him, leaped, struck with her soft slippers on the point of his shoulder and seemed to run up the sleek of the powerful shoulder muscles until she stood partly on his withers and partly on the working shoulder itself, slanting in at a sharp angle to weight against the speed of the circling stallion.

Orchard Creek, which knew a lot about plain horsemanship and something about fancy riding, also, yelled at the top of its lungs, but the stallion simply shook his great head and went on at the same unvarying stride.

"By the jumpin' thunder," said Daves Bates, "that kid has got something in her head or she couldn't 'a' trained the gray like that. Look at the way he keeps to his circle. Dog-gone me, he seems like he enjoys it, sort of!"

"That's nothing. She ain't started," said Harry Quinn. "Look at that!"

She had begun her dance in time with slow music into which the very movement of the horse seemed to be working with a perfect rhythm. Those perilous angles of her swaying threatened every moment to let her drop to the ground. One would have said, many times, that she was suspended by an invisible wire which supported her around the circle, regardless of the horse.

Orchard Creek began to grow hoarse with enthusiasm.

"Can nobody else handle that horse?" asked Reata, suddenly standing up.

"Nobody else," said Harry Quinn. "Nobody else can even lead it, without havin' a terrible fight on his hands!"

"What happens at the end of this show?" demanded Reata.

"Why, she gets back on the geldin', and she leads the stallion away at the head of the procession," said Dave Bates.

"We're going down and get our horses," said Reata. "You fellows that wear guns, get ready to shoot—but do your shooting in the air."

CHAPTER 34

Dave Bates was ill content. As he went down the stairs, he said to Harry Quinn: "He starts right in and gives commands. He makes a boss out of himself. As if he had the right. The kid kind of makes me sick!"

"Everything makes you sick, hombre," answered Harry Quinn. "Hold yourself down for a while, will you? I never seen Reata miss yet, and I reckon he ain't goin' to miss today."

They had their horses in front of the hotel, with the packs already tied on behind the saddles. Quinn paid the hotel bill on the way out, and then found that Reata was already in the saddle on Sue in front of the building. As Quinn tumbled into place on his own horse, he found Reata looking them over.

Reata said quietly: "You two fellows fall in behind me. The gypsies are passing the hat now, and they're getting a lot of money out of this crowd. They're going to feel a little careless as the parade starts away again. But don't forget that they've all got knives, and a lot of 'em have guns. When I start working, you fall in behind me and pull your guns. Keep the crowd back, if you can. And have your spurs in your horses. You've got the best nags that Dickerman can give you. Use 'em. You'll need to!"

With that, he rode straight off through the crowd, letting Sue pick her way gingerly through the press, while Rags stood upon the saddlebow and barked softly to clear a way.

It was easy to see Miriam leading the gypsy parade as it began serpentining, for she stood upon the back of the quiet old gelding, bowing and kissing her hand right and left.

Reata worked forward until he was out of the press of the townspeople and near the girl. Then a wild yell beat on his ears. He saw the cat-faced strong man leaping forward at him. The gypsy jargon that the giant shouted was, of course, to warn the rest that the old enemy was on them. And once the grip of the big fellow was on the bridle reins of Sue, it would need the strength of four men to loosen his grasp.

Reata, jerking around in the saddle, slashed a fourfold coil of his lariat right across that catlike face. The fellow howled and leaped straight up into the air, his hands clapped to his eyes. Reata, straightening, flung the snaky noose of his rope and snared Miriam under the arms, right around the waist.

"You fool. You fool!" she was screaming at him. "Go back, Reata, or they'll kill you! Ride for it! Ride for it!"

"Ride with me, then!" cried Reata. "Change to the gray and ride with me, or I'll try to take you on Sue!"

She pulled once, desperately, at the rope that held her. She looked back, and saw the gypsies rushing forward toward Reata. And then she made up her mind.

She was off the gelding and onto the gray in a flash. The big stallion lurched away through the open gap down the street. Sue, sprinting with all her might, kept up.

Reata, as he looked back, saw the brandished guns of Harry Quinn and Dave Bates make the crowd reel back, shouting.

There were other guns brightening in the air on either side of him. A bullet shaved the very back of his neck. But he heard one deep voice shouting: "Leave 'em! The gal wants to go—so leave 'em be!"

Perhaps that commanding voice saved the scalp of Reata for the first thirty seconds. After that, he was off the square and running full pelt with Sue after the stallion. Right to the very end of the lariat the stallion was leading, but long-bodied Sue, straining to her utmost, made the line slack, began to gain. The stallion ran gloriously; Sue ran like a low roan streak, and as the last houses of Orchard Creek whirred away behind them, the mare was running level with the tall gray.

Then Reata loosened the noose, and the girl threw it away from her. She was sitting down like a jockey on the broad back of the gray. The slender brown arms stretched out straight to the reins, and the ruffles at her shoulders were blowing and shuddering with the wind of the gallop.

Behind them many horses pounded; leaving the rest comfortably, still guns in hand, came Dave Bates and Harry Quinn.

They had done their part well. They would do it still better, perhaps, if once they had to shoot to kill. But they were well mounted on the best horseflesh that Pop Dickerman could give them, and it was very doubtful if any of the riders from Orchard Creek could keep pace with the kidnapers.

No, now the crowd fell away. A few shots were fired. A dust cloud began to envelop the riders far in the rear. And still Sue and the gray drew away rapidly from Bates and Quinn, and the men of Orchard Creek were hopelessly last of all.

The girl began to laugh. She cried over her shoulder to Reata: "You're a crazy man."

"Sure I am," said Reata. "Bring that whale down to a lope, and we can talk."

"What did you want to see me about?" asked the girl. "Talk fast, Reata. I've got to go back with the gray. Everybody will be wild. It was a crazy thing to rope me like that—it was just crazy! Talk fast—I've got to go back."

He looked at her with a faint smile. The ragged blues and browns of the mountains went storming up against the sky, just beyond them. The sun was turning golden in the west. Continents of wild space enclosed them, and through it rode the girl in her shimmering blue tights and golden ruffles.

He had been a fool to use the rope, with that threat of snatching her away on Sue, if she would not ride the gray on her own account. He could see now that she would have come, as readily, merely at a word from him. It was to save him from danger in the crowd that she had changed to the gray.

"I can't talk yet," said he. "I want to look a while."

"You like it," said the girl. "Bullets—you like to hear 'em! While you're looking, take a slant at your hat."

He took off that good Stetson and saw the great rents where two .45-caliber slugs had torn through the strong, white felt. That was preeminently a fair-weather hat from now on.

"You've got a pair through the tail of your coat, too," she said. "You *are* a crazy man, Reata. Now what have you got to say? I can't keep on."

"Keep on a little while," said Reata.

"You didn't need to do it," she insisted. "If you'd whistled from a window, I would have noticed, and somehow I would have come to you. Reata, they almost had you. The gypsies—and most of all, the men of Orchard Creek. They didn't know. They thought it was a kidnaping. How were they to tell, anyway?"

"One man knew," said Reata.

"I heard him bellow. I saw him knock down two or three guns that were ready to salt you away," said the girl. "Heaven bless him for that. Now tell me what it is, Reata."

He looked back. Far away, the dust cloud of those riders from Orchard Creek rolled small and dim, a golden mist under the sun. But close up came Bates and Quinn, their guns out of sight now, their horses at merely a brisk canter, with the dust funnels shooting back from beneath the beat of the hoofs and spreading out wide and high.

Then this picture was lost as the trail bore them behind the shoulder of high ground. They were entering the foothills. A deep valley, with one wall of gold and one wall of velvet black, opened before them, cleaving a way into the heart of the mountains.

Reata turned back to the girl.

"Have you got a knife?" he asked.

"Yes," she said.

"Give it to me."

"Why?"

"I need it."

She produced from somewhere a vicious little icicle of a knife with the light dripping off its needle point.

"That's better," said Reata, taking it. "We can pull up here and talk. Because after what I say to you, you might want to put that knife into me."

They halted their horses. The dust came softly, slowly, up behind them. Bates and Quinn came swinging into view. Reata stopped them by lifting his hand.

"What is it?" asked the girl, frowning. "I don't like the way you're leading up to something, Reata."

"You'll like the something a lot less than the leading up to it," he assured her. "I'm going to ask you to take that gray horse off into the mountains. Just where, I don't know."

"Into the mountains?" she demanded, staring. "What do you mean by that?"

"What I say. I want to take that gray so far into the

mountains that nothing but a turkey buzzard or a Bill Champion can find it again."

She cried out. There was no music in the sound. The soft velvet was rubbed from her voice, which Harry Quinn had said was more poisonous to men than her looks. It made Reata think of nothing but the squall of an angry gypsy. If she had had the knife then— Well, he knew her just well enough never to be sure of what she would do next.

This time she swung the big gray around as though she intended to drive the weight of the horse trampling over the smaller mare and its rider.

She leaned out and caught Reata by the wrist, and shook his arm savagely. Her whole face was savage, twisting with anger.

"D'you mean that you came for the horse?"

"And you, Miriam," he told her honestly. "I wanted to have a look at you. You know that. But I had to get the gray. It's fish bait, d'you see? And Bill Champion is the fish."

"Bill Champion!" she echoed. He was amazed to see the anger go out of her in one sudden ebbing.

Very pale, she stared at him.

"You—and the other pair—that thickhead of a Harry Quinn—you've come to trap Bill Champion? Reata, you fool, he'll kill you all!"

"He'll try," said Reata. "And we'll try. Or maybe I'll try alone. I don't like big odds on my side, because it takes the fun out of the game. And this is a game, Miriam. Straighten out the gray and we'll start traveling."

CHAPTER 35

When she obeyed him, he could see that it was an instinctive reaction only. Her mind was working desperately. Her lips were parted. Words kept trembling in her throat for a time before she said, still half stunned: "Reata, you don't know Bill Champion. Tell me—did you ever so much as see him?"

"I never saw him," he admitted.

At that she groaned and struck her hands against her forehead.

The stallion made a leap ahead. She, in an instant, was crouching forward, ready to send him speeding on his way, perhaps irrecoverably beyond the pursuit of the mare. But, with her backward glance, she saw the noose ready in the hand of Reata, and she surrendered to the coil of that almost living, snakelike presence.

Reata joined her, the mare jogging softly. They walked on into the gold and the shadow of the big valley. It was a huge thing. The trail wound along halfway up the steep side. Trees stuck out angling from the wall of the cliff. At the bottom of the gorge, water boomed or sang with a hollow voice. And that despair which had come over the girl seemed to mate the bigness and the wildness of the scene.

"You never saw him, but they raked you into this job—Quinn and the other one. No, I know the old devil behind all the trouble. Dickerman, the rat man. Dickerman! He's the one, Reata. Admit it!"

"Well, even suppose that I admit it," said Reata.

"But Bill Champion will eat you the way a cat eats a mouse. You don't know him, Reata. You've never seen his horrible face. You don't know anything about him. I've seen men. I've seen fighting men. I've seen blood. I've seen about everything, but nothing like Bill Champion. I've waked up at night and screamed, dreaming about him. Reata, it's not too late. Let me go. I'll go back to the band!"

"Sure you will," agreed Reata. "You'll go back to the band when we've hit a comfortable place to wait—out here in the hills."

"You're going to go through with your crazy scheme?" she asked him, beating her hands together.

"I'm going through with it, unless you know another idea that's a better one," he answered.

"I know a better thing for you to do," she declared. "It's for you to let me go back, and you never stop riding till you've put a thousand miles between you and this neck of the woods, and you never come back here for a year or so, till Champion has a chance to forget that there's anybody like you in the world. And every day of the year, get down on your two skinny knees and thank God that you're still alive!"

"He must be quite a noise, this Bill Champion," said Reata ironically.

The irony did not affect her.

"Once," she said, "I was walking along through the woods—that was weeks ago, near the place we were camping. And something came over me. A chill, you might call it. A chill in the pit of the stomach. But it was a hot day. And I turned around, wanting to get right into the hot of the sun, and there, behind me, I saw Bill Champion leaning a hand against a tree, and just looking at me, and I couldn't move. Mind you—I couldn't move. My knees began to sag. I yelled out: 'Bill, go away! Go away!' I screamed it out. His face moved into what he might have called a smile. His face stretched a little at the sides, and he went out of sight through the trees. But I kept on wanting to scream. I got out into the sunshine, and for an hour I couldn't feel the heat of it. There was a darkness that kept welling up inside of me."

She paused, her eyes closed, her hands gripping the flowing silver of the gray's mane.

"Well," said Reata when he could speak, "there are a lot of men who are pretty good hands at scaring the girls."

"Bah!" she snapped at him. "Don't tell me you're such a fool! Don't tell me that you think I'm a squealing, silly, fainting, rattle-headed dummy, like other women. I'm not, and you know I'm not!"

He knew it very well.

"You're not like the rest," he admitted. "But just because Champion has a funny-looking face, he's got on your nerves."

"Nobody could tell you," she sighed, shaking her head. "But I'm going to find some way. Somehow I'll find a way to tell you what he's like, and then you'll let me take the horse back. Listen to me."

"I'm listening, and I'm looking, Miriam."

"Don't look. If you keep seeing my fool of a pretty face, you won't hear what I have to say. Ah, men have no brains. Because I've got red lips and blue eyes and a body hitched to them, you can hardly follow what I'm talking. But I'm talking life and death. Reata, let me tell you that I've seen Bill Champion take the hand of our strong man—and he *is* a real strong man—and in half a second our strong man was down on his knees, groaning, his bones almost breaking in his hand. Does that mean anything to you?"

"Yes," admitted Reata. "That means something."

"He's lived with guns all his life. He doesn't do tricks. He shoots what he wants to eat. But he likes small birds. You hear, Reata? He likes to get a mess of small birds to fill his stomach, and he shoots the birds. He doesn't trap them, but he shoots them. I've seen him shoot them on the wing."

"Just nips off their heads, eh?" Reata smiled.

"Reata!" she cried out.

He shook his head. "It's no good," he told her. "I believe everything that you're saying, but it's no good. I've started this trail, and I've got to come to the end of it!"

"He'll kill you!" cried Miriam. All at once she began to sob, though her face was fierce. "Reata, he'll kill you, he'll kill you. That's why I had the horrors when I saw him. That's why I've wakened at night and screamed till the whole tribe came running to my wagon. It's because I knew that he was the man who would kill you, Reata! And you—like a fool, you sit there in the saddle, and you sneer, and you smile, and you shrug your shoulders—and I hate you! I hope he does kill you! I hope he puts his hands on you and breaks you like a stick. I hope that I'm standing by, and I'll laugh! I'll cheer him on. I'll tell him to go ahead, slowly, so that I can taste the screaming better. That's what I hope!"

He kept watching her, smiling a little still. He could not tell what part of her was woman and what part of her was cat.

"Well," he said aloud, "what part of you is woman and what part of you is cat, Miriam?"

"I don't know," mourned the girl. "But if I'm a cat, you're the king of the cats. Reata, tell me honestly—aren't you afraid after what I've just told you?"

"I am," he admitted. "I've got the chills up my spine."

"When you have a chance to think it over, you'll see that you don't need to be ashamed," said the girl. "Nobody needs to be ashamed for running away from Bill Champion. Any more than a man needs to be ashamed for running away from the devil. Reata, let me go back now! Please, please, please let me go back now."

He said nothing. The softness went out of voice and

172

eyes as she demanded suddenly: "What do you think that you could do if you ever met Bill Champion? What do you think he'd make of your silly reata? He'd break it with his hands. He'd bite it in two with his wolf's teeth. And he'd laugh as he got at you. What would you do, even if you had a chance to meet him?"

"I don't know exactly," said Reata. "But the more I think about it, the more I think that I'm going to enjoy killing him."

"You're what?"

"I never wanted to kill a man all the days of my life," said Reata. "Not even Dickerman, and that's a strange thing. Dickerman ought to be killed, but I've never wanted to. But Bill Champion seems mostly beast, and I'm going to choke the breath out of him one day."

She started to make a savage protest, a scornful laugh beginning on her lips. But after a moment she began to weep instead.

"You know what it's like," she managed to say through her sobbing. "It's like a silly pet rooster that's bossed the barnyard for six months—it's like that silly little fool of a rooster flapping up into the air to meet an eagle stooping out of the middle of the sky. Well," she cried, angry again, "find him, then! Find him! And I'll have the burying of you. But I won't cry over your grave. I'll laugh. Because that's all that a fool ought to get out of life—just laughter—just laughter! You hear?"

They were deep in the valley. The sun no longer fell around them but only shadow, yet the light was glowing on the upper eastern slope. The voices of the stream in the bottom of the gorge called faintly about them. It seemed to Reata that he was riding in a dream, or that his ghost was here, come back from the other world after being killed by the terrible hands of Bill Champion.

But that was not entirely bravado, that speech he had made to the girl. He began to smooth the head of Rags with the palm of one hand. He began to remember the horrible description of Bill Champion which he had heard from Pop Dickerman. And he had a very sure foreknowledge that he and Bill Champion could not live much longer in this world.

Another thought came to him.

"Miriam," he said, "you loathe Bill Champion, eh?"

She shuddered for answer.

"And the fact is," said Reata, "that the brute left the gray with you. It wasn't because he really needed to leave it with the gypsies. It was because he wanted to please you. Eh?"

She said nothing.

"He showed you some ways of making friends with the gray, and you've gone on and found others. But the fact is that he likes you pretty well, eh? That's why you screamed when you saw him behind you that day in the woods?"

She put up both hands and covered her eyes. She said nothing. She did not need to say anything.

CHAPTER 36

They traveled straight south, out of the big valley, through the foothills, through the first range, and out of the day and into the night they followed beneath the stars whatever fortune might bring them, until at last they came to what all three men agreed was a perfect spot. It was a smooth valley laid across a soft hump of brown hills like a gun barrel's indentation across a sack of wheat. One end of the valley pointed at the mist of the western desert. The other end pointed at the big mountains through which they had passed.

They were very tired, because it was after midnight. They could hear the thin murmur of a little creek; they could even, after they dismounted and got away from the breathing of horses and the creak of saddle leather, hear the faint slapping of waves on the shore of a tiny lake.

The girl was so tired that she threw her arms up over the back of her stallion and leaned her face against the surcingle. Her whole body sagged in.

However, the gray devil would not let a hand touch him except her own. When Reata came up, he tried for the head of the man with his teeth, with his striking forehoofs, and then, whirling, with the long drive of his hind legs.

Reata had to order the girl three times to get the surcingle off the stallion and put the bridle up, and hobble him out, since he could not be tethered to a rope, having the habit of throwing himself headlong back against any restraint.

She stripped the surcingle and the bridle from him and put the hobbles on. Then she slid down into the grass and lay with her face on the cross of her arms.

The three men went on making camp. Every instant, as they could examine the ground more carefully under the starlight, they were better and better pleased with their choice. When the great Bill Champion found them here, he would have to come at them through the open, where rifles tell against might and main. There was a bit of woodland pouring darkly out from between two hills on the left, giving them wood not fifty yards away, an easy distance to drag fuel with a willing horse and a strong rope. They had water. They had with them, in their packs, plenty of food, besides what accurate rifles would bring down for them in this virgin country. Altogether, they could hardly have chosen better with all the brightness of the sun to help them. There was even a scattering of small brush near the shores of the lake which they could tear up to make tinder for their fires. Out of this, in fact, they built their fire for that night. They fried bacon; they made coffee, of course; and they had hardtack.

When the food was nearly ready, Reata got out of his pack the change of shirts and the pair of overalls that he carried with him. She could furl these things and get into them. He went over to wake her up, but even when he shook her shoulder, she still lay like one dead.

So he put Rags down to watch her and returned to the fire. He was through with a bacon and hardtack sandwich when the yipping of Rags summoned him, so he took a cup of the hot coffee over to her.

"She ain't so dead as she seems, if you just know how to wake her up," said Harry Quinn.

Reata patted her shoulder, for he found her lying exactly as before.

"You're awake," he told her. "Rags has been telling me all about you. Wake up, Miriam."

She lay like a log. When he shook her, her whole body wobbled. He got hold of her and sat her up, and made her head spill over against his shoulder, since it had to spill in some direction.

"Listen," said Reata. "If you won't stop this pretending—if you won't wake up—I'm going to put this coffee to your mouth, and if you don't sip it, it'll burn you, it's that hot. I'll keep right on pouring till it blisters your mouth for you."

He put the hot tin against her mouth, and she winced her head away. She rolled her head back on his shoulder and looked up at him.

"All right," she said. "I was trying to think while I lay there. I couldn't make up my mind whether I loved or hated or laughed at you most, but I guess I do all three together. Give me the coffee. It smells pretty good! Give me a hand up and I'll go over there and toast some of the dew out of me. The dew falls pretty thick in this neck of the woods, doesn't it?"

He half lifted her to her feet. She sighed again. The fatigue seemed to have run out of her, and the new strength was filling her.

"I'll go over there and get some bacon under my skin," she said. "It smells pretty good."

"Put on this shirt and these overalls," he commanded.

"Yeah? Why should I put on a pair of old overalls and a shirt of thirty summers?" she asked him.

"Just because I tell you to," said Reata.

She shuffled the shirt over her head. Then she stepped into the overalls.

"Where do I take in the reefs?" she asked him. "Give me that coffee again. I need a drink."

She walked to the fire with an ambling stride. Cup in hand, she scowled down at the two. "Hullo, Harry," she said. "How's the old boy? The last time I saw that red neck I thought a rope was going to stretch it the next day. How does it feel to be sitting up and swallowing coffee and bacon like a real man instead of a ghost?"

"Hello, sister," said Harry. He stood up and held out a hand, which she shook cordially enough. He grinned at her. "Every time I swaller, I say to myself: 'Reata done it! Reata done it!' What do you say?"

"He done it, all right," she answered, nodding. "Introduce me to your friend."

"This is Dave Bates, Miriam. Miriam what, I dunno."

Bates got up and shook hands in his turn, silently, staring.

"I haven't got a headache, doctor," said the girl. "No

use giving me the long look. Wait till I furl these sails, and I'll sit down and be one of the boys."

She sat down cross-legged. Reata gave her hardtack and bacon. She began to munch contentedly.

"That was a pretty good song and dance back there at Orchard Creek," she said. "Who thought it up?"

"Reata done the thinking," said Harry Quinn.

"He would," she answered. "That idea had Reata all over it. It was so crazy that it rattled. It rattled so much that I knew it was Reata, and so I came along to keep him from getting the spot he stood on all red. All that saved you two was the crowd having him to shoot at, and all that saved him was luck and a long chance. If Reata was a poker hand, it would take a poker-faced bluffer to lay a ten-cent bet on him. But here we are, boys, out under the stars, waiting for Bill Champion. Nice and cozy, isn't it?"

"Listen to her," said Harry Quinn, grinning. "You know Bill pretty good, don't you, Miriam?"

"I know the chills of him, but you fellows are going to know the fever," she answered. "When he sees the three of you waiting for a fight, he may laugh himself to death."

"Yes, she knows Bill Champion pretty good," said Dave Bates. "She's a help to have around, too."

"The way you boys throw away good advice, you must be great spenders," said she.

She stood up suddenly, having finished her bit of the food.

"Why don't you all turn around three times and make a wish, and wish yourselves home in bed? You have no right to be out here in the open with all the trouble walking around waiting to find you out! Listen, Reata, when am I allowed to go home, or do I have to stay here to make the gray horse feel at home?"

"You're too tired to go home tonight," said Reata. "You can start in the morning. I'll take you through the hills. You can ride one of the horses—Quinn's, maybe."

"Hey, hold on," said Quinn. "How do you get that way? She rides my horse means I walk how far?"

"There's always the gray for you," said Reata. "Besides, when Bill Champion comes, he'll have a horse under him. I'll break up some of that brush and build you a bed, Miriam."

He cut down a quantity of the brush with a small ax which he always made a part of his pack. On that soft and springy bedding he rolled down a blanket. The girl sat on the bed, sinking deeply into it.

"How do you make sure that I don't slide away from you during the night and get onto the gray?" she asked, studying Reata by the starlight.

"I put Rags here to watch you. He'll bark every time you so much as lift a hand," said Reata.

"I'll have him quiet enough after a while," she said. "I'm an animal tamer, Reata. Look at the gray."

"You train the wild ones; you're no good with the tame," said he, smiling at her.

"This is about the last time that I'll ever have a chance to say good night to you," said the girl. "The most I'll ever see of you after tomorrow is maybe a finger bone that Bill may be wearing for a watch charm the next time I meet him. Well, the sooner it's said, the sooner I'm asleep. Good night, Reata."

"Fresh, ain't she?" said Harry Quinn when Reata went back to the fire.

"Sure she's fresh," answered Reata. "And the best of it is that she's not going to spoil in our company. You boys get that?"

They got it, staring steadily at him.

He had given his blankets to the girl. So he made a heap of the soft brush, burrowed into it, and went to sleep.

CHAPTER 37

It was a broken sleep. He wakened twice out of frightful dreams in which he was seeing a faceless man with eyes that seemed to be staring through a scar-tissue mask. Each time he sat up and made sure that the girl was in her place, with Rags beside her.

A third time he wakened, not because of a dream—at least, there were no floating shreds of the sleep images left in his consciousness—but because something seemed to have plucked at him from the outer night. He stared wildly around him, his heart thundering, and braced himself to see the silhouette of a man coming toward the single red eye of the camp fire.

But he saw nothing of that. Instead, he made out Rags coiled in perfect slumber near the bed of the girl, and from those empty blankets a slinking form was stealing away toward the gray stallion.

Reata stood up and called softly: "Before you can get the hobbles off him, I'll be able to reach you with this rope, Miriam."

She did not turn at once. She simply stood, facing the horse, and gradually she turned.

He walked slowly toward her, and she said: "Where do you keep the extra eyes, Reata? You were snoring, soft and low, a while ago."

"I keep an extra ear for Miriam," he told her.

She had a way of coming up close to people and looking them up and down. She did that now to Reata.

"All right," she said. "You notice that Rags is still asleep, eh?"

"I notice it," admitted Reata. "You can train them, wild or tame. But you haven't trained me yet."

"I didn't have time before Bill Champion came and got him," she answered. "So long, Reata."

She went back to her blankets, but Reata knew that there could be no more sleep for him. Once a fugitive instinct had touched and wakened him; a second time it might fail, and she would be gone, and the trap for Bill Champion would be sprung before he entered it.

Luckily the dawn began a little later. The big mountains turned black against the east, and then the soft color began all around the horizon. He forgot Bill Champion and the girl and the two crooks who completed the company at that camp. For a little while he was alone in his own country, then the day commenced more brightly, and the voice of Dave Bates shattered the time of peace.

They had for breakfast a pair of mountain grouse which Harry Quinn gathered in by the briefest of walks up the slope of the eastern hill. The meat was broiled on the ends of wooden spits. They had coffee and hardtack again with it, and everyone voted the meal prime. Afterward Reata started at once with the girl.

Quinn made no real difficulty about his horse. He gave it up with a shrug and a squint.

"How do I know?" he asked. "Maybe I ain't ever goin' to ride out of this here place, anyway. Maybe Bill Champion is goin' to show me a way to go down a longer trail."

The girl shook hands with the two men rather solemnly.

"After he's gone, you'll have a good chance to get out," she said to them.

She went cantering down the trail with Reata. They were over the eastern ridge of the valley before he pulled up Sue and said to the girl: "You understand, Miriam, I turn you loose because you promise not to make any trouble for me in this job?"

"What sort of trouble could I make?" she asked him.

"If you've got the devil in your mind," he answered, "you could do anything to stop me. You could even let the sheriff at Rusty Gulch know where I am, if you'd rather have me in jail than dead. But you're promising, word of honor, that you won't make any trouble."

"Sure, I promise," said she.

"Word of honor?"

"A gypsy's word of honor—that would mean a lot!" she said.

"I want your word of honor," he commanded, "or we turn about and go back to the camp."

"You can't do it!" she argued. "You can't hold me out there in the hills—a girl and three men."

"I'm doing what I have to, not what I want," said Reata.

"It's what you want. It's what you're crazy enough to want!" she told him. "You *want* to meet Bill Champion. It's like telling a fool of a young horse wrangler about an outlaw horse. He can't wait till he's had a go at it and got himself a broken neck. That's the way with you. You want to show Bill that *you're* the champion!"

"I'm waiting for your promise, on your word of honor," he told her.

"Oh, well, take it, then."

"Give me your hand with it."

She obeyed gloomily.

"Look at me," he directed. "Now say it over. You promise on your word of honor."

"All right, I promise," said she.

He released her hand.

"A lot you trust me." She sneered. "You'd rather trust

Rags—even if he does go to sleep in the middle of things, the way he did last night."

"I trust you," said Reata thoughtfully. "I don't know why. But I trust you, all right."

"Tell me how you trust me?" she asked.

"Well, in the last pinch—if there were life or death in a job—you'd risk your neck."

"For you?"

"Yes, for me."

She made no answer to this, and sulked steadily for at least two hours as they rode into the east. They were not going north, toward the town of Orchard Creek, because he wanted to get her out of the rough hill country and onto the flat, where he could leave her and return. For there were more habitations there on the flat, and he would feel safer about her. He offered her his Stetson to keep off the sun.

"I don't want your hat," she said. "I don't want anything of yours."

"You'd rather have sunstroke?"

"I swore that no man would ever do what you've done to me—kick me around like a dog!" she cried at him. "I hate you, Reata! You're not even a man. You're only a slavey that Dickerman sends around to do his dirty jobs. But you've been man enough to drag me around by the nape of the neck. That'll make you proud. That's enough to set you up for the rest of your life."

There was nothing to say to this. He had to set his teeth and endure. And suddenly she broke out: "I'm sorry, Reata. I didn't mean that last."

"It's all right," said he.

"But why don't we go north, straight off?" she asked. "That's the shortest way to Orchard Creek."

He repeated his thoughts. "I want to get back to the camp as soon as I can. I suppose it's too soon for even a Bill Champion to get on the trail, but I can't be sure. I want to get back there before trouble starts. And the best thing I can do is to take you out of the hills into the flat. There are more ranches there. I'd feel safer about you."

At this she insulted him with loud laughter.

"Chaperoning me, eh, Reata?" she said. "You drag me in the dirt and then you chaperon me, eh? That's pretty good!"

Rags turned his head suddenly as he ran ahead of the

horse, and snarled over his shoulder at her. The thing struck Reata heavily. It was as though the dog sensed evil in her.

"You might as well worry about a hawk in the sky as about me," she insisted. "What's the matter with you, Reata?"

"I don't know," he said. "Maybe I'm being a fool, all right. But this is the way we go."

She softened again just after that, and tried to be friendly, but he was overcast with a gloomy doubt.

They came through woods to the top of the last ridge, and below them lay the plains, dotted with cattle, and with ranch houses, here and there.

He pulled up Sue, dismounted, loosed her cinches, took off her bridle, and turned her out to graze and rest for a short time before he started the return journey. It was already past noon.

"There's the way for you," he told her. "You head down into the flat, and then you pull gradually north, and you'll hit Orchard Creek in the eye—and you'll be at home with Queen Maggie and the rest again."

She felt the grimness underlying his words.

"Tell me something, Reata," she asked. "Since you were a little kid you've been falling in love and out again?"

"Yes," said he.

"It's the practice that counts," she said bitterly. "And what a man learns the easiest is the falling out."

He, staring at her, tried to think forward to that time. He wanted to have it come soon. They could never get on together. He kept telling himself that.

"This time it won't be easy," he said. "Not for me. But what about you, Miriam? If I've looked at one girl, you've looked at ten men."

"And let 'em pass," said she.

"Sure," said he ironically. "I'm the first man that ever meant a thing to you."

"You are," said the girl. "The first one that ever meant a thing."

Then she added: "Ask me to say that on my word of honor, too!"

But in his bewilderment he knew that what she told him had been perfectly true. He was still stunned as she waved him a brief farewell, and, without another word, rode her mustang down the slope of the hill toward the flat country beyond.

Even Rags stood up on a rock to watch her go.

CHAPTER 38

The girl, as she went down the slope, kept her teeth locked hard together in order to master the trembling of her lips. She had done everything wrong, she felt. She should have poured out tenderness on him in this last meeting. She should have showed him clearly how completely he dominated her world. Instead, she had left him on a wrangling note.

Would she ever learn to check herself and express only the pleasant thing which men may care to know? No, there was a savage in her that made her burst out against the things she loved the best.

What did she love? she asked herself then.

Well, she loved to sway and dance on the back of a horse with plenty of people looking on, applauding, finding her beautiful.

She loved to lie in the grass and look up at the sky through the brown-and-green branches of a tree, while the gypsy music hummed and throbbed somewhere not too close.

She loved a good horse, and sandy ground, and to ride against the rain.

She loved these things, but last of all she loved Reata, and most of all. He was neither magnificent nor handsome. He was not rich. He had none of those qualities of fairy prince about which she had daydreamed. But he had an eye that washed her clean.

Those two men who were back at the camp, they were formidable enough to have been picked out of any crowd. They were dangerous fellows, dangerously trained, but they were nothing compared with Reata.

As she thought of this, an agony came over her. There were two mighty forces in this world, and one was Reata, standing for the right, it seemed to the girl; and one was Bill Champion, standing for all that was foul and dark. And the evil would conquer the good. Surely, if ever they met, Reata could not stand against that monster. It would be like asking a child to stand against the devil!

The devil in every way was Bill Champion, and most of all in that secrecy which he had maintained so perfectly that there were hardly a dozen men in the West who knew about his revolting crimes. A sheriff or a Federal marshal here and there patiently and steadily searched for that master devil among men. The others knew little or nothing about him. And his deeds were so monstrous that they were quickly forgotten, like nightmares that dissolve from the mind in the brightness of daylight.

She alone, in this world, was able now to make a gesture to protect Reata, yet she had given her word and her honor that she would not do such a thing.

Word? Honor?

Suddenly such things were breath to her. Reata was already saddling the mare behind her, no doubt. Reata was already turning back toward the camp on Sue, and the little dog Rags was scampering ahead, happily running down every attractive scent that crossed the trail.

Something had to be done. It was in her hands. It seemed to the tormented girl then that the voice of Reata himself had told her the proper thing. Her word and her honor? She waved them away. It was for the life of Reata that she would have to struggle.

Reata had told her that the sheriff of Rusty Gulch would be glad enough to ride long and far to put hands on him.

Then, it seemed to her, settling her mind of all doubt, that fate must have chosen the course in which Reata had ridden.

For the way had been around a corner toward Orchard Creek, to be sure, but it had been almost on a straight line for Rusty Gulch.

She gave over her thinking. The thing to do, it seemed to her, was to make her horse fly to Rusty Gulch as fast as she could, and then start the sheriff galloping back toward the spot where Reata would be waiting, and his two companions beside him.

Let Reata curse her and rage at her. It would be better,

far better, to have him resting safely behind bars than to have him stretched out as food for the buzzards!

Those were the things that she kept rehearsing to herself as she urged her horse on. Then, at last, the miles fell away from before her, and she saw the sun flaming on the windows of Rusty Gulch.

It was late in the afternoon already. But by twilight, if the sheriff could start at once, they could be up there into the mountains in full power. They could find Reata and close on him, and hold him fast in the great, safe hand of the law!

So she stormed into the main street of the town.

The sheriff? He was at his house. His house was down there on the corner—and look! She could see the sheriff himself sitting out on the front porch in his carpet slippers!

She spurred the mustang cruelly, till with a switching tail it raced that remaining small distance, and she flung herself down in front of the fence of the sheriff.

Lowell Mason had what a sheriff needs in his face. He had a sense of humor, too. And when he saw the girl in those flopping clothes of a man, he smiled a little. He wiped the smile away as she raced up the steps to him.

"You're the sheriff?" she said.

"That's my job," he said.

"I want you. Come fast. Reata!" she called to him.

"Reata? What about him?" said the sheriff.

She had turned away to the steps again, burning in haste. Now she paused and stamped with impatience.

"Reata—you want him here—he broke out of your jail, didn't he?"

"Yes," said the sheriff, unhurried, casual, watching every detail of her.

"Well, I can show you where he is. I can lead you to him. But you'll need men. You'll need a lot of men. Will you come, or are you just going to sit there and stare?"

"A girl like you," answered the sheriff, keeping well inside his maddening calm, "would never sell Reata. Never to the law. Not for money, either, I take it."

"I tell you, I can show you where he is!" she cried.

"What sort of a put-up job is this?" asked the sheriff. "You'd be more likely to fight for him than to sell him like this—without a price, either! Come on, now, and tell me the straight of it!"

This calmness of his seemed to her like a vast, a metal monster. But she had to be reasonable. Suddenly she saw that it was necessary for her to tell the whole truth, incredible as that might seem.

"Did you ever hear of Bill Champion?" she demanded.

The sheriff leaned forward. Then he stood up.

"What are you talking about?" he asked sharply.

"Bill Champion, you know about him?"

"Aye, but you don't—you can't," said the sheriff.

"I'm wasting time—*you're* wasting time," she cried desperately. "But he's up there in the hills—Reata's up there—and Bill Champion is coming for him. Do you hear that? Does that mean anything to you? Oh, if you want to get famous—maybe you'll get Bill Champion, too. Will that budge you?"

Budge the sheriff? It made Lowell Mason walk up to her and stare fixedly into her eyes, as though he had to get at the inner truth.

"I'm tryin' to understand and believe what I hear," he said. "You say Bill Champion is comin' into the hills to meet up with Reata?"

"He's going to meet Reata—they're going to fight—Reata will be murdered! Does that mean anything to you? Will you come? Will you get men and come?"

"And Reata's going to be a lot safer in jail, eh? Is that the angle? I can foller that, all right," said the sheriff.

"Are you going to do anything?" she cried at him.

"Oh, aye! I'm going to do something! I'd take a trip around the world on my hands and knees if I could lay hands on Bill Champion! You know the way, you say?"

"I can take you there—I could take you in the dark. But when will you start?"

"As fast as I can get hosses and men," said the sheriff. "Because I ain't fool enough to think that this here is any one-man job!"

"One horse for me!" she begged. "One fresh horse for me!"

The sheriff, once he was in motion, moved very fast. He had a horse ready at his hitch rack. He flung himself into the saddle on that horse and galloped up the street. Here and there and again he checked his mustang and shouted; men came to doors, listened, and then flew into action in turn.

The sheriff was quite right when he said that it was not

a one-man job, but neither did he intend to take an entire crowd with him. Men are willing enough to volunteer for posse duty, but they are also likely to make such a noise that they would frighten away the eagles from the mountaintops, to say nothing of the hunted criminals.

What Lowell Mason got for this work was a small party of six men. Every one of them was a fellow able to ride and to shoot and to follow a trail. Every man of them had proved his nerve in more ways than one, but above everything else, with guns.

It was not a pretty party, at that. Old Lem Oliver was sixty-two, but his tough rawhide and whalebone would still stand a hundred-mile ride in a day.

Young Terry Craig was a fat lad of eighteen whose swollen, red face made him look as though he were about to burst into laughter every moment, but he was as good a shot and as brave a man as rode with the sheriff that day.

And the girl, as she swung into the saddle on a strong, fresh horse, looked over the faces of those men, read them beneath the skin, and was content.

CHAPTER 39

Back at the camp, beside that small lake in the valley, Bates and Harry Quinn did not spend a peaceful day. The trouble was that Quinn chose to boast about the prowess of Reata, and this boasting hurt his companion to the quick, for the nature of Bates was such that he could not endure to hear another man praised.

"I told you what he would do, and he done it," said Quinn. "He went in and he grabbed the hoss, and he took it away, and he brought it out here."

"You heard the girl say—Reata—he rattles, Reata!" Bates sneered. "Yeah, the girl was only kidding. What did she say about you, hombre? 'Doctor,' she called you; poison face is what she meant!"

"Did she?" said Bates. "Me, I wouldn't waste my time

187

on no black-headed, black-eyed gypsy gal, like you and the kid would."

"She ain't got black eyes. She's got blue eyes," said Harry Quinn. "You oughta look twice before you talk. The trouble with you is that she let you pass so fast that you been seein' black ever since."

"She didn't linger none over you," remarked Dave Bates.

"Me? What claim would I put in? Not with Reata around. That hombre has to come first, and I've got sense enough to know it. But a gent like you, Dave, you wanta see yourself first or you don't want to see yourself at all. It'd choke you to see the facts about what folks think of you. But my throat's too big to be choked. I know what they think, and I swaller it and have another drink."

It was well on in the afternoon as they chatted in this jolly vein, and the gray stallion, by this time, had wandered, in spite of his hobbles, rather close to the edge of the woods that spilled down from between the two hills. The pair had watched him fairly steadily all the day; not that they expected Bill Champion, to be sure, but because the great horse represented to them a focal point on which danger would at some time be directed.

They were so busy with their argument now that they did not see the shadowy form that moved among the trunks of the trees, stealthily and soundlessly as a hunting cat, a huge being who strode, and paused, and shifted from one shadow to another.

For Dave Bates was saying: "The trouble with this gent Reata is that he's all wide open and lookin' for a sock on the chin, and he's goin' to get it. You seen the holes in his hat? Well, they might as well 'a' been a coupla holes in his head. Is that brains? No, it ain't. He's ripe to get punched, and when he gets it, it'll be a hole that'll spoil the ticket. He'll ride one way, and there ain't goin' to be no return."

"I tell you," said Harry Quinn warmly, "that the only thing to it is the luck that he's got, and he knows how to ride it like a dog-gone jockey."

"Wait a minute," muttered Dave Bates. "It looks to me like the gray was steppin' along without those hobbles. I think he's broke the rope!"

For, a moment before this, the knife of the man in the woods had slashed the rope that made the hobble. And he had stretched out his vast arm from behind a tree to grip the mane of the stallion.

It was at this instant that, as the horse turned his head, pricking his ears, Dave Bates had a glimpse of the white slab of that face, and he screeched suddenly: "Hi! Harry—it's him!"

There was a rifle not two steps away, and Dave Bates knew the importance of accuracy in dealing with that monster, but he knew the importance of speed, also.

Harry Quinn, gaping, paralyzed by the suddenness of the danger, dragged out his own gun slowly. And he saw a huge man leap out of the woods onto the back of the gray stallion—a man so big that the gray horse looked as small as an ordinary mustang. As he sprang, a snarl issued from the beast face of the creature. He could have drawn back among the trees to safety, but, seeing battle, the sudden lust for it had mastered him.

He had sprung onto the back of the gray, and now, with the gigantic pressure of his knees alone and the sway of his body, he turned the head of the horse straight toward the men by the lake and charged, his spurs gouging the flanks of his mount.

He had a Colt in either hand. Fast as Dave Bates had been on the draw, that charging monster was faster still with his bullets.

The first of them struck Harry Quinn and hurled him violently back against his companion, so that both went down, and only that fall prevented the second slug from the guns of Bill Champion from flashing through the brain of Bates.

A howl came out of the throat of the giant as he saw the victory already almost accomplished. That howl gripped the whole body of Dave Bates with cold. He knew what was coming. He strove to wriggle from beneath the pinning body of Harry Quinn, so that he could use his guns, but Bill Champion dived from the back of his halting stallion and hurled himself on the two men.

He knocked the wits from the head of Harry Quinn with a backhanded stroke. He picked Dave Bates up by the throat and stripped the Colt out of his grasp as though it had been in the fingers of a child.

Then Bill Champion sat down on the rock beside the ashes of the dead fire and began to laugh.

It was not a real laugh, in fact, but a brooding chuckle,

long continued, and the sun played on the scar gristle that made a flat of his face as though on the quicksilver of a mirror. The eyes seemed deeply buried behind that mask, looking out through profound holes.

Bill Champion, in his hands, held the scrawny body of the gunman, and turned it this way and that, curiously, as a monstrous ape might have done.

"Why," said Bill Champion, "if it ain't the friend of the gent that eats fire. It's the friend of little Gene Salvio, ain't it?"

Dave Bates, half strangled, made no effort to reply, but the giant added suddenly, gruffly: "Talk, you fool!"

He got Bates by the hair of his head and easily bent back his head and forced him to his knees.

"Yeah," gasped Bates. "I'm a friend of Gene Salvio."

"It's a kind of a funny thing that I'd bump into you up here," said Champion. "What I'm wonderin' is could I cut the scrawny neck of you clean off with one swipe with the old bowie knife. What do you think, eh?"

Bates said nothing. Being about to die, he gathered his nerve. He did not look into the frightful face of Champion for fear of going to pieces.

Here Harry Quinn recovered enough to sit up with a groan. The bullet had struck him through the body, and he was sick with the pain of the wound, and gasping for air.

Bill Champion kicked him deliberately in the face and knocked him flat and senseless again.

"Went over like a ninepin, all balanced fine," said Champion, grinning. "Now, you—what's your name? You big enough to have a name?"

"Bates," he answered.

"Bates, eh? First name?"

"Dave."

"Dave Bates. A little wizened runt like you, and yet you wear two names, just like a real man. Dave Bates, tell me something. There was another gent in this job. There was a gent by name of Reata, they tell me. And he grabbed the gal and he grabbed the gray at one wallop. What's become of him?"

"He's gone," said Bates.

"Sure, he's gone. I ain't a fool. I can see he's gone. But where's he gone to?"

"He took the girl away," said Bates.

"And is he goin' to bring her back?"

"I dunno. I guess not. I guess he took her back to Orchard Creek."

"You lie. I come down by Orchard Creek way."

"Then I dunno where he took her."

"She went free and willing with him, did she?"

"Yes."

"There ain't a woman in the world that's worth anything," said Bill Champion. "All that they can see is faces. They ain't got brains enough to look behind faces and see facts. They can't see no heart and soul. Am I right?"

"By thunder," exploded Dave Bates, "you *are* right."

"You agree with me, do you? A lot it means to me to have a monkey like you say that you agree with me. It sure makes me a lot happier. Now, tell me something. When does this here Reata get back to the camp?"

"I don't know."

"He's coming back pretty soon, ain't he?"

"I dunno," said Dave Bates. "Maybe he's not coming back at all."

"You wouldn't lie to me, would you?" asked the giant, freshening his grip on the hair of Bates until it almost came out by the roots.

Suddenly the little man, in his agony, smiled. "I might lie to you, you gristle-faced baboon!" he said.

Bill Champion closed his eyes. When they were closed, it was not even a semblance of a face that he wore. It was a deformed stone, rather, horribly white with the sheen of flesh.

"Say it again, kid," said Bill Champion. "Dog-gone me, but I sort of like to hear you!"

"I've said it; I'll say it again. I might lie to you, you gristle-faced baboon!" repeated Dave Bates.

"Good!" said Champion, opening his eyes and his formless, crooked slit of a mouth. "Plenty good! Why, I been hearin' about men with the real nerve, but I had to find a monkey before I could find anybody that would talk like a man. You know what I'm goin' to do to you for this? I ain't goin' to take you apart bit by bit. I ain't goin' to unravel you, so to speak. I'm just goin' to tie you up and throw you in the lake, and there you'll choke peaceful and pronto, and go wherever the apes go. Maybe they's a special heaven for the runts and the half-faced monkeys that wear clothes—and two names, just like men!"

CHAPTER 40

Champion wound the entire length of a forty-foot rope around Dave Bates, saying: "Looka, Bates. This is kind of a big honor that I'm doin' you, wastin' the whole of a pretty good rope on you. I could tie you up with twine, and that would do all right, but dog-gone me, I don't mind what I spend on a good man and a real man like you."

Bates, to this compliment, merely answered: "If you're goin' to throw me in the lake, go and do it, but if you ain't hurryin', put my hat back on my head. I hate the sun in my eyes."

Bill Champion bit the corner off a fresh plug of chewing tobacco and spit out the loose shreds of the leaves. He was gap-toothed. The teeth of upper and lower jaw looked to Bates as though they would fit into one another like the teeth of a shark. He munched his tobacco quietly, considering his captive. His lips seemed stiff and uneasily compressed; they kept pulsing in and out as he chewed.

"Yeah, yeah," decided Bill Champion, "I kind of like you. I'm near sorry to drown you. I gotta fix up your sidekicker, and then I'll talk a minute to you."

With that he tied Quinn securely.

"I wanta know something about this Reata," resumed Bill Champion. "Why not tell me something about him? It'll give you a little more time on dry land."

"Reata? Don't you know about him?" asked Bates.

"No," said Champion.

"Yeah, you know about him," answered Bates. "Everybody knows about him!"

"I'm tellin' you straight. I never heard of him till the other day." Champion spit and folded his vast hands, prepared to listen.

"Aw, well," said Bates very seriously, "I dunno what I could tell you. You wouldn't believe it, because he ain't so big."

"That's what I hear. That he ain't big."

"Not more'n a hundred and fifty pounds, maybe. So you wouldn't understand."

"Why wouldn't I?"

"You wouldn't know what he could do. You wouldn't believe it. But maybe you've seen a hornet and a tarantula?"

"What you mean? Sure, I've seen 'em."

"How much bigger is the spider than the wasp?"

"Why, I dunno. Three or four times."

"Yeah, or five or six. But the hornet gets the spider into the open, don't he?"

"Yeah. I've seen that. And then tackles him, and the dog-gone tarantula don't seem to know what to do. Pretty soon the hornet stings him, and he turns into a wet rag, and the hornet drags him away."

"You know what happens then, Champion?"

"No, I dunno, then."

Harry Quinn began to groan. He would still have fought back those groans if he had been aware of them, but he could hear nothing. With every breath he drew the groan shook his body. Bill Champion canted his head to listen and to grin.

"I'll tell you what the hornet does with the big spider. Drags it off to a hole in the ground and lays an egg onto it, and the egg hatches into a worm. And that spider ain't dead. It's only chloroformed, like you might say, and the worm pitches in and starts eatin' the spider, d'you see? And it eats that spider for days and days, and gets bigger and fatter, and the spider feels every bite, but it can't move, because its legs and its mouth are all paralyzed. It has to lie there, and finally the worm, it takes and feeds on the vitals of that tarantula, and that's the finish of the spider, and the grub is ready to turn into a hornet."

"Dog-gone me, but that's a good idea. Where'd the wasp come to think about an idea like that?" asked Champion, full of admiration.

"That's what you wanta watch out for," said Dave Bates. "Don't you let Reata get you into the open."

"Why not?"

"I'm just tellin' you," said Bates. "Don't you let Reata get you into the open, is all I'm tellin' you. Because he'll paralyze you, like the wasp paralyzes the spider. You stay in a hole in the ground, if you got any sense."

"What does Reata do, eh?" asked Champion.

"You wouldn't understand," said Dave Bates, shaking his head. "He'd sting you numb so fast you wouldn't know nothing."

"I can sting 'em now and then," said Champion, tapping one of his big Colts.

"Sure. You're all right," said Bates. "But I was just telling you. You're big and you're fast, and you can shoot pretty straight. There ain't many like you. You're one of the best that I ever seen. And you got strength enough to bend iron. I've seen that, too. Only—don't you let Reata get a hold on you. Understand?"

Bill Champion frowned. He spread out his huge hands and looked down at them.

"That's right where I live—in the hands," he said. "Why wouldn't I wanta let him get a hold on me?"

"I'm tellin' you," said Dave Bates.

"But he ain't so big," said Bill Champion.

"The hornet's a lot smaller than the spider, too. But you know what happens. I just been tellin' you."

Bill Champion scowled, but in thought rather than in anger. Men who are about to die tell the truth, and there is even an old proverb to say that they tell it. Bill Champion had a belief in proverbs, now and then.

But what could the mystery of Reata be?

"Well," said Champion, "that's all you can tell me, eh?"

"That's all you'd understand," said Dave Bates.

"You think I'm a dummy, eh?"

"No, you're bright enough. But ordinary gents like you and me, we don't understand. I seen him work, and even then I couldn't understand. You take a gent that rides right in and takes a gal and a hoss out from a whole crowd—could you understand that?"

Champion pursed his frightful mouth and said nothing.

"I couldn't hardly understand, neither, but I seen it. Maybe it's hypnotism. But there ain't any use for gents like me and you. We don't know enough. We couldn't understand."

"The devil with him," decided Bill Champion suddenly.

A little chill had run into his blood, into his nerves. He stood up and took a breath, to make himself realize his own size and strength a little more vividly. Then he picked up Dave Bates.

"Got any last requests, son?" asked Champion, beginning to sway the burden back and forth, ready for the toss.

"Not me," said Dave Bates. "This is as easy as any way. That's why I been givin' you the good advice. That's why I been tellin' you to get into a hole when you see Reata comin'. So long, Bill."

"So long," growled Champion, and heaved the weight of the body far out into the water. It struck, threw up a crystal flash into the slant sunlight, and then the body of Dave Bates disappeared.

Champion, content, turned and leaned over Harry Quinn for a moment. The mouth of Quinn had sagged open; his eyes were popping.

After that, Champion saddled the gray, took the horse of Dave Bates, plundered the camp of the food that he needed, threw the rest into the lake, and then mounted and rode down the narrow valley toward the end which pointed out at the hot mist of the desert beyond.

He did not look back till he was on his way, and then he scanned the horizon with a certain doubt in his mind.

The tarantula, to be sure, is bigger than the wasp.

Also, dying men tell the truth.

A little shudder of cold ran again, swift as quicksilver, through the blood of the giant. He turned back and put the gray into a strong gallop, because he wanted to get from the view of that valley as quickly as possible.

Dave Bates, as his body cleft down through the ice of the water, knew that he had come to the end of his way, but instinctively he had drawn in his breath, so as to hold it when submerged.

Falling, his shoulder struck the hard ridge of a submerged rock. He could see the vague, sloping shadow of it rising toward the sunlit brightness of the surface. The lake was very shallow. If, perhaps, he could manage to roll his body up that inclined surface of the rock he might be able to project his nostrils and mouth into the sweet heaven of life-giving air.

He could not move hand or foot, but he could roll, and he could twist and thrust with his entire body like a half-frozen serpent.

So, stifling, his lungs bursting, a fist opening in his throat, he worked his way patiently up the rock—and slipped off it to the slimy bottom!

He tried again. A last long effort, and he gained a distance up the rock. He sat up, and the air burst from his lips above the surface of the water!

He drew in the sweetness of the air, incredulous. His life had been given back to him—but for how long?

There was a decided current flowing down the lake. It moved against him. It threatened, every instant, to buoy him up and swing him away from his perch of safety.

In the distance, he could hear Harry Quinn groaning more huskily, more faintly with every breath.

CHAPTER 41

Reata was two thirds of the way back toward the valley, with the sun rolling red in the west, when he saw a horseman swing over a hilltop and drive suddenly down into the hollow where he was traveling. The rider saw Reata and swung instantly toward him.

Even the weariness of his mustang could not prevent this stranger from showing an essential dash. His style in the saddle was straight without stiffness. He seemed to be all lightness and strength. His hands and his head moved with unusual quickness. There was a decision and a certainty about him. If he had ridden up in a group of a hundred cow-punchers, one could have picked him out in the distance. Even a novice would have said: "That fellow is a real man!"

As he came up to Reata, there was another thing worth noticing, and that was an air of perfect poise. He seemed ready to drop the reins and ride with his knees only, leaving the hands free for other things. And as he came, driving, with the wind of the gallop furling up the brim of his white Stetson and his bandanna fluttering out behind his neck, Reata thought this stranger one of the finest sights he had ever spotted in all of his days.

A moment later, he recognized the dark, handsome face which he had seen in the photograph. It was the third and greatest of Pop Dickerman's men. It was Gene Salvio, who twice had gone down before Champion, and still clung like a savage hawk to the chase of that greater bird of prey.

Once, Reata had seen a swift duck hawk dropping again and again from the dim zenith at a wide-winged eagle, making the huge king of the air flop over on its back to wait clumsily, foolishly, with talons and beak prepared for the attack. Still the hawk kept stooping and shifting at the last moment from the grasp of those deadly feet so they had flown out of sight into the horizon.

And Reata thought of that now, as he looked at the lithe, strong, swift body of Gene Salvio. For all his good looks, the savage showed in him, and the wild freedom. He said, as he came up: "Hullo, stranger. What's the good word?"

"The goose hangs high for somebody," said Reata. "How's things for you?"

"I'm looking," said Salvio, "for an hombre with a gray horse—a whale of a stallion, and a whale of a man on the back of him. He oughta be over in this direction somewhere. Have you seen him?"

He fell in beside Reata. He was nervously alert. With his high head, he seemed to disdain all things around him. He seemed to be wishing to rush over the thin mist of the horizon into a new view of the world. He kept his horse prancing and dancing uneasily for the spurs, which on the heels of Reata were rather an ornament than a tool, were useful instruments to Gene Salvio. There was a red, round spot in the tenderness of the flank of his good gelding. Pain and fear and labor had widened the nostrils of the horse, and its eyes were red.

Reata looked hastily up from the horse to the man. He hated to give pain, and he hated to see it given. That doubt which he had first felt when he looked at the fine face of Salvio in the picture returned now with a fuller strength.

But what could one expect of the men of Dickerman? Keenness and courage and strength, one could hope to find in them, but that was about all. In Harry Quinn, also, a certain faithfulness, perhaps.

"I don't know where Bill Champion is," said Reata. "But I can show you the gray, Salvio."

Salvio, thus recognized, jerked about suddenly in the saddle, and could not help darting a hand down to a holster beside him. He kept the hand there, staring at Reata.

"Steady!" said Reata, smiling.

"Who are you? I never saw you before," said Salvio.

"Not even in a crowd?" asked Reata, still smiling.

The bright, black eyes of Salvio flashed over him.

"No," he said. "I'd remember you. You're easy to remember."

"I never saw you, matter of fact, except in a picture," said Reata. "Dickerman showed you to me."

Salvio tossed back his head with an air of instant understanding.

"Dickerman, eh? Old Pop Dickerman, eh? You're with him?"

"I'm with him on loan," said Reata. "My time's about up, I hope."

"What were you talking about—Bill Champion and the gray—what's the meaning of all of that?" demanded Salvio.

"We've got the gray. We're waiting for Champion to show up on the trail of it. Quinn and Bates and I have the gray, and we're doing the waiting."

The facts went home behind the eyes of Salvio, and at last he brightened with understanding.

"All right," he said. "I see the idea. You grab the horse; that's bait for Bill Champion; and when you have him— well, I'm free to go home to Pop. Is that right?"

"You've got the idea," agreed Reata.

"Brains!" said Salvio. "Pop always shows the brains, when it comes to pinches. How far away is the gray and the camp?"

"There'll still be red in the sky," answered Reata.

Salvio rode hard, but the long roan mare flowed easily along over the ground behind him, while little Rags sat up before his master and squinted his eyes into the wind of that ride. An extra strap gave Rags a foothold for his forepaws, and he balanced himself like a circus dog.

That was how the two men came swinging up the narrow little valley, with the blue gleam of the lake still tarnished by the last of the sunset colors.

"They're gone!" exclaimed Reata. "They've pulled out, Salvio!"

"Maybe they're in the trees," suggested Salvio anxiously.

"In the trees? Where Champion could get 'em in the dark? They wouldn't be fools enough for that! They're gone!"

Silently the two increased the speed of their horses, and rushed to the stain of ashes on the ground.

198

Beside it they saw Harry Quinn stretched out in the welter of his own blood; he was still groaning feebly.

It was Salvio who got to the ground first and slashed the cords that were torturing Quinn. It was Reata who heard, before he dismounted, the voice of Dave Bates that called weakly from the cold waters of the lake.

He rode Sue straight into the pool, and carried out Bates to the shore. Even when the ropes were cut, Bates was helpless for a time. But he made no complaints. When he could use his hands, he started massaging his numbed body.

He merely said: "Get a fire going, and work on Harry. He needs you a lot more than I do—or else he don't need you at all!"

Salvio and Reata worked almost silently. Each knew what had to be done, and there was no need for orders to be given or advice asked. They had Harry Quinn stripped to the hips in no time, and a fire burning to give light and warmth. They washed the wound. And when Reata saw the location of the bullet hole, before and behind, his lips pinched hard together.

It looked hopeless. It looked as though even help given at the first moment would have been useless in the end.

But they bandaged the wound and stopped the bleeding. They gave Harry Quinn water, and water again, and more water, until the thickness of his tongue was lessened, and his eyes popped out of his head less horribly.

He was out of his head, at first. Only gradually sense came back to him, and when he made out the voice of Reata, his wits cleared up almost at once. He made a reaching gesture, and Reata gripped his hand.

"You got back," muttered Harry Quinn. "Things'll be all right then. I didn't think that you'd ever get back, but here you are. Reata, it's good to have you around ag'in. It makes things sort of safe, I'd say."

Salvio, at this, looked sharply from the face of the wounded man to that of Reata. He knew Harry Quinn perfectly well and, therefore, his respect for Reata suddenly climbed to the top of a very high ladder.

A good drink of coffee and then a short whisky poured a bit of strength into Harry Quinn. He kept his eyes closed and he kept on smiling.

Salvio said to him, rather brutally: "You're hit pretty bad, Harry. This might not turn out very good."

"You think that I'll be cashin'?" said Harry Quinn. "Ain't you got any sense, Gene? It's a joke; that's what it is. Bill Champion comes and slams me, and pegs me out to die, and I don't die. There wouldn't 'a' been any sense of you fellers comin' along, if I was to die. There's a meanin' and a purpose in everything, Gene. But you're too young and so you don't understand. Besides, Reata, he knows how to pull a gent through a tight fit."

"Aye," said Salvio thoughtfully. "He must know a lot—because Dickerman liked him well enough to give him Sue to ride." A sudden flash of jealousy gleamed in his eyes. "It's more than he ever done for me!" he added.

Then he said: "Bates, can you talk now?"

"It's easy," said Bates. "We sit here, watchin'. Champion comes out of the woods, near where the gray is chewing the grass. He jumps the stallion and rushes us. He bowls over Harry, and Harry falls into me, and we go down in a heap. And then up comes Champion and picks me out of the heap by the neck. He ties Harry up, talks a bit to me, and then swaddles me up in a rope and chucks me into the lake. I manage to roll myself up the side of the rocks and hitch onto the fresh air ag'in. Then you hombres arrive, and there you are. How much nearer are you to Bill Champion than you were back there in Rusty Gulch, Reata?"

"I'm nearer," said Reata. "I know the trail the gray leaves. Where I can't see it, Rags can smell it. I'm going to find Champion!"

"All by yourself, eh?" asked Gene Salvio critically.

"Your horse can't keep up with Sue," explained Reata.

"That," said Salvio, "is why I'm goin' to ride Sue. This here is my job, partner. And I'm goin' to have the hoss that'll gimme a chance to catch up with Bill Champion. Right now he ain't ten miles away! Bates, you must 'a' seen which way he rode!"

"Out straight at the desert!" said Dave Bates.

"I'm off!" exclaimed Salvio. "Take care of Quinn, you two. And luck to you!"

With that, he sprang into the saddle on the back of the roan mare.

CHAPTER 42

There was the snaky length of the lariat which could have pitched Salvio out of the saddle in an instant, but Reata did not wish to use it. Instead, he merely whistled, and the good mare answered the spur of Salvio by suddenly rearing, wheeling, and coming down facing Reata.

"You whistled that mare back to you?" shouted Gene Salvio, in a rage. He controlled himself a little. "Maybe you've done a good job, Reata. But here's where your job stops off! Here's where I begin. Champion's my meat, and you know it!"

"Why be a chopping block?" asked Reata. "He's cleaned you up twice, already. Get off that mare, Salvio!"

"You mean it, eh?" asked Salvio.

"I mean it."

"Why, then, the devil with you. Come on, Sue! We're off!"

The lariat shot from the hand of Reata, almost invisible in that dim twilight. The underhand flip was hardly a threatening gesture, even, but the narrow, hard coil of the noose struck over the shoulders of Gene Salvio and the blinding grip of the rope suddenly imprisoned his arms at his sides.

"Let me go!" yelled Gene Salvio. "I'm goin' to cut you in two for this, Reata!"

He leaped from the saddle, springing down with wonderful lightness in spite of the fact that he could not help himself with his hands. But there was sufficient play in his forearms to enable him to twitch a revolver out of a thigh holster that hung low down on his leg. In the madness of that instant, Salvio would have used the gun, too, but he stepped at that moment into a flying coil of the reata and tripped forward on his face.

Reata stooped over him, took his guns and knife, and loosed him from the rope.

As he worked, he talked to a face which was frozen with incredulous rage.

"If you want to fight for the mare, you can fight with your hands, Salvio," he said. "There's no use shooting each other up for the sake of taking the first crack at Bill Champion. Likely, there's enough of him to go around for both of us, or two times both of us. There you are. Now you can have all the fighting you want!"

Gene Salvio, springing like a wild cat to his feet, balanced an instant on tiptoe. He was bent forward, his crouched body ready to hurl at Reata. But something in the quiet expectancy of Reata—not aggressive in the least, and not at all inviting trouble, and yet calmly ready for anything that might happen—something in this fearless and quiet attitude worked so on the mind of Salvio that he broke off to exclaim: "I'm a dummy! I start fighting the gents that have come out to help me, and I'm a fool. Take the mare then. I'll take my own nag. He's got some good work left in him, and I'm goin' to have it out!"

He flung into the saddle as he spoke, and rushed the gelding straight down the valley toward the desert night beyond the hills.

Reata waited for a short time.

He took the bridle from the mare, led her to the lake, and gave her a few swallows of water. Then he brought her back, and opening one of her canvas saddlebags, he gave her a small feed of crushed barley. She devoured it greedily, then started to graze. Reata, lying flat on his back on the grass, paid no heed to her. One would have said that nothing was farther from his mind than the pursuit of Bill Champion, now riding far away on the gray stallion.

But Dave Bates said: "It's brains that wins the race. You got the brains, Reata."

"He's got the brains," said Harry Quinn softly.

"How d'you feel, Harry?" asked Reata.

"Better. Better, and sleepy. I'm goin' to sleep. I'm goin' to get well. I'm goin' to get so well that I'm goin' to be able to laugh. I'm goin' to—laugh—hard—"

His voice trailed away. And Reata smiled at the stars. The coolness of the grass was soaking into him, and the fever of the sun was soaking out. The stars burned down brighter and closer. Under the last arc of them, the girl was rounded in. She was back at Orchard Creek, by this time. She might be looking up at the same stars, hating him calmly and steadily. Or, perhaps, she was looking up at them and forgiving him. That was more like it. When people have been through many things together, they are more apt to forgive, and distance softens resentment. If he lived, he would find her, somewhere, and take her away. If he had her and the roan mare, and Rags to find a way through the world—well, there would be nothing but happiness. And he, Reata, would reform.

He made that resolution almost sleepily, so complete was the relaxation of his body.

At last, he sat up and lighted a cigarette. Dave Bates silently offered him coffee, but he refused it.

"I can live on the thought of Bill Champion," said Reata, inhaling a cloud of the smoke and breathing it out slowly. "What he did to Harry Quinn is better than food and drink to me."

"You're right," said Bates. "And when you catch up with him, you're goin' to find that he expects something big."

"How big?"

"Big as a hornet is to a spider. I put some ideas in his head. But watch yourself, Reata. If he lays hold on you with one finger, he's goin' to smash your bones."

"Thanks," said Reata. "I've been guessing that."

He stood up and saddled the mare and bridled her. Then he took Rags and, by match light, picked out the bigger hoof marks left on the grass by the stallion. The little dog sniffed at those prints until he filled his tense, sleek body to trembling with the scent. Then Reata put him upon the saddle and prepared to mount.

First, he kneeled by Quinn and took the cold hand of the sleeper for a moment.

When he stood up, Bates said: "It's a funny thing. When a gent is down, you get to thinkin' about the good side of him. I never knew that Harry had no good side, till now. He didn't do no groanin' till he was out of his head. He put up a good show, Reata."

"There's something right in him," agreed Reata. He held out his hand. "I wish I could have you along with me," said he.

"There's no place where I'd rather be," answered the other earnestly. "But maybe I'd only make a bigger spot for Champion to see. Mind you, Reata, he's got everything. He's big, but he's as fast as a cat. He's as fast, almost, as you are. And he can't miss with a gun. He had his hoss at a full gallop when he slammed a slug into Harry Quinn. And nobody's shootin' straight off the back of a runnin' hoss. Nobody but Bill Champion."

"I'll go after him," said Reata cheerfully, "with both my eyes wide open. So long, Dave. Be seeing you later, I hope."

He mounted. He did not put the mare into a canter. Although he rode on that long trail to catch Bill Champion, he let the mare drift down the valley at an easy trot.

And Dave Bates, seeing and understanding, shook his head with a wordless profundity of admiration.

CHAPTER 43

A loping horse will catch a blooded racer; a trotting horse will wear down the one that lopes; and the walking horse, if the distance is great enough, will surely finish off all the others.

Reata knew the span of that desert into which the valley had pointed like a gun barrel. He had not crossed it, but he knew the look of it from the surrounding mountains and the width of it on the map, and he could judge it by its fellows. The result was that he kept the mare at a trot, and out of the valley they passed into the desert itself.

There he swung down from the saddle. The ground was not firm. A lot of it was the sort of blow sand which shifts like mercury underfoot and kills the heart of man or beast. Ten minutes of running will kill a cow-puncher in his ordinary riding boots, but the boots of Reata were as supple as kid and made for running as well as riding. So he struck out at his own dog-trot and took the killing burden of his weight off the back of the mare.

He grew tired. His legs ached. His very arms ached at the shoulders from the constant swing. But he stuck with the work like a day laborer who knows the pain of extended effort.

He had a mare which already had covered a great distance that day. He was pursuing a man on a powerful and fresh horse. And if he was to wear Bill Champion down, he would have to use every device known to him, and in every way supplement the strength of Sue. He had one element fighting for him, and that was the weight of the gray itself on these treacherous sands, and above all, the crushing burden of Bill Champion himself, which must be killing the stallion.

In order to take advantage of this factor of weight, he had to keep traveling not fast, but steadily. There was time. By the brightness of the next dawn they would be among the painted mesas on the farther side of the desert, and after that they would get into the mountains. Before the mountains were reached, he hoped to be at Bill Champion!

Mile by mile, the desert flowed slowly behind him. In the painful illusion which came to him, it seemed as though the earth were in motion beneath him, bearing him back on a vast treadmill. But he had strength to draw upon in various ways. He could remember old Pop Dickerman's description of the frightful face of Champion. He could remember how the girl had covered her face at the thought of him; he could remember, last of all, how he had carried Bates like a drowning rat out of the lake, and how he had taken the cold hand of poor Harry Quinn in his and seen by firelight the gray death invading the face of the man.

When he thought of these things, they did not oppress his spirit. They gave him power which he could translate into more miles.

They crossed the shifting sand and gained, at once, a firmer footing and a belt of greater heat. It seemed as though the fierceness of the sun had soaked deeper into the ground here, and therefore, it was radiated for a longer time. The soil was more rocks than earth, but little Rags rarely had to drop his muzzle to the surface. He could read the scent easily with his head up, and his small feet kept twinkling on.

The moon rose. Its silver light seemed to be bringing the suffocating heat down through the windless air, but it showed the way to Reata's own eyes for the first time. He could see, here and there, the big imprint of the hoofs of the gray horse. And he knew that Rags was running true.

Thirst began to parch his throat. Well, they would have to come to water before long. The bigger Bill Champion was, the huger his horse, the more need there was of water for them, and their trail would touch at water holes.

He had filled two canteens before starting. He made a brief halt now, and took a swallow out of one canteen. Then he held it at the mouth of the mare. She took hold of it as though she were trained in drinking from a bottle, and swallowed down the contents.

That was fuel against the time to come, and the mare needed that help not long after when they came again to soft sand.

Reata had ridden across the firm ground; he forced himself to go on foot again, when they came to the soft. He was still very tired. His left foot was chafing badly. There was blood in that boot, or else he did not know the meaning of pain. But small things like that had to be taken for granted. If his whole body were roasted in fire, it would not keep him, he knew, from going forward.

Then he saw a strange silhouette before him. It grew clearer. He made out a man seated on the prone body of a horse, and he knew what that meant. It was Gene Salvio, who had rushed into the desert thinking that his horse could live on the red of the spur. That horse was dead, and Salvio was there with his head in his hands, grinding his teeth, cursing life.

Well, there was nothing to be done for Salvio, and therefore, Reata called Rags in and took a deliberate detour to the side.

A shout challenged him before he had gone far. He looked and saw that Salvio was on his feet, running, waving his hands in wild gesticulations, and calling out, again and again:

"Reata! Reata!"

Reata swung into the saddle, snatched up Rags, and put the mare to a canter. He knew that Salvio was desperate, but he was not prepared for what followed. Salvio dropped to one knee, steadied his revolver with a rest, and fired a bullet that whined in the air right across the face of Reata!

That was it. For the sake of a better chance at Bill Champion, Salvio was ready to murder any friend!

The mare did not need heel or hand. She was instantly running like the wind, that wire-strung body of hers stretching out as straight as a string. Another and another shot followed, all whirring frightfully close. And then the shooting ended.

Looking back, Reata saw Salvio throwing up his hands into the air, and then running like a madman to overtake the horse!

In a sense, no doubt, the man *was* mad. He was one of Pop Dickerman's poisonous rats, cornered and savage for the fight!

But Gene Salvio dropped away in the distance, and again Reata was on foot, driving ceaselessly forward. The heat was so intense that already he was beginning to have the water dreams. Little moments like sleep overcame his weary body and his brain, and he found himself starting back to full consciousness with a sound of water in his ears, not the faintly musical trickling of a little stream, but the chiming and gushing outpouring of whole cataracts that cooled the winds and gave a delicious savor of wetness to the air.

Always, of course, the hot, narrow horizon of the desert closed in upon him again with its remorseless fact. But again and yet again the delirium returned and brought him one high-hearted instant of hope, insane hope, to be followed by the realization of the truth.

Then they found the first water at which Bill Champion had stopped.

Rather, it was not water but seethed mud. For Champion, after watering himself and his horse, had ridden the stallion around and around the banks of the hole and trampled the alkaline soil into the water.

It was fouled and spoiled.

And that was murder. Men might come to this place on their last legs, their blood and their brains on fire with desperation, and they would find a slimy mess instead of life.

Reata trembled with hot anger. But he was almost glad, because Champion had to die and he was the appointed executioner.

He poured from his last canteen a bit of water on a clean bandanna, and with it swabbed out the mouth of the mare. He parted her teeth and reached far back and washed off the scum and the grit from her tongue and the roof of her mouth, and then he cleaned the nostrils as deeply as he could. Afterward, he poured some of that precious fluid into the palm of his hand. At the touch of it, a frightful desire came to dash the liquid down his own throat. But he set his teeth and grinned back the temptation. He lowered his hands, and Rags whined with delight as he drank. Again, and again, he emptied the hollow palm of that hand.

Then Reata stood up and poured the rest down the throat of the mare, and he struck on again through the desert.

It had been right, he felt. Without the strong legs of Sue, without the faultless nose of Rags, he would be a useless wanderer along this trail. And as for himself, no matter if the fire were mounting out of his throat and into his brain, he had human thought and invention to feed him and to give him drink.

So, through the endless softness of the sand, he kept plugging along at his work, remembering what he had heard an Indian say, that the way to keep breathing is to keep the chin tucked down a little. Let the chin rise and the head begins to fall back, the throat muscles strain, the whole body bends and labors before long. So, no matter how he felt his strength giving way, he jogged on with chin down, breathing deeply of the acrid air.

After all, there would have to be another water hole before very long. Bill Champion would never take a trail that he did not know by heart. There would be more water, and Champion, of course, would not spoil the second drinking place. He would depend upon the fouling of the first one to discourage any hunters who might venture along his trail; not even a Bill Champion, beast though he might be, would venture on ruining two water holes in the parching middle of the desert!

That hope kept Reata swinging along in his stride, until they reached a firm footing, once more, and he climbed dizzily into the saddle again. He picked up Rags to rest the little dog, also, since it was certain that Rags could not endure this pace forever.

Rags kept shuddering, as though in pain. It was the pain of terrible thirst, Reata knew, that tormented the poor little dog.

So they crossed the desert to the second water hole and found—that it had been destroyed, exactly like the first.

In the vagueness of his mind, in his desperation, Reata drove his hands to the wrists in the mud. It was warm. The water would have been warm. It would have been as hot as blood. Aye, and it would have meant the blood of life to them!

Champion had done his work again. If he had killed men before, he had killed treble the number now, for men who trusted the second water hole would die of sheer despair when they came to the place and found it ruined.

But Reata did not die of despair.

His throat and mouth were so dry that he could have bitten his own arm and sucked the blood like that fevered wretch in the poem. But he sat cross-legged and put his chin on his hands and made himself swallow, and wondered how long it would be before the swelling of his tongue forced him to open his mouth to the air!

If the sun had been shining— Aye, but under the sun there is always a brighter hope and a wider horizon, with new visions always rolling in upon the mind. But here, the moon radiating in a small circle through the misty air of the desert, it seemed to him that he was traveling in the very country of death.

Rest was the next best thing to water.

He rested therefore, lying on his back, his arms outstretched. And little Rags came and sat down beside his face with his tongue hanging out, shuddering back and forth with the rapidity of his panting. And now and again, as though on a drawn breath, Rags moaned with the greatness of his despair.

Only the mare seemed brave and hopeful. Queer cartoon that she was, she kept her ears pricked as though she knew good things about the future, and Reata loved her for her courage.

He could remember how that Dickerman had promised her as a gift, a great bonus, if the three men were actually brought back to Rusty Gulch. Well, he would have her. The thought poured a bit of new strength into him.

He got up and resumed the way, not walking, but always at the shambling run. For walking would not overtake the great Bill Champion in the width of this desert. He put up Rags on the saddle, only taking the little dog down, now and again, to solve some riddle in the disappearing trail. The nose of Rags had become the second most important thing in the world!

CHAPTER 44

Sometimes it seemed to Reata, as he went on, that this was the fire of torment which purified mind and soul as metal is purified before the forge hammers begin their play—well, he would have the hammering, too, before very long.

Time went out of his mind.

There were ways of measuring it, however. He could count his burning footsteps to a hundred and then another hundred. He could tell himself that he would mount the saddle after another hundred strides, and then another hundred, and then another.

Or he could listen to the thudding pulse in his temple which plainly told of an overworked engine. Queer crowds of words and thoughts and memories bumped roughly into his mind, each thing repeated to the verge of madness. He had to keep his chin down and run. He had to keep his chin down and run. Chin down—run; chin down—run; chin down—run!

That was the way phrases took possession of him and beat out the words slowly in his mind, one for every stride he took.

Then he found himself running open-mouthed, babbling the words, and staggering as he ran.

This frightened him back to soberness. He mounted the saddle and told himself grimly that he would see how long the mare could last. But there was no wearing Sue out. She kept on with her wire-strung body, her gaunt, swinging legs as though she did not know what fatigue might mean.

Dickerman had once said that she could get fat on thistles. Get fat—thistles; fat—thistles; fat—thistles!

Well, why not?

A fellow could chew the green stalk of a thistle, and the sap would be like water. It would be better than water. It would be better than wine. The green sap of thistles would be life. Thistles—life—thistles—life.

And then they struck soft going again.

He slid from the saddle. His knees sagged when his feet hit the ground, but he began to run. Those refrains which had been maddening to him were now a help, a comfort, a strength to lean upon. He welcomed them into his mind, and suddenly he found that the words would come no more. All that he could think about was the twinkling feet of little Rags as the dog made the way sure, and the sliding crunch of the hoofs of Sue behind him, and the pain of breathing. He was sure that the membrane was peeling inside his throat, inside his lungs.

He saw Rags stumble, recover, stumble and recover again. Rags was going out. Rags was near the limit. But the little dog always recovered and went on with a suddenly fresh spurt.

He realized, in a golden burst of feeling, that they were both heroes—the mare and Rags. Not beautiful, but heroes.

They knew nothing about the goal toward which he was driving them so remorselessly, but they were sticking to their jobs, blindly, without complaint.

The going began to be firmer once more. He pulled himself into the saddle again, and this time, not only were his knees nearly numb, but there was so little strength in his arms that they shuddered and shook under the weight of his body, which he was pulling up.

This was a thing to worry about. This was a frightful calamity—if the strength went out of his arms and the cunning out of his hands. For all that he had was the strength of those arms—worthless, almost, against the brute force of the great Champion—and the cunning of his hands.

Brains will win. That was what Bates had said. Yes, but brains will not win without hands to serve. And his hands were going. They trembled, even when he rested them folded on the pommel of the saddle.

Sue carried on, while the head of Reata bobbed sleepily. The mare went on, like a ship of the desert, carried by winds, without effort. It was for this that all flesh was stripped from her. She was simply heart and lungs mounted on wire-strung legs that would not fall.

Well, Champion had a big start, a long start, but how far away could he be, even now?

At that, Reata looked up, and suddenly he saw what seemed to him the mighty parapets of heaven, with all the gates flung wide and dim, gold shining out!

His staggering mind realized, in a moment, that he had come to the verge of the great painted mesas at the foot of the mountains. And this was the golden dawn that was pouring out through them, gilding the canyons.

It was beautiful. He told himself that only a man near to death could realize how beautiful it was!

And then he remembered another thing. Through these canyons, men said who had traveled through the desert, small streams of water ran and passed a little distance into the desert, and there were drunk up and wasted.

He glanced to the left. There ran a streak of faint gold far out into the desert for miles and miles.

In a moment, he realized that it was water, with the dawn color reflecting from it. Water that he had been running so near all this time—that he could have had an hour ago, a sweet eternity ago, perhaps!

But he had stuck to the trail!

He began to laugh hysterically, and then he was aware, like the old illusion which had haunted him so often during this nightmare of a journey, that there was a sound of gushing waters. No, it was no illusion, but the mighty truth. There, at the entrance to the first canyon, making its last leap down from the mountains, there was a little crystal cataract—and both his own will and the trail of Bill Champion led straight for that point.

It grew bigger. The mare was cantering of her own will, stretching out her head. If that brilliance of flinging water had been composed of fine diamonds, it could not have been half so beautiful, so bright, so invaluable!

Reata flung himself out of the saddle. He plunged his face into the water—and he could not drink!

He was merely stifling himself, but he could not swallow a drop!

He had to sit up and take the water in his hand and let a bit of it flow into his mouth and so trickle, little by little, into the burning heat of his throat. He could swallow then.

He gathered handfuls of the water, laughing crazily, and drank from his hands.

What was that story in the Bible about those soldiers being chosen, who, in the water famine, when they came to the river drank like men from their hands, and not with lowered heads like beasts?

Somehow, he found an omen in that. Bill Champion was a beast, and Reata would have to play the part of a man.

And always there was that shaking laughter in his breast.

Afterward, he sat up, dizzy, and looked around him at the unreal beauty of that world of the dawn. He stood up. Strength had returned to his body and steadiness to his hands. Actually it was as though he had been drinking not water, but the very blood of life.

The canteens were not filled. There was no need for them in a world of many waters, a blessed mountain world. There was no need of anything now, except to hope that the nose of Rags would be able to follow the sign of the gray stallion over the naked, the iron-hard trails that wound along the sides of these canyons. The big, flat-topped mesas stood out against him with a degree of scorn, forbidding him to carry his petty hopes and his malice into their great domain. But presently, he was traveling up a sharp slope along a narrow, jutting trail, with Rags, head down, working hard on the sign of the gray horse.

The way wound upward dizzily. And still Rags kept true, where the trail forked at the coming in of a greater ravine. They turned down the side of a very narrow valley, its walls of red rock with the gold of the dawn dripping over the polished surfaces. Above them was the sky, golden, too. Beneath them the waters of the creek that had carved out these rocks was gilded, also.

Heaven help the man for whom existence was blotted out in a world so beautiful!

The trail wound steadily. He had a glimpse of a place where the creek had tunneled through the base of a giant wall, on the face of which the trail crooked back and traveled again across the opposite side of the ravine, hardly twenty-five or thirty feet away.

That was when he heard the clang of the rifle, monstrously loud, and felt the sting of a bullet that drove through his left thigh cleanly.

He fell forward on his hands and his right knee. Even in falling, he had snatched out the reata from his pocket, but it slithered out of his hand and dropped not over the

213

edge of the cliff but down a ragged gap in the floor of the trail.

He was helpless, and from the other side of the ravine a vast, beastly, booming voice was roaring down at him.

CHAPTER 45

He turned his head slowly. He was seeing clearly through this trick of fate, which brought him gloriously across the desert, gloriously into the presence of his enemy, and then let him be blind! Why, fool that he was, had he not realized that Bill Champion must be very close? For how else would Rags have been able to follow a scent over those rocks of red iron?

If there had been half a wit in his head, he would have known that he was on the very heels of his quarry!

Then he saw the man. The gray stallion was there, also, a weary horse with a downward head. If only he, Reata, had been in the saddle when that rifle spoke, instead of saving the mare by taking the steep of that strong incline on foot, she would have carried him swiftly past the danger of rifle fire around the corner of the next rock. And, after that, wounded as he was, he would have been able to shift for himself.

Little Rags came whining back and stood upon his hind legs to lick his master's face.

Reata merely muttered: "Fetch it, Rags! Down! Rags! Fetch it, boy!"

Rags jumped back and canted his head to one side. How would the poor dog be able to understand that his master wanted that slenderly coiling snake of a lariat back in his hand?

So, calmly, despairingly, Reata looked up and across the ravine at the face of the rifleman.

Even death was made more horrible by the sight of the featureless slab of gristle. It was like standing half in hell and half out to confront the monster.

Bill Champion was laughing, but not enough to shake

the aim of the rifle at his shoulder. It was hardly a sound of laughter so much as the snarling of a happy wolf. It was not the look of laughter, but a writhing of the face only.

"Hi, Reata," said Bill Champion. "I'm glad to see you, boy!"

"Hi, Champion!" said Reata. "I'm seeing you, too."

"How does it feel?" asked Champion, behind his rifle.

"Like a hammer stroke, and a wasp sting in the center of the bruise. Sort of numb, Champion."

"That's a pretty good description," said Champion. "That's what a bullet through the leg feels like. I wasn't sure that I'd sock the slug through your leg, at first. I thought that I'd put it through your head. But I didn't want to have only one mouthful of you. I wanted to *see* you die, Reata."

"That's natural," said Reata. "What made you doubt your rifle, Bill?"

"A fool of a dead man," said Bill Champion. "He went and talked you up like you was somebody. And when it comes to travelin', you are. You're a travelin' fool, all right. I didn't think that nobody would show up on the trail behind me as fast as this. And then I seen you. And I had to laugh, Reata, when I seen you ridin' right up, blind as a bat."

"Yes, I was the fool," said Reata.

"You was the fool, all right. By the little dog that I'd heard about from the gypsies, I spotted you."

"They told you all about me, eh?"

"Not Queen Maggie," said Champion. "Dog-gone me if she ain't sort of fond of you. The others, they talked plenty. But Queen Maggie, she wouldn't talk none. What would she be seein' in a sawed-off runt like you, eh?"

"Women are queer," said Reata.

"That's a true word," said Bill Champion. "But bust loose and tell me something. Dog-gone me if I don't always learn something from my dead men."

"What'll I tell you?"

"Why, the last dead man that I left behind me, he told me that you was hell on wheels, and he told me to keep in a hole when I seen you coming. Well, I kept in a hole, all right. I pulled in out of sight, and just looked over the rim of the rock to slam you. But there ain't nothin' to you.

You ain't no kind of a fightin' man, Reata! Bates, he's as sure a liar as he's sure dead!"

"All right," said Reata. "You'll have to choke that one down, because he's not dead."

"He's as dead as water can drown him."

"He's not dead. He wormed his way up on a rock on the lake. That lake was only a shallow pool, Bill. If you'd had good sense, you would have made sure of that. You want to drop a man out of his depth before you are so sure of drowning him."

"I ain't got good sense?"

"You're too big to be very bright, Bill," said Reata. "All you big, beefy boys depend on your hands instead of your head. That's why you don't have a chance in the long run."

"A chance? What sort of a chance have *you* got?"

"I'm not dead yet."

"You're goin' to be, and pronto, too!"

"I'll believe that when the lights go out," said Reata.

As he said this, out of the tail of his eye he marked the fuzzy head of little Rags appearing out of the gap in the floor of the trail with the end of the lariat gripped between his teeth. Reata had it instantly in his fingers.

How much could Bill Champion see? In that beautiful but uncertain golden light of the dawn, how much could he see? Reata raised the hand that now held the end of the thin lariat and knotted it swiftly inside the stirrup leather that hung down close to him. For the mare had halted in place and remained there, motionless. Now the rope was anchored.

Without motion of his arm, with the working of his dextrous fingers, he began to gather in the sleek, meager coils of the reata.

"How long, brother, you think you're goin' to live?" asked Champion, his wide mouth actually gaping.

"Why, I don't know," answered Reata. "There are a lot of things that can happen to you, Bill."

"Are you bleedin' a lot?" asked Champion eagerly.

"Not a lot. A rifle bullet doesn't tear a fellow up the way a forty-five-caliber slug does."

"You would 'a' used a revolver, would you?"

"No. I never carry a gun."

"You never what?" shouted Champion.

He stepped forward to the edge of the rock, with the perilous drop down the canyon wall unheeded, at his toes.

"You mean that you never carry a gun? What you talkin' about?"

"I'm telling you the truth. Now and then it pays, Bill."

"How would you 'a' done anything to me even if you *had* caught up with me?"

Anything to keep the monster occupied, while that forty feet of line gradually retreated into the hand of Reata, gradually gathered in, as a spider gathers in its longest thread of silk with rapid claws!

"Didn't Bates tell you what I could do?" asked Reata.

"No. He didn't tell me. Hypnotism, or some fool thing like that, he talked about. You might as well try to hypnotize one of these here cliffs as to make a dent in me with your eyes, Reata!"

"That's right," said Reata. "A fellow has to have a brain to work on."

"Look here," complained Bill Champion—and Reata could almost have smiled as he listened— "you think that I'm some kind of a wooden dummy, do you? You don't know nothin' whatsoever about me, do you?"

"Oh, I know enough," said Reata. "You've got hands big enough to break a neck or two, now and then. That's all you have. And you're willing to shoot from behind. That's why you've killed your men."

"Did I shoot Gene Salvio from behind?" shouted the giant.

"That's what Salvio told me," lied Reata smoothly.

"He told you that? The—why, the sneak! He won't give me no credit, eh?"

"Why should he," asked Reata, "when you're running away from him all over the lot?"

"Running away? From him? Who said that he was after me?"

"He's back there in the desert now, and you know it," replied Reata. "And that's why you humped across the desert so fast and even smashed in the water holes on your way. You're afraid of Salvio. Why don't you make yourself easy and tell the truth?"

"The truth? It ain't the truth! It's the worst lie that anybody ever wriggled his tongue around. Why, I was kind of sorry, almost, to step on you after you come so fast across the desert after me! I was goin' to ask you how you managed to come through that hell without no water for two whole stages—but the way you yarn and lie, dog-gone me if it ain't goin' to be good to sink a chunk of lead into you and finish you off."

"Now?" asked Reata.

"Yeah, right now!"

"I'll take it standing up then," said Reata.

He had gathered in the subtle coils of the lariat by that time. He had spread, with the magic of his fingers, a sufficient noose. And all he wanted now was to stand erect for a single instant. So he grasped the stirrup leather and pulled himself halfway to his feet.

The rifle clanged. A bullet slid like the thrust of a hot needle through his right thigh, and the numbed leg let him down with a thud on the rock. He sat up and stared at Bill Champion, and with a gesture pushed the coils of the slithering rope behind him. His right hand hungrily fingered the noose.

Champion was shouting: "I'll learn you to try to move before I want you to! I wish that I could make you die the way Quinn died! That'd do me a lot of good, to tie you up like that and let you stare at the sun till you died!"

He added: "Are you ready?"

"I'm ready any old time," said Reata. "But don't think that you killed Quinn. He's a tough hombre, that Quinn."

"Dead? I got him right through the body!"

"That's what you think. The bullet just kind of glanced around his ribs, that's all, and then came out his back."

"What you mean?" roared Champion.

"I mean that he was sitting up with coffee in one hand and a smoke in the other, when I last saw him. Does that sound dead to you?"

"By thunder!" muttered Champion, and even that muttering wakened a sullen echo up the wall of the ravine. "I pretty near believe what you say!"

"You ought to. The truth ought to be pretty fine for you to hear, Bill."

"Would you take and swear on your word of honor that Quinn was alive at sundown?"

"I'll swear that."

"And Bates, too?"

"I'll swear that."

"What's the matter with me?" exclaimed Bill Champion. "I dunno what's the matter today!"

"You don't understand," said Reata.

He had struck on a sore chord.

"Don't understand? What don't I understand? First Bates talks about me not being able to understand, and then you begin to yammer like a fool at me about not understanding. What don't I understand?"

"There's not much good explaining," said Reata. "It's too deep for you, Bill. It's one of those things that a big, beefy fellow like you wouldn't be able to understand. Didn't Bates tell you what it was that was too deep for you?"

"Bates? What would Bates know that might be too deep for me?"

"He didn't tell you, eh? Why, Bill, it's hard to explain. But everybody knows, the minute you've said two words—"

"They know what?"

"They know what's wrong with you, Bill."

"I've got a mind to come around there and wring it out of you. Talk out! What you mean, Reata?"

"You've never seen people laughing at you?"

"Laughing at me? I'd tear their hearts out!"

"Think back, Bill. You're not very bright, but you ought to be able to remember. You've walked past people, and felt 'em smiling behind you?"

Bill Champion seemed stunned.

"I dunno," he muttered, the words carrying dull and thick to the ear of Reata. "I dunno what's behind it all. Maybe they've smiled. But why would they smile at me?"

"You ought to be able to see. It's why I'm smiling now, Bill!"

"You're goin' to stop laughin'," shouted Bill Champion. "You're havin' your last laugh now! Rifle bullets don't mean so much, eh? I'm goin' to chop you up with slugs out of a Colt. I'm goin' to whittle you away, Reata, little by little!"

He turned, as he spoke, and wrenched a long Colt out of the saddle holster on the gray stallion.

It was for that moment that Reata had talked and worked and waited, with the sharp agony of the wounds growing momentarily greater. Now he swayed his body forward until he pitched up onto his knees, the torn legs shuddering under the weight. And with a wide, underhanded sweep, he hurled the noose of the rope.

It carried like a flung stone. He thought, for a moment, that the noose would not open, that he had hurled it too flat, but at the last instant, as though a snaky brain worked in the thing, it spread out and dropped as the big man turned.

It seemed to Reata that there was not even time to let the coil settle. The instant it was over the head, he snatched the grip of the running noose tight around the throat of Bill Champion and with his wrench on the line made the monster totter on the verge of the abyss.

That moment would have been the end of Champion, but grasping wildly back, the gun falling from his hand, he caught the gray horse by the reins, and that pull steadied him.

"Sue!" Reata screamed, and slapped her with his hand.

His own strength of both arms was a mere nothing against the power of Champion. With his one free hand, the monster snatched the line quite out of the hands of Reata, and then jerked the noose open. He was free—no, for at that moment the trotting mare brought the line tight. The noose jerked hard in, imprisoning the one hand of Champion. He was thrust forward by the pull. Still, with his other hand he gripped the bridle of the gray and actually brought the stallion slithering forward and down the shelving surface of the trail until the gray, as though disdaining fear, as though familiar with frightful needs in following its master, suddenly rose and leaped far out into the ravine.

The two bodies dropped out of view. Reata then heard the sound of the body of the hanging man as it thudded against the side of the cliff. Next, he heard the crash of the horse beneath. And faintly, out of a strangled throat, Reata halted the mare with a word.

CHAPTER 46

He had to loose the lariat, when he had dragged himself to the mare, from the stirrup leather. And he heard the second sound of the fall of Bill Champion on the red rocks of the ravine below. After that, he had to make the bandages for his wounded legs. Finally, there was the need of pulling himself up into the saddle. He managed that, his body limp as a sack, his legs quite useless. Balanced in the saddle, he turned the mare down the old Spanish trail and passed to the bottom of the ravine, then up beside the foaming waters until he reached the place where Champion lay.

It was hard to loosen the reata, it had sunk so deeply into the thick of the neck, but he managed it with weakening hands. Afterward, from his saddlebag, he got out the ration of hardtack and raisins, and slowly munched it.

The pain from his feet was much greater, even now, than the pain of his wounds, which were merely a dull, numb ache. He worked off his boots and dipped his raw and bleeding feet in the cold water.

His shirt and undershirt had been torn to bits to make the bandages for his wounds. And that was the way they found him, sitting with his back to a rock, calmly smoking a cigarette and looking up toward the bright sun which was now flooding that narrow street which the edges of the cliffs fenced through the morning sky.

The yipping of Rags, when he heard hoofbeats, was what called the attention of the sheriff and his men; but as they came up the ravine, a haggard set, with their horses staggering under them, Miriam fled before them, galloping her mustang among the boulders.

She was on her knees when the sheriff came up. She was babbling out things that had not a great deal of meaning, and Reata was smiling up at her in a curious, detached sort of way.

The sheriff looked at this scene with a frown, as though

he derived great pain from it. Then he went to the body of the gray horse, and last of all stood with his three men— all who had managed to keep their horses going across the desert—and looked down at the last of Bill Champion.

The mark of the reata was around his neck, sunk in deeply, marked with red and purple.

"It ain't possible," said the sheriff. "The way I see it, Champion was able to sink two bullets through him. And yet he was able after that to shake that reata around Champion's neck—and do this. It ain't possible—but here's the dead man laying!"

He went back to Reata and leaned over him.

"The hoosegow for you, son," said the sheriff.

"I have to lie up for a while, anyway," answered Reata.

"Don't talk to him," pleaded the girl. "Not till you've told me if you forgive me, Reata!"

"Why, all that anybody can do is his best," said Reata. "You did your best and brought along the sheriff, and the sheriff wants to take me where I can find a doctor and stretch out long and lazy, till I've got two good pins under me again. What could be better than that? You knew I'd need an ambulance, and I wouldn't want a better driver than ol' Lowell Mason!"

In fact Reata was "stretched out long and lazy," in Rusty Gulch, but not in the jail. They put him in the hotel, instead, while letters and telegrams poured in on the governor of the state. A Federal marshal spent forty minutes telling that governor a few details concerning the life and times of Bill Champion, and after that a free pardon came down for Reata.

It must be admitted that he enjoyed his convalescence immensely. His visitors ranged from the sheriff up and down through various degrees of the community.

Salvio came in one day and stood turning his hat in his hands and staring at the wounded man, and asking his forgiveness, and getting it. Then Salvio gave one keen, bright flash of a look at Miriam, and went out.

"What did that look mean?" asked Reata.

"It means that I'll see him again. He knows that, too. It means he'll have some trouble—and that he *doesn't* know," said the girl.

Reports came in that Bates was still caring for Quinn, who was progressing very favorably.

And then, one day, two strange personalities met at

Reata's bedside—Queen Maggie and Pop Dickerman. They walked in at almost the same moment, and Reata introduced them. He used phrases which had been in his mind long before.

"Maggie," he said, "I want you to meet Pop Dickerman, the king of the rats. Pop, this is Queen Maggie, the queen of the cats. You two ought to know each other."

They did not make a foolish gesture at shaking hands. They merely stared and grinned.

"How come you wasn't hanged a long time ago?" said Maggie.

"They wouldn't bother," said Pop Dickerman. "They been too busy lookin' for you."

And he stroked his long, furry face.

"Get out and leave me talk business," said Queen Maggie.

Pop Dickerman got out, grinning, for he felt that he had had the best of the encounter, and Queen Maggie sat down and put her spurred heels on the edge of the table. She lighted a thick, oily Havana and closed her eyes during the first few, sweet puffs.

Then she said: "Things is all gone bust with the tribe, Miriam. The boys are gettin' out of hand. They get drunk; the police slam 'em in jail; and there ain't any Miriam to talk 'em out again. We give our show, and we get pennies instead of dollars, because Miriam ain't there to give us a cymbal crash at the wind-up. Honey, why don't you come back to the easy life?"

"There's the reason," said the girl.

"A rotten reason," said Queen Maggie. "Listen to me, Reata. Ain't you a rotten reason?"

"Sure I am," said Reata.

"He knows he is," said Queen Maggie, puffing around her words thick clouds of strong tobacco smoke. "You wouldn't have no kind of a life with him. It'd be marriage, wouldn't it?"

"That's what it seems like," said the girl.

"He'll keep you toeing the chalk mark," advised Queen Maggie. "Wouldn't you, Reata?"

"Yes," said Reata.

"In his house there'd be only one boss. Wouldn't there, Reata?"

"Only one," agreed Reata calmly.

"He's been around so much that he knows things, and

you couldn't cut no corners. Miriam, it'd be a bust. Can't you see that?"

Miriam said nothing.

"And ain't there no cravin' in you for gypsy stew and gypsy days and gypsy nights, honey?" asked Queen Maggie. "Don't you kind of hunger a bit to hear old Maggie cussin' around the camp and watchin' the pots over the fire?"

"I hunger pretty bad for all of it," said Miriam, "and the tights and ruffles and . . . and the flounces and the people yelling. But I don't know. I guess I'll stay here while I'm wanted."

"Hi!" shouted Queen Maggie, leaping to her feet. "You mean to say that you've found your boss? You found your master?"

"It looks that way," said the girl. "It's mighty hard, but it looks that way. I'm going to be a sick cat a lot of the time, but it looks as though I've found my boss."

"I see it in your eyes," said Queen Maggie heavily. "You used to be a wild young heifer cutting up capers. But I can see the heavy look, the cow look, all over your eyes. Reata, treat her fine, but don't keep sharp knives in your house."